DAUGHTERS

OF

DASHEEN

THE CHOSEN ONE

Series One

A NOVEL

Sandra Davis

CHOCOLATE ROOTS PUBLISHING
Marietta, Georgia

CHOCOLATE ROOTS PUBLISHING

Chocolate Roots Publishing,
Registered office: 178 Roberts Trail, Marietta, Georgia 30066
Copyrights © 2018 by Chocolate Roots Publishing

Sandra Davis
DAUGHTERS of DASHEEN Series/First Installment
THE CHOSEN ONE

1. Young Women - Crimes Against - Fiction
2. Murder Mystery- Fiction
3. Human Trafficking - Fiction
4. Drug Smuggling - Fiction
5. Witchcraft - Fiction
6. Romance- Fiction

Library of Congress Cataloging in Publication Data has been applied for.

ISBN 978-0-997-1627-0-7 Paperback
ISBN 978-0-997-1627-2-1 Hardback
ISBN 978-0-997-1627-1-4 (eBook)

Book Interior design by Slim Rijeka

Cover design by Alexander Von Ness
nessgraphica.com

Author's Photograph by Deelee Productions

Printed in the United States of America
10   9   8   7   6   5   4   3   2   1

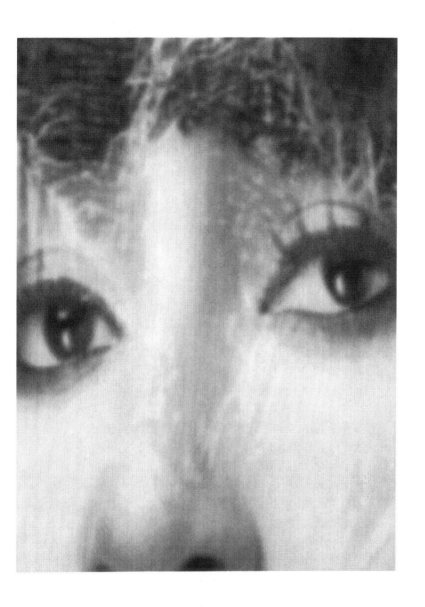

THE CHOSEN ONE

CONTENTS

ACKNOWLEDGEMENTS

This story is my second child. It came with excruciating labor pains and numerous sleepless nights. It's been a different kind of journey for me. However, I am eternally grateful for the knowledge, guidance, and support from my Heavenly Father and my extraordinary family and friends.

Love and Blessings to my one and only son, John Davis. You are God's greatest gift to me, and I thank him each day for you. You are the air in which I breathe.

Love to my amazing sister, Carol Sue Harris, who spent a multitude of laborious hours editing numerous revisions. I am eternally grateful. You are the gift that keeps on giving of your talent, love, and support. You are my hero.

To my original wildflower and reader in progress, Debra Hudson. Thank you for being the wind beneath my wings, my most loyal and best friend. Without your support, this journey wouldn't have been possible.

Ken Hutchinson, my friend and the coolest guy in Texas. Thank you for giving me a place to rest my mind during the creation of this book. It was always a pleasure to plant my feet under your dinner table and enjoy the best darn steak in the world.

Si King, author and friend, always came through instantly when I called on her. Thank you for never being too busy to take my calls.

My gratitude to my graphic designer and brother, Alexander Von Ness, for his valuable assistance in creating my New York Times best seller book cover. Your creative genius and commitment to this project helped maintained my sanity.

To Cynthia Jones. Thank you for encouraging me to pursue my dreams and join a local writing group—the best decision ever.

Thank you, Virginia Clairmont, for giving me access to your brilliant mind. Meeting you thirty-five years ago was a blessing.

My gratitude to Jedwin Smith, my instructor and father of my second child, who taught me that lots of red marks on a manuscript was a great way to improve your craft.

Continuing thanks to Marianne Stefanelli, founder of Writers High, who shared priceless advice and introduced me to the Atlanta Writers Club, George Weinstein, and Patti Callahan Henry. You are the best.

My enthusiastic beta readers: my little sister Sally Turner, Elana Turner-James, Stephanie Horton, Debra Hudson, and Carol Sue Harris. Thank you for your valuable time and feedback.

Always thanks to Gaby Aguliar, for being the best friend and Hispanic translator in the world.

Love to my friend, Joyce Kean. I am truly grateful for your encouragement and longtime friendship.

Kudos to Bernice (Tasha) Millin, my kindred spirit, who kept my inbox full of insightful information and spiritual motivation. Namaste!

To Jerrie Thomas-Hardwick, my amazing spiritual friend. Thank you for always believing in me.

Kudos to Attorney Driskell, for his advice in matters of investigation and detection.

My eternal love to my beautiful granddaughters, Shakira Davis, Areill Davis, Jasmine Jones, Kristian Brandon, Jaleyah and Jaleesa Davis. Thank you for blessing me with five beautiful great-grandchildren, LeArea, Camille, Adrian, Ayden, and Zander. I'm so grateful their life on earth will extends far beyond mine.

Blessings to Apostle Barry and Doretha Dunn for their prayers, friendship and encouragement, and to all my beautiful family and friends who have been waiting for me to complete this book, so we can discuss it!

My love always to all my sisters Jean Darnell, Connie Davis, Vera Robinson-Watson, Berna Lang, Robin Miller, Ruby Breaux-Parks and Charlene Ndi-Jones. Your love, support and friendship is priceless.

Love and gratitude to Gerald Davis, you have been a great father, brother and friend. Thanks to you and Betty for rising to the occasion with your love and support. You are loved.

Love to my nephew Anthony Turner aka Ynot, thank you for making me smile and encouraging me to never stop living the dream.

Thanks to my solider Bradley Brookes for teaching me how to fight on the battlefield of life.

It's ready!

In Loving Memory of

Marion Turner & Lonnie Davis,
the best parents ever

and

Dedicated in Love to My Son,
John W. Davis

Chapter 1

"Mother, where are you taking me?"

The old woman turned slowly, shaking uncontrollably, as she pulled her daughter towards the top of the steps. Despite the crooked smile that etched across her weathered and wrinkled face, her daughter could still recognize the strange look in her eyes that signaled something was wrong, and she hesitated.

"What's the problem, Danielle, don't you trust me? Haven't I always looked out for you and your sister?"

"Yes, Mama."

Danielle was bewildered. She glanced around the damp wooded area and felt a coldness come over her entire body. No matter how fast she walked her legs seemed to be moving in slow motion. She noted the sounds of footsteps coming their way. Stopping, she begged her Mother to tell her what was going on. "Mama, wait...wait...wait... I hear footsteps."

Trying to get her daughter to move swiftly, she grabbed her by the arm, speaking firmly under her breath, "Come, Danielle, there's no time to waste. Just know that I'm doing this for you."

The old woman paused for a moment, looked into Danielle's eyes and said, "You, my daughter, are a gem. You're a beautiful woman and deserve much more than I can provide. If your father had not left us in debt with the government, God rest his soul, things would be different. But I've run out of time and money, and it looks like God's too busy to help, so we have to do whatever we can to survive."

Danielle snatched her arm out of her mother's grip. "Mama, what are you talking about?"

"I refuse to watch you waste your life away as I did. You can have everything the world has to offer. The beauty God blessed you with will soon bring you a life of wealth and happiness."

"I am happy, Mama. I love you and Dior, and next year Jon and I will be married."

Dasheen's eyes saddened as she whispered harshly, "Hush child! Mama's not going to let you marry Jon. He's a fine young man, but he's as poor as a church mouse. I didn't have a problem with you marrying Jon until his father died. Did you think his daddy's wife was going to give that boy and his mother one red cent of Downing money? From the moment old man Downing got her maid pregnant, everything changed for the worst. Jon and his mother have been an embarrassment to Ms. Downing for over twenty years."

Dasheen held out her hand in supplication to her daughter. "Don't you understand?" she whispered. "Downing's body wasn't cold before she schemed both of them out of their inheritance. Now Jon is just another bastard child left to provide for himself and his poor old mother."

Emotion overtaking her, Dasheen began shaking harder. "If I allow you to marry Jon you'll be trapped on the island of St. Thomas barefoot and pregnant for the rest of your life. It's my responsibility, as your mother, to get him out of your life. I have an urge to write that boy's name on a piece of paper, place it in my shoes, and walk all the way to Haiti with it."

"Mama, stop talking nonsense. Please don't send me away. I love Jon and he loves me. Times are changing. This is the twenty-first century. You can't send me away. We both have dreams and plans to go to college, and make a better life for everyone, including you and his mother."

"Hush child, I have a better plan. There will be no more talking. Wipe your eyes and remember the old West Indian proverb, 'hot lub soon cool.' One day you'll look back and thank me for this."

"I don't think so, Mama. I don't think so."

Wise beyond her years, Danielle had always obeyed her mother's every wish. But not tonight. She leaned towards her mother with a sad smile and engulfed her in a hug. She looked over Dasheen's frail shoulder and saw four men standing by a row of stately swaying palm trees. The swift movement of the trade winds caused the trees to dance in the tropical breeze.

Surprisingly quiet and still was Alex Gunn, Governor of the U.S. Virgin Islands. His bigger than life stature and loud, boisterous voice could easily give one the creeps. Beside him stood two local men she faintly recognized. The fourth man was a tall handsome white man; a stranger to Danielle. He looked American. All eyes were facing her with a shocking look of disbelief.

Staring questioningly at the men, Danielle stepped away from her mother and started walking backwards. In a trembling voice Danielle asked, "Governor, what are you doing here?"

The stranger walked directly towards Danielle, took her long slender hands into his and slowly turned her around admiring her from head to toe. Danielle's smooth bronze colored skin was covered with tiny drops of moisture causing her skin to glisten. Her full succulent lips of red and her expressive amber colored eyes caught the stranger's complete and undivided attention. He voice was low and strangely captivating. "Stunning, young lady. Absolutely stunning."

Turning to the old lady, the stranger said quietly, "Dasheen, your daughter is a beautiful woman. She shines from within. I would be pleased to have her by my side." He turned to the man beside him, "You did well, Governor."

"Indeed, I did," he replied proudly.

Struggling to get a grip on the situation, Danielle pulled her hands away from the handsome stranger and gave her mother a questioning glance. She took one step forward and spoke firmly, "What in the world is going on here?"

Dasheen stepped forward. Clearing her throat, she then addressed the men, "Gentlemen, I practically dragged Danielle here, I didn't have the opportunity to explain all the details of our meeting."

Governor Gunn moved toward Dasheen clumsily through the lush bushes. Puffing on his black cigar, he leaned back on his enormous feet. Gunn's cigar smoke hung like a cloud in the still of the night. He bellowed, "Then tell the damn girl why she's here."

The two local men laughed; that did not improve Danielle's disposition. She went from confused to angry as their laughter echoed and lingered in her ears.

Attempting to comfort Danielle, her mother spoke firmly, "Pay these clowns no attention, my dear. I brought you here to meet your future husband. He's a rich and powerful man and can provide you and our family with the life we rightfully deserve."

Once again, Danielle faced her mother, this time with tears streaming down her beautiful face. She pleaded, "Don't do this, Mama. Nothing good will come of this. You love money so much that you're willing to sell me to the highest bidder?"

The men covered their ears as Danielle screeched, "Dog run fo' he character, hog run fo' he life. Tonight, I am the hog." She turned to her mother. "My spirit is saddened, and my heart belongs to Jon. I beg you mother to abandon this craziness and return home with me, and we'll forget this ever happened. "

Laughing, Governor Gunn approached Danielle and said, "Young lady, you are as foolish as you are beautiful. You have been given an opportunity of a lifetime. Women all over the world would sell their souls for the charmed life you will be living."

Glancing at her mother, Danielle tried hard to find a glimpse of the woman she loved and respected so dearly. She turned her attention to Gunn, a man she felt was the most despicable person in the world and spoke rudely, "Then by all means give the opportunity to one of them and leave me out of this horrible nightmare, I'm not for rent or for sale."

Danielle whispered hoarsely, "Since we're quoting West Indian proverbs, here's one for you, Mother, 'What eye don' see heart don' grieve fo'.'"

"Be careful young lady," warned Gunn. "Let me make one thing perfectly clear. This is not your decision. Your mother has given you a chance for a better life, and the opportunity to rid your family from the large debt owed to the government. If it was left up to me, your backside would be on the boat to who knows where with the other girls."

Stunned, Danielle replied, "Girls? What other girls?"

The governor, now agitated, said, "Don't worry your pretty little head about that. I'll tell you one thing for sure, you got the wrong damn man. If you cause any more embarrassment to me or your mama, someone will suffer."

Danielle looked at him and laughed.

Full of rage, Gunn replied, "When rat see cat he nebber laugh."

Danielle saw her fate was sealed. She sunk into a deep state of sadness. Feeling alone and defeated she replied, "And cane don't grow like grass."

Gunn yelled, "We're not growing cane here, missy. Now stop your foolishness and prepare for the biggest day of your pitiful life."

Danielle rolled her eyes in exasperation, then stared at his pitted face and oversized belly. "I can't go with you now. I have unfinished business and I didn't pack any clothing to travel. If you allow me to bid farewell to my friends and family, I will meet you here tomorrow at the same time."

Rocking back and forth on his heels and polluting the air with clouds of cigar smoke, the governor said, "Just how foolish do you think the Governor of the Virgin Islands is, young lady?"

"No, Governor, no," the American stranger yelled. "I'll handle this."

Danielle watched as the stranger walked slowly towards her. She did her best to shield herself, but his body invaded her space so closely they shared the same oxygen.

He lowered his head and whispered softly into her left ear, "Allow me the pleasure of introducing myself. I'm Robert Kelsey and I'm sure this has been quite an emotional day for you. I assure you I mean you no harm. I'm doing everything in my power to protect you. Unlike this present situation, you will be granted the opportunity to make your own decisions and chart your own destiny. As for now, I need you to just trust me and understand my intentions are completely honorable. I will personally give you the chance to take care of your business and communicate with your friends later in the week. I can't guarantee you happiness, but I can guarantee you freedom. It will take some time for you to understand, but when you do, your opinion of this situation will definitely change."

Danielle could no longer control her emotions; she had no dignity. With her head lowered, looking at the ground, tears flowed like the morning rain. She replied, "It's hard for me to imagine good in a situation arranged like this. I feel like my ancestors who were sold like animals on the auction block."

Robert replied, "I assure you, beautiful lady. The life which awaits you will never resemble the life your ancestors had to endure."

She glanced into his eyes and said, "Wha' yo' do me nobody see, wha' I do yo' everybody see."

He removed a handkerchief from his pants pocket and gently wiped the tears from her eyes. Robert wanted to offer some comfort to Danielle, so speaking respectfully he said, "I promise you I will be as understanding as I possibly can, but I will never tolerate disrespect from you or anyone else. I will never disrespect you. We will both require time to get to know each other. I'm hoping that you'll at least test the waters before you refuse to take a swim. You might not realize it now, but eventually you will understand the methods to my madness, which I can honestly say are for your well-being, Danielle."

"Oh, how silly of me," Danielle said in a low sarcastic voice.

Robert laughed and replied, "Then let's go, sarcasm and clothing are not needed on this trip. There's plenty of clothing at my estate. If you are not satisfied with what you find, we'll take a private jet to New York or Paris to shop. The choice is yours."

Reluctantly, Danielle replied, "I'll keep that in mind, sir." As confused as she was about her current situation, she felt she had no choice but to trust the words of the American, since he was the only person who genuinely seem to be concerned.

With a puzzled expression, Robert replied, "Sir? A little formal isn't it? You may call me Robert or Kelsey, whichever suits you. Why don't you take a moment to compose yourself? You've had an exhausting day."

Chapter 2

Danielle studied the situation before she replied again. Dasheen had power over Danielle. Governor Gunn had power over Dasheen. And Robert Kelsey had power over Gunn. Everyone but Governor Gunn was stepping blindly into the business of sex slavery.

Danielle tried to back away, but they were behind her and around her. She stood with her head lowered, trembling and afraid. For the first time Danielle was speechless. As unhappy as she was to be in her current situation, she couldn't help but wonder how Jon would react to her disappearance. At that moment she turned to Robert, requesting to speak to her mother alone.

"Very well," he replied.

Danielle walked towards her mother, who was just a few feet away. Still crying, she pleaded, "Mama, I simply can't go without speaking with Jon. Please help me. I need you to convince them to let me return home tonight."

Bound tightly by her commitment to the governor, Dasheen replied, "That's not a good idea, baby. Jon will only interfere in your departure. I can't risk that happening. I'm here for you, but I must leave you now. When you get to your new home and everyone is asleep, write Jon a letter explaining everything to him. I will collect it and deliver it to him."

"Will you, Mama?"

"Yes, Danielle, I will be the link between you and Jon. Now, please go, Danielle. I pray you have a safe journey. We will meet tomorrow at 12 noon at Red Hook Marina."

Taking her mother at her word, Danielle complied and cried out, "I love you, Mama."

"I love you, too, baby. Please don't worry. Everything will be just fine. Fo' night bring day."

A sobbing Dasheen turned her head, took a deep breath, and disappeared into the overgrown bush. She had left her sweet Danielle with Robert Kelsey in hopes of him affording her a better life, now she had to live with her decision.

Even though Danielle had a close relationship with her mother, she had promised her father on his death bed that she would never abandon her mother and sister. She considered the commitment to her father to be a badge of honor and had every intention of wearing it until the day she died. But never in her wildest imagination did she think she would be sold off like an animal to provide and protect her family.

For a second all was quiet, then in a loud and obnoxious voice Gunn said, "Women. They are so fickle. They never know what they really want. Let's get this show on the road."

The governor's men hurried Danielle along the edge of the damp, overgrown bush and crumbled pathway to Red Hook Marina. As they reached the end of the path she spotted a beautiful white yacht waiting at the pier. She had no idea of her destination, but it became clear that to return home again, she would have to travel by air or sea.

The captain was casually standing in front of the yacht, awaiting their arrival. He was tall, slender, and, from a distance, it appeared he was wearing dreadlocks. She stood with her head lowered glancing down at his sparkling white shoes, and slowly worked her way up to his neck. His crisp white uniform was shining as bright as the morning sun. Danielle's eyes shifted to his name tag and saw the name Bill engraved in gold.

In a pleasant and friendly voice, Captain Bill greeted Danielle, "Good evening, Ms. Harrigan. May I help you aboard?"

Danielle was too embarrassed to look into his face, but he spoke in such a respectful tone she couldn't help but wonder how he knew her name. All she could think of was everyone on the island of St. Thomas would soon know that she had been sold into slavery to the highest bidder. She slowly raised her head and recognized a friendly face. She recognized him as Bill Nikko. He had one arm extended towards her, as if he was preparing to catch her if she fell.

Danielle gave Bill a quick smile but pretended not to know him. She didn't want anyone to know he was the husband of her good friend, Robyn, and that she trusted him. For the first time since the unfolding of her bizarre night, she felt God remembered who she was and how much she needed his help. All she could say was, "Thank you, God, thank you."

As everyone took their seats, Danielle began to make small talk with Robert. She was trying to find out in a discreet manner if Bill Nikko was the regular captain of his vessel without disclosing her association.

11

"So, Robert, do you have your captain's license as well?"

"For God's sake no," he replied. "I have enough to worry about. I leave the safety of my family and friends in the capable hands of Captain Bill. I'm really quite lucky to get him. My last captain returned to the states. But I had the good fortune of running into Bill at the same time he was looking for a job. We've been sailing together now for a little over a month. He's a great guy and takes his job very seriously. I hope he'll be around for a long time. Then I can continue to focus on enjoying my guests."

Danielle was relieved to hear his response. This gave her hope that she would be able to escape when the time permitted. This was an insurance policy she was sure she could cash in on. It immediately relieved the stress that was weighing heavily on her shoulders.

Large swollen waves moved the yacht away from the pier. Danielle couldn't help but notice how the still-blue sky was lined with clusters of sparkling stars. It was hard for her to imagine how instinctively beautiful the night was even though she had just participated in a battle for her freedom with her mother, the governor, and a white stranger. Danielle had no idea of her destination. She could only assume it was St. John. Either way, it was much too far from home.

Danielle breathed a momentary sigh of relief as she observed that Robert had left Governor Gunn and his two clowns at the pier. She had always found Gunn to be obnoxious and egotistical. It was hard for her to understand how he was elected to the position of governor. All she knew was that not spending another second in his company was a much-needed gift from God.

Robert sat quietly, but he felt uneasy. He was conflicted. The spoiled, egotistical Robert had occasional thoughts of intimacy, while the passionate, sensitive Robert played a huge role in rescuing this beautiful young woman from her demonic mother. Robert was ashamed of his egotistical behavior. He knew his intentions were honorable; however, it was becoming very clear that he was smitten with the beauty and grace of Danielle. For the first time, he felt completely without power. Something strange was happening and he was afraid of what the outcome would be. There was something mystical about the woman that sat beside him on the brief ride to James Island. As the yacht got closer to the dock, Roberts's anxiety rose as Danielle sat quietly observing the seamanship of Captain Bill.

Danielle blurted, "I thought we were traveling to St. John?"

Robert replied, "No, beautiful lady, we're traveling to James Island."

"I've never heard of James Island."

"Oh? It's a private island that's been in our family for over thirty years. I certainly hope it meets with your approval."

"I'm sure it will."

As they drifted toward the dock, Captain Bill secured the yacht. "We've reached our destination. I trust you enjoyed your trip, Ms. Harrigan."

Robert stood up immediately to assist Danielle off the yacht. She turned to Captain Bill and thanked him for a safe journey. Tipping his cap, Captain Bill replied, "The pleasure was mine, Ms. Harrigan."

Robert looked at her and smiled, "You're not only beautiful, Danielle, you're also a lady of class and elegance."

"Thank you, Robert," she replied. "I see your unorthodox ways still have a bit of chivalry in them."

Danielle had no problem with small talk with Robert, all she could think about was her plan to escape with the help of Captain Bill.

"It's been a long day," Robert said. "Maria will show you to your villa." He leaned towards Danielle to kiss her goodnight, she turned her head and his lips landed on her left cheek.

"Goodnight, Robert."

"Goodnight, Danielle."

At that moment, a smiling, short, small framed Hispanic woman appeared at the dock. She reached for Danielle's hand and said, "Hola. ¿Cómo estás? my name is Maria. This way please."

Robert smiled at Danielle. "You might not find me appealing, but I promise you'll find Maria irresistible."

As Danielle stepped up to the entry of the estate, her eyes and mouth were both agape. She never envisioned such beauty. It was like turning the pages of a prestigious home magazine. James Island resembled a luxurious resort in the middle of nowhere. Captivated by the beauty of the island, Danielle paused in disbelief and said, "How impressive, Robert. It's absolutely breathtaking."

Pleased with Danielle's response, Robert responded, "I'm glad you like it. I can't wait until morning so you can see every intricate detail."

Robert stayed behind, placing her in Maria's capable hands. But his eyes followed Danielle's every step, until the ladies were no longer in view. Maria directed Danielle past two large white villas. At the third she was prompted to enter.

It was a lovely, romantic villa. In the middle of the room stood a bleached mahogany handcrafted poster bed draped with layers of airy white gauze which danced around the bed like floating ballerinas. The air was fresh, and the scent of the flowers were captured in every corner of the room.

The entire villa was designed in pure white and filled with fragrant lavender and bouquets of pink roses, which adorned the top of a beautiful marble console.

For the first time, the evening's despair began to fade into the night. Danielle found herself in a peaceful state of mind. She took a deep breath and danced around every inch of the villa. When she opened the exquisitely designed walk-in closet, she found fashions fit for a queen. Linen and silk dresses framed the back wall of the massive closet, while shoes in every hue were placed neatly along mahogany shelves. Everything was beautiful like the replica of a Parisian high-end boutique—a dream come true. But at the same time, it was her worst nightmare. She found herself thinking about how wonderful it would be to share life with Jon on Robert's amazing island.

Aware that morning would soon come, Danielle decided to take a long hot bath. She wanted to fill the tub, but couldn't find the faucets. At that moment there was a knock on the door.

She heard Maria's voice, "Hola, goodnight, Ms. Danielle."

Danielle responded, "Maria! I'm so glad to see you."

"Ah! Is something wrong?"

"Yes, very wrong indeed. How do I fill the bath tub?"

Maria laughed, pointing to a silver plate on the wall. "Touchy, touchy."

Danielle touched the silver plate lightly and magical streams of water fell like rain from the sky. Laughing like a child, Danielle turned to Maria and said, "Now I've seen everything."

"Not quite, there's more to see," replied Maria.

Maria removed three scented candles from a large wicker basket and placed them around the sunken tub in the bathroom, then carefully placed three glass globes over each one to prevent the flames from dying. She walked quietly to the side table, turned on a beautifully crafted chrome radio where soft and soothing music escaped from each strategically placed speaker.

Maria leaned toward Danielle, gave her a big hug, and said, "Goodnight. I hope you like living here, Ms. Danielle."

Danielle replied politely, "Goodnight, Maria. Thank you."

Maria dimmed the lights and walked swiftly out the door.

Danielle knew exactly what Robert meant. Maria truly was irresistible. She was warm and caring, scrutinizing every little detail to ensure others were happy and comfortable. Danielle was beginning to enjoy the enticements of her imprisonment, as the sweet sounds of Jon Lucien flowed softly from the speakers. She sat on the bed unbuttoning her white cotton blouse. Peeling away every layer of fabric that draped her flawless body, then emerged herself in a tub full of lavender scented bubbles. The spa treatment was so therapeutic that within a matter of minutes Danielle had forgotten that she had been sold into the care of a man she knew nothing about and into a life she found momentarily fascinating.

Thinking over Robert's conversation, Danielle realized he was absolutely correct. There was nothing a woman could want that couldn't be found at his estate. She even found stationary. The night had been filled with chaos and confusion. As much as she needed to communicate with Jon, she didn't know where or how to begin her letter, so she retired for the night in hopes of having a clear head in the morning.

Danielle nestled peacefully into the majestic mahogany bed for the night. A wonderful sense of peace filled the room. She laid her head down on a cloud of pillows and fell fast asleep.

But on the other side of the estate, Robert was again in conflict with himself regarding the methods he had used to bring Danielle into his world. He had no idea what morning would bring, and what action he would take if Danielle requested her release. His night would be filled with uncertainty and vodka tonics. Just as he decided to retire, the telephone rang. He hesitated momentarily, then lifted the receiver.

"Goodnight."

Now that she had Robert on the phone she panicked, not knowing what to say.

"Goodnight," he repeated. "Who is this?"

"It's Dasheen. I'm calling to check on my daughter. How is she?"

Robert exhaled and replied, "Danielle is fine. She has retired for the night. I promised I would take care of her, and that's exactly what I plan to do. What's the matter?" he asked in an irritated tone. "I find your call perplexing. We both agreed that you would not contact Danielle, or me, at this number until we were able to establish a bond. You have the money you requested, and your daughter has the life you wanted her to have."

In a lowered voice Dasheen replied, "That's all I wanted to hear, sir. I pray that you do the right thing. If you don't, my ancestors from hell will rise up against you and Governor Gunn, and no island in the entire Caribbean will be able to protect you."

Robert set up abruptly in his chair, spilling vodka on his sharply creased pants. With a trembling voice he replied, "What the hell is that supposed to mean, Dasheen?"

"The meaning isn't important unless you fail to do right by my daughter. If you don't, I promise you the meaning of my words will invade your world for all the days of your natural life."

He heard the click of the phone hanging up on the other end. Robert now found it harder to relax. He wondered if Dasheen's conversation was that of a helpless mother trying to scare him into taking care of her daughter, or if she really did have demonic family members waiting patiently to cast spells of witchcraft on him.

Robert was no fool. Although he wasn't a native islander, he knew not to dismiss the harsh reality that witchcraft was alive and well in the Caribbean.

Chapter 3

As the morning sunlight peeked through the white partially opened plantation shutters, Danielle opened her eyes to her reality. She tossed the covers aside and threw her toned legs over the edge of the bed and gently rubbed the back of her long slender neck. A flash of depression came over her as she realized she had fallen asleep without writing one word to her beloved Jon.

Wrapped snuggly in a fluffy white terry cloth robe, Danielle began to play back the events of the night before. She tried desperately to grasp an understanding of how things had come to be. As a dutiful daughter she had accepted her mother's request, but at the same time she had abandoned Jon and Dior. She knew that writing a letter to Jon would ease the blow of her departure and soothe her own conscious until she could escape her captor.

She rose and walked slowly towards the mahogany desk next to a beautiful picture window. She opened the center drawer and picked up two sheets of ivory linen stationary. She held the stationary in her trembling hands, and found her mind racing on what to say. She took a deep breath and began writing. Tears dropped from her beautiful amber-colored eyes.

My dear Jon,

I'm sure this letter will come as a surprise, as I left without a word. However, the truth is that I have much information of the highest importance to share with you, my love. Where do I begin? It appears that father left a large tax debt with the local government, and mother has been working to pay it off.

The problem with all of this is the outstanding debt and interest, tacked on by the government, has made it an impossible task for mother to bear. More importantly, Governor Gunn has advised Mother that the government will seize our home in Eastside Bay unless she complies with his request for me to wed Robert Kelsey.

Robert Kelsey is a wealthy white American who lives on James Island, where I was taken by boat last night and now being held hostage. The money my family owes the government will be paid to the government only after the wedding ceremony.

I have no idea how much time we have, but we must move with a sense of urgency. Jon, you must find a way to free me from this craziness, but please be careful, my love, for evil often lurks around people with evil ways. I can only hope you know how much I love you, and I would never leave your side for anything or anyone. If Ms. Downing would agree to loan you the money for the delinquent taxes, Mother would be free to live without fear of losing our home and her daughter.

My darling, Bill Nikko is the captain of Robert Kelsey's yacht. It is my intention to steal a moment to speak with him regarding my escape from James Island. Mother will be the communication link for us, so please remain in touch with her, as I will simply die if I'm unable to share my thoughts with you.

Loving you to distraction,

Your Danielle

Danielle felt a sigh of relief once her letter to Jon was complete, but now she had to find a safe place to hide it. She knew it wasn't a good idea to leave it in the room, not knowing what level of privacy she had. She felt the safest place would be her body. She placed the letter into a matching linen envelope and sealed it with a kiss, folded it in half, and attached it to the inside of her bra with a safety pin.

When the task was completed, she washed her face in cold water to help reduce the swelling from her crying eyes. As she looked in the mirror, she wondered, for the first time, if her God-given beauty had been a curse. It was difficult for her to understand how a person could look upon another human being and decide they would possess them without winning the heart and the approval of that person.

Danielle glanced at the clock and realized that time was moving quickly. She knew she had to get in motion if she was to meet her mother at Red Hook Marina. Just as she started towards the closet, she heard a light knock on the door. It was Maria.

"Good morning, Ms. Danielle, breakfast will be served in thirty minutes on the front terrace."

"Good morning to you, Maria. Thank you, I will be there shortly."

For a moment, Danielle thought her heart would stop beating. She didn't know who or what to expect when she left the villa. She immediately fell to her knees and prayed for God to direct her path and protect her from all who tried to harm her and her family. The only thing she was sure of was clothing wouldn't be a problem, and if she was going to be humiliated, she would do it in style.

After carefully examining all the clothing she selected a white linen dress, which highlighted her slender but shapely body. She accented her tiny waist with a braided leather belt adorned with enameled seashells, and allowed her beautiful black hair to fall freely on her shoulders.

She looked in the mirror to make sure everything was fitting properly. Fashion was something she loved to play with, and Robert Kelsey had given her an opportunity to play beyond her wildest dreams. Danielle's skin was flawless, so she only required a little moisturizer and gloss to help protect her lips from the sun. She slipped on her own shoes, and immediately kicked them off when she spotted a pair of Tory Burch white ankle-wrapped sandals embellished with tiny sea shells and a two-inch heel. They were the prettiest sandals she had ever seen.

Danielle heard footsteps approaching her door. This time the knock was heavier. When she opened it, she saw Robert standing before her. She was surprised to see that he was more handsome this morning than last night.

Robert stepped backward with delight and greeted Danielle. "Good morning, beautiful. I trust you slept well last night?"

"I slept as well as I could under the circumstances. And you, Robert, did you sleep well?"

"Not really, I was slightly uncomfortable having you here against your will."

"Really! Does that mean I'm free to go home?"

"You are always free to go, Danielle. We can discuss it over breakfast? Are you hungry?"

"Yes. A little."

"Great! Allow me to escort you to the terrace, one can easily get loss if you don't know where you're going."

Danielle pondered for a minute, then calmly said, "Robert, if I didn't know better, I could confuse you for a charming gentleman, but your behavior yesterday makes me believe otherwise."

Robert nodded, "Alright, I deserve that. I've had my way for so long sometimes I forget that I can't control everything."

"Absolutely."

Upon arriving at the terrace, the ambiance was soothing and relaxing. All one could see was crystal blue water and white sandy beach behind the backdrop of the bright morning sun. The table was set in a rainbow of colors with cascading runners of bright red bougainvillea taking center stage.

Danielle's face broke into a wide smile and she nodded approvingly and said, "All of this for me?"

Robert, happy to see a smile on her face replied, "Yes, beautiful lady, all of this is for you. You know, if you give me half a chance you just might get to like me."

"If you're trying to win me over, Mr. Kelsey, it will take more than a few charming words and a fabulous veranda."

Robert extended his right hand over his heart and muttered, "Oh that hurts, and I thought we were making progress."

"Rome wasn't built in a day, and neither will our friendship."

Robert pulled the chair out for Danielle, then took the seat directly across from her so he could look into her amazingly almond shaped eyes. There was something he found so captivating about her eyes. He took advantage of every opportunity to look into them.

"Please don't take this the wrong way, but I'm surprised that you speak so eloquently. Your style and grace are unbelievable."

She sat her fork down, looked Robert directly in his eyes and said, "Is it unbelievable because you feel that rich white Americans are the only group of people who appreciate being educated and poised. This isn't the 1800s, Robert. I may not have traveled the world; however, when you live in paradise, you're exposed to various cultures who bring their knowledge with them and graciously share it at your request. I don't have your resources, but I possess the same thirst for knowledge as you. One day my dreams will become my reality."

"Really?" Turning his attention towards the ocean Robert asked, "What are your dreams, Danielle?

"I won't tire you with my dreams over breakfast, I will save that conversation when we're at a loss for words."

Taken aback by Danielle's response, Robert inquired, "Are you sure you're only twenty-two? Your behavior is so mature."

Danielle paused to think about her reply. "I have to attribute my maturity to the death of my father. He died from a fall when I was fifteen years old. It was impossible for me to remain a child. I promised my father on his death bed that I would look after Mother and Dior. I had to grow up to help our family survive. I was expected to attend school, work after school, clean the house, and cook. There were times I wanted to give up and do nothing, but watching my mother work so hard to make sure we had the same opportunities girls with two parents had, made me stronger and wiser. My only regret is that my childhood disappeared before I had a chance to enjoy it. Now I'm no longer in control of my destiny."

With a concerned look on his face, Robert picked up Danielle's delicate and slender hands and said, "That's not true. You're more in control than you realize. If you think that telling me these things will make me want to change my mind about having you as a guest, I assure you the more I converse with you, the more I admire you and appreciate your company. There is so much more to you than your beauty. I've never met anyone quite like you. I'm afraid to let you go, in fear of losing your friendship. Yet, I fear that if I hold you against your will, I'll also lose you. I'm in a hell of a jam."

It was a beautiful day. The sky was lined with dripping clouds as time passed swiftly. The two became relaxed in each other's company, talking, laughing, and watching the boats sailing slowly at sea while eating salmon, cream cheese with bagels, washing it down with an occasional sip of lemon-flavored water. It was apparent that the circumstances Danielle and Robert found themselves in created the opportunity for them to know each other faster than normal. The quiet of the day was interrupted by the ringing of the telephone.

Robert hesitated momentarily, then reluctantly answered the call. "Good morning. Robert Kelsey."

"Good morning, Robert, this is the governor."

"Yes, Governor."

"I will not be meeting you today. I'm sorry, but something more pressing has come up."

"Not a problem, Governor. Give me a call later in the week."

"Very well," he said and hung up.

"Gunn will not be joining us today, so I guess you have to spend the day with me."

Robert was taken by surprise by Gunn's announcement. However, he was all too happy to spend the day alone with Danielle. As for Danielle, she didn't care. She was more concerned about meeting her mother and sending the letter to Jon.

Danielle spoke in a lovely and quiet voice, "Will you ask Captain Bill to take me into town to see my mother?"

"I'm sorry, Danielle. Bill has already taken the yacht to St. Thomas to pick up supplies. Why don't we send for your mother? We can continue our conversation, and your mother will see for herself I'm taking good care of you. Would you like that?" he asked directly.

She smiled shyly as she nodded. "I would like that very much."

"Very well," Robert said. "I'll call Dasheen and tell her to meet Captain Bill at Red Hook Marina."

Robert grabbed the phone off the table and began searching the directory for Dasheen's number. Danielle's eyes were focused on him as he picked up his cup of coffee, then sat it back down without taking a drink. He hesitated about his decision to call Dasheen. He looked at the sadness in Danielle's eyes and made the call without further hesitation.

Dasheen was shocked to receive a call from Robert. She couldn't help but wonder what was going on. Governor Gunn had given her instruction not to contact Danielle until Robert had established a strong bond and agreed on a wedding date. Dasheen's excitement was now replaced with concern. To make sure she didn't miss the boat, she grabbed her purse and rushed out the door, without telling anyone where she was going.

Robert had made Danielle happy by the invitation he extended to her mother, but what he didn't know was if she would want to remain on James Island or return home. He knew another attempt had to be made to persuade Danielle to stay with him before Dasheen arrived.

Robert gathered his thoughts. He knew in order for Danielle to stay out of the clutches of the human trafficking, she would need to remain on the island. There was no getting around it, the truth had to be told. Although he had no idea how Danielle would be affected once she found out it was her own mother who arranged to sell her for compensation. Even he was sickened when he found out about the plan. It was at that very moment he decided to purchase her freedom from Dasheen. In a way, they both were victims of a well-thought-out plan by her mother and Gunn. He knew it would be a risky thing to do, since Danielle was so loyal to her mother. All he could think of was what would happen if she didn't believe him. It would only be a matter of minutes before she would discover that Dasheen would never allow her to leave the island.

Faced with this dilemma, he discloses to Danielle the treacherous details of the entire plan which were orchestrated by her mother. He watched as her expression changed drastically. Robert expressed to her that she had two options only: one—remain here with him and live a good life, or two—go back home and be sold into the sex trade business.

Chapter 4

It had been a long and informative morning. In total disbelief, Danielle retreated to her villa, reclined on the pillow, and cried herself to sleep. When she reopened her eyes, the villa appeared dark, except for a candle Maria had lit. Danielle sat upright to gain her bearings. She heard two sets of footsteps approaching the door. There was a light knock, and she recognized Maria's voice.

"Ms. Danielle, your mother has arrived."

Danielle was anxious. There were so many things she wanted to discuss, and finally she would be able to send her letter to Jon, but she wouldn't need the letter if her mother denied Robert's accusations. She would simply return home with her mother, if there were no delinquent taxes to be paid. The thought of returning to St. Thomas with her mother brought a boost of energy to her tired body. Danielle swiftly jumped from the bed, ran to the door, and embraced her mother with vigor.

Dasheen took a sharp deep breath and said, "Danielle, you're squeezing my old bones."

"I'm sorry mother, a part of me is so happy to see you, and another part of me is furious."

"Furious, why are you furious, child?"

Danielle spoke firmly, "This morning at breakfast Robert told me it was you who arranged to sell me for $100,000. You made me believe that I was brought to James Island against my will to help settle a family debt. I begged you to take me back home, and you refused. You lied to me. Mother, how could you?"

"Robert is a foolish man. I guess your undeniable beauty has gone to his silly rich head."

Danielle fumed. "What does that mean? And what does it have to do with the lies you told?"

"It was only a little white lie. I did what any mother would have done for her child. I just couldn't sit back and watch you throw your life away with Jon. Honey, you are pure magic and you have been blessed with powers that you have yet to discover. I would never place you in harm's way. Believe me, if someone did bring harm to you, they, and anyone associated with them, would suffer beyond their wildest imagination. Danielle, you are twenty-two in body and thirty in mind. I beg you to let the thirty-year old woman lead the way. As I've told you before, Jon is a fine young man and will make someone a great husband one day, but until that day, you need to set your sights on someone else. Jon isn't going to give up his opportunity for a better life; he would leave you behind in a heartbeat."

Dasheen walked around the room, hands stretched in the air, shouting, "Look around you, look how you're living girl. In this world you must take advantage of every opportunity that comes your way. Remember smart girls marry for money, foolish girls marry for love. They are the girls who get left behind with a broken heart, a house full of babies, and a spoiled belly and broke. Do you think I'm going to let that happen to you?"

Danielle sprang up, hands tightly together. "Jon and I will earn our own money. Once we graduate from college and start our careers, everything will be fine."

Dasheen took Danielle's head into her hands. "Girl, please stop your foolishness. You can marry more money in five minutes than you can make in a lifetime? Robert Kelsey is a very wealthy young man. He's connected politically, he's charming, and he's white. That's a powerful combination and every white American woman's dream. You are a beautiful African star. You can have it all. Robert worships you and will provide a life you'll one day come to appreciate. Danielle, I'm pleading with you to stop acting like Jon is the catch of the century. I spoke with that boy yesterday."

Danielle's eyes lit up. "You did, what he said?"

"He was jumping around like a headless chicken. Excited about traveling across the ocean to Babylon to tour New York University, and find housing. I told him we had a family emergency and you would be away for a few weeks. He's leaving in the morning. Which will give you time to explore your options. I will take your letter to him tonight."

"Oh, my goodness, Mother. You're lying to everybody. So much has happened, I forgot about his tour. I want to return home and speak with him myself."

"Danielle, both of you appear to be getting in each other's way. Allow Jon to make a good life for himself. If it's meant

31

for you two to be together, the separation will do you good. Remember, a kick to the mare does the stallion no harm. It will either strengthen your relationship or determine that you weren't meant to be together. If you continue this relationship with Jon before you are able to provide for yourself, the day will come when you will both resent each other. Tell me you're not a bit excited about this whole situation."

"No, Mother, I'm not excited. I'm intrigued, but who wouldn't be? It's like a dream."

"Exactly, so why would you allow a dream like this to slip away from you without giving it a chance?"

"Because it's not my dream, it's yours. I wish you were younger. Then you could stay here with Robert Kelsey, and I would be happy."

"Nonsense. You're talking nothing but nonsense. While Jon is away, take the time to get to know Robert, see what he has to offer you. When I see Jon, I will tell him you will communicate with him by mail until he returns."

Feeling low and without hope, Danielle hung her head in shame. "Mother, I understand your desire for me to have a better life, but what I don't understand is the disgraceful measures you were willing to subject me to. You were willing to sell the life I love so I could live the life you love. I have always respected your wishes, but this time I'm not sure I can."

"Sure, you can. You can choose to either stand on top of the world, or let the world stand on top of you. Do you realize that if Robert Kelsey hadn't told you that it was me who made this arrangement, you would be singing a different tune this evening? What does that tell you about him?"

"For one thing, it tells me he knows this whole arrangement is a crock of shit."

"You watch your mouth, young lady. I'm still your mother."

"Then why don't you act like a mother. You're acting more like a madam!"

"I can't believe you feel that way. What I'm doing is making sure my daughters have a better life than I did."

"All you're doing is selling me to the highest bidder so you can have the life you never had. Obviously, it doesn't matter what makes me happy. I'm not like you mother, and I'm not looking for money and power. It doesn't make you happy, it only pays the bills."

"You're right. It only pays the bills, and when you can't pay the bills and you have no food and no home, no clothes and no pride, you have nothing. I'm tired of selling fruit and vegetables at the market square to keep a roof over our heads. How do you think I feel with people passing by sticking their noses up in the air acting like they're so much better than me? We've lost many ancestors on that very block where I sell vegetables. Now we have an opportunity to regain some honor for the family."

"I'm not sure we're on the same page, Mother, because I see no honor in the selling of one's body for money."

Dasheen opened her purse. "How much money do you have to pay bills with, Danielle? Do you see any money in my purse? In time you will see. Until then, swallow your pride and help the family any way you can. I don't understand why that's so hard for you. You're just like your damn father; full of stupid ass pride. All he had to do was swallow his pride and go to

Anguilla and get what was rightfully his. But no, he wouldn't do it. He kept saying money wasn't important, that he would take care of his obligations without his family's money."

Danielle walked away, shaking her head.

"Don't walk away from me, young lady. You listen to what I have to say. Never once did your father think about me or the fate of his children. And after his death, he took his selfish pride and his obligations to the grave and left me to provide for the family he created the best way I could."

Crying, Danielle said, "Ok, Mother. I'm sorry Father died and you weren't able to live the life you dreamt. I know having money makes life easier, but having the love of your family and friends is far greater. If you're able to have both, then that's the icing on the cake. I'd rather have the love of my family than any amount of money the world has to offer. I will abide by your wishes and remain on the island with Robert, but only because I have no desire to return home with you, and I'm honoring my father's wishes. I'm confused by your behavior and I feel a little distance will be good for the both of us."

Dasheen grabbed Danielle's arm, pulling her toward her, "Danielle, what are you saying?"

"Mother, I'm saying you're right. Based upon our conversation this evening, I need time to reevaluate my relationship with everyone—including you."

Tears welled in Dasheen's eyes. She couldn't believe that her faithful and loyal daughter wasn't able to understand that everything she was doing was for her. "Very well, have it your way. Be ungrateful and persecute me for wanting you and Dior to have a better life."

"Speaking of Dior, Mother, who do you plan to sell her to?"

Dasheen turned around with a look of rage in her eyes, and before Danielle could say another word Dasheen's hand fell hard across her face. Danielle was in shock. Her face burned like hot coals. She couldn't believe her mother struck her. That was the final straw. Danielle escorted her mother to the door, handed her the letter addressed to Jon, and bid her a goodnight. Danielle was too traumatized to take a breath or shed a tear. She found it ironic that her place of captivity was now her place of solace.

Eventually the face of her mother faded from her memory. For the first time she realized her mother's unspoken sorrow had made it impossible to recognize the underlying unhealthiness that had rooted in their lives. It was obvious things would never be the same. They had reached a crossroads, and it was now time to choose the direction in which she wanted her life to go. Danielle was frustrated, her emotions were as explosive as an active volcano. She knew she needed to speak with Robert, although she wasn't sure what she would say. Her life was spiraling out of control; coupled with periodic fragments of contempt for her mother.

Despite her uneasiness, she pulled herself together and walked regally around the estate looking for Robert. On the main terrace she saw Robert dining with a beautiful American woman. She was petite in stature, and spiked blonde hair framed her face perfectly. As the woman picked up her glass of wine, her freshly manicured fingers were adorned with the most amazing jewels. Danielle paused and turned back towards the villa.

Robert noticed her and called out, "Danielle, come join us. Allow me to introduce you to the first girl to steal my heart, my little sister, Debra."

"Debra, meet my beautiful friend, Danielle."

"Hello, Debra. How are you?"

"I'm fine, darling. You are far more beautiful than my brother described you."

"Thank you, that's kind of you to say."

"Oh my, Robert. Danielle is drop-dead gorgeous and charming. Where did you steal her?"

Robert cleared his throat, "Now, that's a secret I'll never disclose. Danielle, Debra lives in New York, and when she gets bored, which she often does, she travels to James Island to worry me and the local guys to death."

"Don't believe a word he says. He loves it when I come to visit. If I didn't come so often he would sit on this beautiful island and be bored and broke. My extensive travel encourages him to work harder."

Robert, laughed uncontrollably. "What she really means is, she spends all the collateral in the family."

Smiling, Danielle interrupted, "Please forgive my intrusion, I had no idea you had a guest. I wanted to speak with you on a matter of importance, but it can wait until tomorrow."

Immediately, Debra said, "Nonsense. I'm exhausted from the flight and would take great pleasure in retreating to my villa. Again, Danielle, it was a pleasure to meet you."

"The pleasure was mine, Debra."

Robert stood up and gave his sister a hug. "Welcome home, honey. You know your way around, but if you need something just ask Maria."

"I'll do just that. Goodnight, you two love birds. See you in the morning."

Robert and Danielle were both eager for Debra to leave so they could continue their conversation.

Robert sighed, "Debra has had one too many cocktails, her lips seem to be speaking about things she knows nothing about. I apologize for her unnecessary remarks. Now, Danielle, you have my undivided attention. I'm surprised you didn't return to St. Thomas with your mother."

Danielle smiled and took a deep breath. "That makes two of us. I was so excited about her arrival all I could think about was returning home, but after we spoke I felt so betrayed."

Tearfully, Danielle said, "I found it difficult to be in her company." Pondering the enormity of what she just said, Robert nodded his head in support. Danielle looked at Robert. "I can't believe I'm asking this, but I was hoping you would allow me to spend a few more days on the island until I can wrap my head around things and figure out my next step."

He was delighted with her request. "You are most welcome to remain on the island as long as you wish. Maybe you can help keep an eye on Debra. She's a free spirit with no boundaries. Honestly? I hope you choose to never leave. But please know you're free to go anytime your heart desires."

"Thank you, Robert. You're slowly redeeming yourself."

Robert looked to the sky. "It has been said that redemption is good for the soul."

Finding themselves in a happy place, they laughed.

Chapter 5

Contrary to what she thought would happen, Danielle felt safe in her immediate surroundings, and, surprisingly, in the company of Robert Kelsey. It wasn't difficult to be in Robert's company. He was handsome, kind, and easy to talk to.

Danielle let out a long sigh. "It's a beautiful night, Robert. Stars are dancing all over that amazingly blue sky."

Robert lifted his head and watched the night. "Yes, you're right, it is a beautiful night. I sometimes have the tendency to overlook God's creations. I'm lucky you're here to bring it to my attention."

"Are you patronizing me, Robert Kelsey?"

"Who? Me? Would I do that?"

"One must never answer a question with a question, and quite frankly, I'm not sure what you're capable of doing."

"When it comes to you, neither am I."

"Tell me, what were the terms of the agreement?"

Robert's nervousness made a repeat appearance. It was the craziest thing, he was afraid to speak in fear of saying the wrong thing. Danielle watched him becoming jumpy and irritable.

He looked into her eyes. "I feel so stupid even speaking about it. After getting to know you, I feel like a complete ass. For some strange reason when I'm around you, it makes me want to be a better man. I seem to be unraveling at the seams. Believe me when I say no one has ever had that effect on me. Not even my parents."

Danielle laughed, "That's because you're a spoiled brat."

He ran fingers through his long blond hair. "You think so, do you?"

"I don't *think* so, I *know* so."

"Would you like the job of changing me?"

"Absolutely not. The job doesn't pay enough for the frustration I would encounter. Besides, change is something one must commit to do themselves. It's up to you to change what behavior you feel needs changing. No one knows you better than you know yourself. The good, the bad, and the ugly."

Robert laughed, but Danielle continued with her interrogation.

"Now, Robert, don't get off the subject; back to the terms of the arrangement."

To buy himself a little time to formulate an answer, Robert readjusted his chair. "Well, their plan was to bring you to the island. Have you fall madly in love with me and the lifestyle. When that was accomplished, we would plan a small informal wedding ceremony attended by a few close friends and family. My plan was to free you from their plan. Give you an opportunity to make your own choices on how and who you spend your life with."

"You mean there was no courting involved? No meeting of the minds. Just the old caveman mentality: find a woman; hit her over the head; drag her to the cave; get her pregnant; make her cook; and have sex with you for the rest of her life?"

Robert chuckled in amusement to her statement.

"What woman would want a life like that? All the money in the world couldn't entice a good woman. I believe you've bought into the hype that money can buy everything and anything. Money can't buy love, freedom, or loyalty. It can, however, buy sex."

"You're right, and you're wrong."

Raising his hand into the air. "Please don't interrupt me. Let me finish."

"Money can't buy love and loyalty. It can buy sex and it can definitely buy freedom. I didn't buy you for sex, and if that's what you still think, then...look, I bought your freedom. Let me remind you that it was your own mother who was willing...no, she was selling you, her daughter, into the sex slave trade. I, the rich white American guy, found out about it. Now, I could not solve the whole problem of the sex trade, but I had the power and means in this instance to save one person."

There was a brief moment of silence as he continued.

"It's really hard to have this conversation with you, because it pains me to even think that anybody can get caught up in the despicable crime of human trafficking. But there you were. I saw you around the island several times, I had no idea who you were. I thought you were the most beautiful woman I had ever laid eyes on. I asked to be introduced to you, Gunn laughed and asked how much I was willing to pay for you?"

She watched Robert stand and pace in front of her, as the horror of the situation sunk in.

Taking a deep breath, Robert continued, "I thought he was being funny, a comedian. Until…until one day he approached me and made it quite clear he was dead serious. I left that conversation bewildered. That's when I started doing a little checking around and discovered that the good old governor has some dirty little secrets."

Knowing the governor's seedy reputation, Danielle listened to Robert's impassioned speech and asked, "Is that what you want do? Buy sex?"

"For your information, I don't buy sex. I'm not that kind of man. Weren't you just listening to what I said?"

"You impress me as a man who wants to remain in control, Robert. You make a call, they come. You have sex. They are dismissed. No emotional connection. I find that sad. Making love is a beautiful experience when shared between two people who love each other. There's a big difference between the old *wham-bam-thank-you-ma'am* and a romantic evening of intimacy with your man."

"You really don't believe a word I'm saying, do you?"

"I believe that you believe it. I'm trying to tell you I know the difference between being loved and getting laid."

"And how do you know all this?"

"My understanding came from God. It was He who gave me the heart to love and the desire to satisfy my man by exploring his desires. I believe your plan was to purchase and bed me until you got bored, then move on to another loveless relationship."

Robert shook his head in disbelief.

Danielle continued, "Regardless of my mother's pathetic behavior, God didn't put me here solely to satisfy a man's sexual urges. I was placed on this earth to be a queen to my king. I was placed here to make our home his castle. To nurture the fruits of my womb and his loins. I am a woman of substance."

Waving both hands in the air, he replied, "Yes, you are a woman of substance. I believe you're far too much woman for me."

Danielle nodded in agreement. "Quite possibly, you are correct. Look, Robert, if all you have to offer a woman is your money and a romp in the hay, then your life is going to be very disappointing seeking women of little or no substance. I have my own beliefs about what determines a person's worth."

Robert stopped pacing and leaned over her. "Care to share them with me?"

"People make the money. The money doesn't make the people."

"When you speak, I feel intoxicated. You have an unusual effect on me."

Danielle chuckled. "It's just your body reacting to the lack of control over a woman. If I gave myself to you, that intoxication would fade into the night without a trace."

Robert sat and hung his head. "I simply don't agree. I believe the impact you have on me will last a lifetime."

In a moment of tenderness, Danielle covered Roberts's hand with her own. "If the proper steps had been taken to meet me, I would have been more inclined to believe you."

Robert nodded. "I understand. Then will you please grant me the time to get to know the woman that sits beside me."

"That opportunity has already been granted, Robert. I'm here on your island, sharing your life, your views, and your hospitality. I would like to know who you are as a man, why you took the actions you did to help me, and why, today, you are offering me friendship through truth."

"All of that will be revealed. I could talk to you for hours." With a mischievous smile on his face he said, "Your voice is so stimulating; it's almost orgasmic."

Danielle shook her head. "Lord, I will never understand why men speak more from the waist down than from the neck up." That got a huge laugh out of Robert, and he laid an arm around her shoulders. "It's getting late, I think we should retire for the night and continue this delightful conversation in the morning. I feel you have the advantage of being completely sober, while I on the other hand have consumed four cocktails."

"I agree that could be considered an advantage point for my side. However, if your thought processes are the same on this subject tomorrow, I assure you my responses will remain the same."

"I can't win with you."

"If winning is important to you, maybe you should contact Charlie Sheen and get some of that tiger blood."

Robert smiled. "Oh, Danielle, you're a hoot. May I walk you to your villa?"

"Your request is granted."

The evening had gone so fast that Danielle had forgotten to get Robert's approval for Captain Bill's wife, Robyn, to visit her. "I would like to invite Captain Bill's wife to stay with me while you're away. Any objections?"

Robert looked puzzled. "Why would you want the company of Captain Bill's wife?"

"Because Robyn is one of my oldest and dearest friends."

"What?"

"Yes. We grew up together. We walked home from school every single day. The locals used to say they could tell time by us. Robyn is funny. You will love her, and she missed her calling. She should have been a comedienne."

"Boy, this little circle just gets smaller and smaller. Actually, it's really good. It can get lonely on the island, and I have no idea how much company Debra will be. She stays on the move; that girl is a gypsy at heart. She loves to island hop. I don't see a problem with that, Danielle. I will speak with Captain Bill in the morning, and you ladies can hang out and catch up on things."

"Thank you. As much as I enjoy Maria's company, it would be nice to spend time with my friend Robyn."

Danielle no longer felt like a caged bird. Robert was keeping his word, allowing her the freedom to express herself, as well as permitting her friend into the world she temporarily called home.

He pulled her chair from the table, extended his hand to help her up, and walked her safely to the villa. This time when he leaned in to kiss her, she stood still and allowed him to place his lips softly against her cheek. Both were smitten with each other.

Robert didn't go straight to his private villa. Instead he took another stroll across the estate meditating on how wonderful it was to have Danielle's company. He had spent so many days without the satisfaction of real company that he'd forgotten just how stimulating it was to converse with someone so engaging. Life for Robert was changing for the better.

After his walk, he retreated to the library to call Governor Gunn. It was a conversation he didn't look forward to. He had already agreed to purchase Danielle's sister, but Gunn reacted negatively regarding his request and questioned why Robert wanted to purchase multiple women who were sisters. Of course, Gunn would think that. He would not believe Robert had another reason.

Spending time with Danielle gave Robert the opportunity to explore her feelings and to understand her desire to be valued by a man, and not merely as a plaything. The only thing he knew to do was to make it right. Going forward, Robert couldn't let Gunn know that all he wanted out of the arrangement was information regarding his father's death and Danielle's freedom. Governor Gunn was shrewd and cunning, so Robert wasn't sure how he would get information out of him. He just knew that he was going to, by any means necessary.

As Robert prepared to pick up the receiver, the phone rang. It was Gunn. "Good evening, Governor. I trust you had a good week?"

"Indeed, I did, Robert. How is your houseguest behaving?"

"Which one?"

"Ah, well, you have more than one?"

"Yes, my sister arrived today."

"I hope her visit doesn't interfere with our plans."

"No, actually I think it may help things a little. She and Danielle appear to have good chemistry. Which means I can leave the island without fear of her attempting to escape."

"That's a good idea. Now you're thinking, son."

"Dasheen paid us a visit today."

"Dasheen needs to keep her butt on St. Thomas and let us handle things. I will speak with her tomorrow."

"No, Governor, everything's fine. She really did me a favor. Danielle was so angry with her mother she elected to remain on James Island."

"Really? Well, I guess you have everything under control."

"Oh, you'll be surprised at the progress I've made."

"I knew once she stepped her foot on James Island and saw the life she'd be living; a change of heart would come into play."

"Actually, the island hasn't phased her one bit. She isn't concerned about wealth. I even had to change plans. I led her to believe I was against everything that had happened to her and she was free to leave the island anytime she desired. We're becoming friends and she's trusting me more each day. Before it's all said and done I will have her eating out of my hands and loving it."

"You're beginning to sound like that old pimp out of Kansas City."

"Who? Greasy? That's not a compliment, so I guess I need to put a different spin on my words."

"If not, at least change your associates."

"I guess," he sighed. "Damn Greasy, huh?"

"You know he has a reputation for being able to slide in and out of everything."

"I'd rather be referred to as smooth."

"Then make it happen, lover boy."

47

"Consider it done. I'm available in the morning. Let's meet at Red Hook around 10:00 a.m."

"That's fine with me. I'll see you in the morning, Silky Smooth."

Robert could hear Governor Gunn laughing at his own joke as he hung up the phone, and Robert didn't like the sound of that laughter, because it was evil? Robert was relieved that conversation had ended. It was so out of character for him to act so big and bad, but Gunn had a way of making one feel less than a man, if he saw you couldn't handle your business.

However, what Robert didn't know was Gunn was already on to him. When Dasheen left James Island, her first stop was to the Governor's office. She didn't waste any time telling Gunn how Robert had disclosed information to Danielle she had no business in knowing, and that he was falling hard and falling fast for her beautiful daughter. Without knowing all the details, Gunn had already put a new plan into motion. He knew that some men would allow a woman to weaken their minds, and one thing he knew for sure was he didn't have any plans of losing control over his golden white boy.

Doing business with Robert Kelsey had been a profitable business for the governor, and the last thing he needed was for him to start trying to make sense out of his life and his inheritance. There was too much to lose. If the goose didn't continue to lay the golden egg, then the goose had to go. Things were slowing down on the islands since the Fed's began poking their noses into every missing girl in the Caribbean. The ring shut down its human trafficking operations and focused more on illegal drugs and weapons. Resources for their criminal enterprises were beginning to dry up. When things get tough, murder gets easy.

Governor Gunn was no one to play with. There was only one person who didn't fear the wrath of his hell. Which was his wife, who he kept under lock and key. No matter how big and brazen the governor portrayed himself in public, when he opened the door at 666 East Bay Road, a submissive man closed it.

Just as Robert was looking out his darkened library window, he saw a light reflecting on the grounds. He reached for his gun then noticed the boat was turning around in the ocean, heading away from the island. He figured some drunken fools had lost their way, so he disregarded the incident and retired for the night.

Chapter 6

Early the next morning, Captain Bill arrived on island with a special delivery package for Robert. Without warning, or an invitation, his sister-in-law, Camille, appeared out of nowhere in a drunken state. The man who lived completely alone was now surrounded with three women, a housekeeper, a groundskeeper and a captain. The island was filling up and coming alive pretty quickly.

When Robert arrived on the terrace, Danielle was already having breakfast. "Well, aren't we the early riser?"

"It's Maria's fault. I kept smelling the sweet aroma of bacon and couldn't stay in bed any longer."

"Well, thank you, Maria, you can expect a raise on your next check."

Both ladies laughed. "What can I expect on my check, Robert?"

"You, my lovely lady can expect a blank check, carte blanche. Whatever your heart desires, you have the power to purchase."

Danielle responded with a smile which charmed Robert completely.

"I saw you in my dreams last night."

Danielle laughed. "I saw you in mine too. You were standing behind iron bars wearing an orange jumpsuit. That was crazy, don't you think?"

Before Robert could respond, Camille appeared on the terrace. "I thought you were getting lonely, so I decided to pay you a quick visit."

"Well, nice to see you. Hmm—for what the third time this month?"

"Danielle, allow me to introduce my sister-in-law, Camille."

"Camille, my lady friend, Danielle."

"Hello, Camille, it's a pleasure to meet you."

"The pleasure is mine, darling. Well, you're a pretty little thing. Robert, wherever did you find her?"

Glancing at Danielle, Robert smiled. "I found her in the dictionary under charming." Danielle rolled her eyes at Camille and smiled.

Robert chuckled. "Camille was married to my older brother, Randall. Whenever she gets bored, which seems to be pretty often these days, she drops in uninvited and unannounced."

"Pay him no mind, Charming. He did say your name was Charming, right?"

Danielle pushed back. "No, he didn't. He told you my name was Danielle, and he found me charming."

"Oh, well, whatever. It really isn't important. As I was saying, Robert loves for me to visit him. If I didn't visit regularly, he would sit on this tiny little island with his tiny little hands, and grow old and lonely."

Danielle smiled. "That appears to be a general consensus."

Robert's face broke out in a wide grin, nodding approvingly. "You know, Danielle is going to get the wrong impression of me."

Camille responded in a sultry and condescending voice, "I'm surprised it matters. I'm in total disbelief. Robert Kelsey cares what someone thinks about him and his tiny little hands. That's a first."

Danielle stood there not knowing what to make of their strange conversation, but she wrote it off remembering how different Americans could be. She sighed deeply, then spoke, "Robert forgive me for the intrusion, but did you have the chance to speak with Captain Bill."

"Not yet, but I promise I will take care of it shortly."

Robert picked up a bottle and said, "Who's drinking so early in the morning?"

Camille rose from the table, picked up her glass, and said, "I'm exhausted from the trip and would take great pleasure in retreating to my villa."

Robert extended the bottle of champagne and told her, "Take the this with you."

Camille, standing toe-to-toe with Robert, pointed directly towards Danielle and asked, "Robert, do you really think I would leave the champagne with you and Danielle? She's charming, but she isn't that charming."

The smile on Robert's face faded. "Was that necessary? On another note, leave the champagne. It's obvious you've had too much already."

Camille walked slowly passed Danielle, and said, "It was a pleasure meeting Robert's new flavor of the month."

Danielle politely replied, "The pleasure wasn't mine."

Robert couldn't stop laughing as he watched Camille stumble up the long path to the villa.

"Now, Danielle, you have my undivided attention. I'm so glad she's gone."

Danielle smiled and took a deep breath. "That makes two of us. I didn't find her company very refreshing."

Robert shook his head. "She's usually not so offensive. I have no idea what's going on with her today."

Thirty minutes later music was blasting through the garden. "Oh Lord." Laughing with his head buried in his hands. "Debra's back and popping."

As Debra approached the terrace, she was wearing a big pretty smile and a sexy black two- piece dental floss styled bikini. Her pale shapely body was heading straight to the pool. "I hate living in New York in the winter. Look at my complexion. I look like frosty the snowman's daughter; white as the driven snow. Fear not, beautiful brown people, it will not be like this for long. Care to join me, Danielle?"

"Heavens no. I've had more than my share of the sun. You, on the other hand, need to be careful with those sun rays. They can do both good and bad."

"I know, but us white girls don't have that pretty brown complexion like you black girls."

Robert just shook his head. "Danielle, please forgive my crazy sister."

"She's fine, Robert. I like her, and I'm not offended. God made us the way he intended us to be, so we can either own it or love it."

"That's right, sister girl. I'm owning mine, cause I sure as hell don't like it."

Robert's sigh was deep enough to be heard. "You're one crazy chick, but I love you to life."

"Thank you, brother. I love you too. By the way, Danielle is cool."

"I think so, too," Robert replied.

While she was not able to compete with the Kelsey's financially, Danielle's looks and sophistication couldn't be denied or ignored.

"Hey, Danielle, I'm going into town later to pick up a few things, would you like to go?"

"No thanks, Debra. I appreciate you asking, but I plan to just hang out on the beach today. But if you'd like some company, Camille might want to tag along."

"Is Camille here again? Good grief. Why doesn't she just move in. Something is up, Robert. She's coming too regular. You might want to check with Randall and find out what's going on."

"As a matter of fact, you're right. I'll give him a call. But you know Randall, it'll take a month of Sundays to get a return call."

"I don't have any business of my own, that's the reason I have to talk about Randall and Camille."

"No, you don't," Robert repeated. "And while we're on the subject, they made the decision that was best for them. So, leave them alone, Ms. Busybody."

Debra, took offense to his statement and replied, "We can't change history, can we? However, we can change the subject. I am finished with that boring conversation. I'm outta her." Debra grinned and headed in the direction of the pool.

Robert was so engaged in his verbal tennis match with Debra he forgot Danielle was present. "I apologize for excluding you from the conversation. Please forgive my little bundle of joy, she is such a live wire. She and I have always been close. No matter her age, she will always be my crazy little baby sister."

"I understand, I feel the same way about my sister, Dior. I think about her every day. I can't help but wonder what plans mother has for her. I certainly hope she's ok. That's another reason I want to see Robyn. I need her to keep an eye on Dior. You see, Robert, we do have something in common. We both love our crazy little baby sisters."

Robert merely nodded. "Don't worry. Captain Bill will return in about 30 minutes. When he arrives, I will instruct him to bring Robyn over, as often as you ladies like. You can make any request of anyone here, this is your home as long as you wish."

Robert's voice was calming and distinctive. Danielle was drawn to his aristocratic and perfectly placed features. His eyes were a perfect shade of piercing blue. She often found herself staring at his wavy blond hair, which he kept pulled back into the cutest ponytail. The more she got to know him, the more she liked him. He was almost perfect, except for how and why their paths crossed. She couldn't help but wonder why a man with so much going for him would fall prey for such a demoralizing scheme.

In total disbelief, Danielle asked, "Why would you want a woman who has no desire to share her life with you?"

"What do you mean?"

"Just answer the question, Robert."

"Danielle, my dear. In my travels I've met many women, and one thing I know for sure is 80 percent of them can be purchased for the right price and the remaining 20 percent can be persuaded to love you, if they feel loved by you in return."

Danielle shook her head and said, "I think your philosophy and data is crazier than you. I assure you, Robert, that my love can't be purchased by you are any other man, regardless of their wealth or power."

Robert hesitated, looking directly into Danielle's amazing eyes. "I know, that's exactly why the chain of events played out as they did. You, my dear, are in the remaining 20 percent. My plans are to love you and wait patiently for you to love me in return."

Robert was conflicted about the role he played in the vicious scheme against Danielle. Initially, it didn't bother him, but after spending quality time with her, he realized that his role in the incident could possibly destroy any hopes of making her an important part of his life. He couldn't help but reflect on how amazingly happy he was to rise in the morning, knowing he would have the entire day to share with Danielle. There was no denying it, she made a difference in his life. She was not only beautiful, he found her to possess qualities which were unbelievable. She was young and wise. His greatest fear would be the day she discovered just how far he had gone to possess what wasn't rightfully his.

Robert sat perched upon a large red boulder, watching the Atlantic Ocean dance slowly around the beautiful bright yellow sun. He sighed quietly, then said, "Danielle, give me a chance to make things right. I'm positive that in time you will come to appreciate your life with me."

Danielle didn't respond, instead she played Robert's words over in her head, trying to decide if he was correct in his assumptions. Would she enjoy living on his private island? Her mind signaled a resounding yes. She would, if she loved him, but she didn't, she loved Jon. Unfortunately for Robert, she knew living in a cramped conch cottage with Jon was more appealing than being held hostage with a spoiled man that believed he could have anything he wanted.

Robert and Danielle talked for a while longer. He couldn't help but notice that Danielle was growing up right before his eyes. His conscious was taking over. The lies were mounting like sand flies on the beach. There was an unusual silence between them for a moment. Robert started to speak, but hesitated. He wanted to say something, but was uncomfortable. He knew he had to be completely honest with Danielle, if he hoped to have any chance with her.

After clearing his throat, he said, "Danielle, please don't get upset with me for what I'm about to say."

She sat quietly, unable to imagine what on earth he could say that would be worse than her being abducted and sold off like an animal."

Robert turned his body away from hers, his voice began to crack. He'd never had a problem speaking before, but he knew it would be a sensitive subject for her. He paused with his eyes closed and said," Danielle, your mother didn't deliver your initial letter to Jon, and all the additional letters you have written to him are stored at your mother's home. It's my understanding that he has already left for New York."

Danielle had always been poised, even under the worst circumstances, but this time was different. She turned to Robert, screaming at the top of her lungs, "Why does everyone believe it is okay to lie to me, and to make decisions that affect my life? Are you telling me my own mother is still deceiving me.?"

Robert listened to Danielle's rantings. For a moment he felt like a jerk, but he knew it was necessary in order to move forward in honesty. Methodically, he was removing everyone from her life that she loved and trusted, with the hopes of her relying and trusting only him.

There was a short intake of air as Robert stumbled to find the right words to confess. "Your mother was depending on you to help her survive, Danielle, but she went too far and so did I. I had no idea that you weren't aware of the arrangements until the night we met. I had no idea that you were deeply in love with Jon. I never meant to hurt you, but I do want to set the record straight, hoping that we could be friends, if nothing else. I know I'm not the good guy here, but your mother is a horrible woman."

Danielle was praying that Robert was lying. She searched his face for a window of truth. In his eyes she saw nothing; in her heart she felt disturbed. She knew he was telling the truth. She felt betrayed once again. The island was quieter than usual. As tears streamed down her face, the bodice of her white silk dress absorbed each drop, framing the magnificent outline of her full and youthful breast. A surge of anger traveled through her slender well-proportioned body. "I dare you to speak ill of my mother. You throw water and it runs, you throw blood and it settles." She wiped her eyes and walked towards the villa. She could hear Robert's voice, but being lost in mind, body and spirit, she withdrew and retreated to her villa, and remained there without conversation or food. Danielle was in absolutely intense pain.

Robert's plan had backfired, he couldn't believe the old Willie Lynch method of divide and conquer had failed. He would have to reevaluate his plan to gain Danielle's trust.

Danielle remained in her villa for six days. She was consumed with grief, refusing to speak with anyone. Everyday Maria would leave a tray of food at her door, only to return and find it untouched. Maria became increasingly worried. Danielle was inconsolable as she struggled with the thought that her mother, the most important person in her life, had completely betrayed her. Her heart was too broken to mend. On Sunday, July 23rd, she vowed never to speak to her mother again.

Nothing in Robert's life prepared him for Danielle's reaction to his confession. He didn't realize the impact his words would have on her emotionally. She wasn't as strong as he thought. He was devastated and needed help, but who would understand his dilemma, without casting blame on his self-serving ignorance?

As Robert was preparing to exit the terrace, Captain Bill appeared.   "Excuse me, Robert. I haven't seen Danielle in a few days. Is she alright?'

"No, Bill, she isn't?"

"Is there anything I can do?'

Suddenly, the light came on. Robert had the perfect solution. "Actually, there is. Will you invite your wife to come and spend a week or two with Danielle? I will pay her any amount she wants. Well, hell, I'll pay her four times the pay she gets from her job."

Bill's eyes bulged. "I don't think that's necessary, Robert. She loves Danielle. I'm sure she'll be happy to spend some time with her."

"Man, if you do that for me, I will owe you big time."

"Consider it done. Robyn can take some vacation days and make sure her position is covered while she's away. But I'm sure she can be here no later than Wednesday morning."

"That would be great. I will be gone on business for a couple of weeks and that will give the girls the freedom to move around without my presence. While I'm away, I would appreciate you making yourself available to take them anywhere they wish to go. Debra is leaving for Aruba on Monday. Camille has been acting really weird. I plan to speak with her later tonight about getting a condo on St. Thomas. She and Danielle are not getting along that well, and I don't want anything else to upset the apple cart. I will need you here bright and early in the morning to take Camille to St. Thomas."

"No problem, sir."

"Thanks, Bill. You're the man."

Robert knew he had to inform the governor of his botched plan, but he didn't care. All he cared about at the moment was mending Danielle's broken heart. He understood he could no longer straddle the fence. He had to choose a side and a direction. Being unsure of where his decision would lead him, Robert retreated to his villa to examine himself as a man.

Chapter 7

Robert lost track of time as the sun went down and dark shades of blue hovered over the beautiful Island. He emerged from the villa and walked out to the terrace only to find Camille sipping on a pineapple martini. He pulled up the white wicker lounge chair and scooted it close to her side. "Camille, what's going on with you? Your behavior has been so bizarre, and I've been so busy lately that I haven't been able to catch you when you were sober enough to talk."

"I'm upset!"

"Upset about what?"

"I'm afraid I don't know."

"Camille, you're not a damn child, you know better than anyone what the hell you're upset about. Come on now, stop tripping and tell me what's going on."

"Okay, damn it. I'm upset with myself. I blew $100,000 up my nose. My condo in New York is in foreclosure. The people I owe the money are threatening to kill me if I don't pay up. Anything else you want to know?"

"I seriously think that's enough."

"Look, Robert, let me set the record straight. I didn't come here to ask you for money. I came to James Island to save my life. I knew that as long as I was here, I would be safe."

"Why the hell did you think that? Did it ever occur to you that you might be putting someone else in danger? "Who let you shove a $100,000 worth of cocaine up your nose?"

"The same people that let me run up a $400,000 cocaine bill."

"You owe someone $400,000 for cocaine?"

"Well, not now. I paid all but $100,000."

"You're lucky they haven't killed you already. Have you looked at yourself lately? Really looked? You're a mess."

"Thanks, Robert. I needed that."

"I'm not going to baby you, Camille. You're smarter than that. I simply don't understand how you got yourself in this mess."

"Why don't you ask Randall?"

"What does my brother have to do with this?"

"Your cheap, lying brother cut me off. I had to make a living."

"Huh! You're making a living snorting cocaine?"

"No, dummy, I'm a mule. I run cocaine from the Caribbean to New York."

"Oh, I'm the dummy? What's even crazier? You're not a mule, you're a fool. It seems like you're snorting more than you're running. How long have you been doing this? Don't you know if you get busted, you're going to prison?"

"Robert, before I get to that, I'm not going to prison. The $100,000 wouldn't even be a problem if you hadn't rolled over on the governor's deal."

"What the hell are you talking about?"

Expecting Robert to be consumed by guilt, she blurted out. "You think I don't know you paid $100,000 for little Ms. Charming, and you were supposed to pay another $100,000 for your next little bundle of joy. But you got caught up and fell for Danielle, and now the governor can't collect his other $100,000. So fast forward, who does he put the squeeze on? Me, poor little me."

Robert had to stop and think. He was preparing to defend his arrangement for Danielle's presence in his life, but he merely raised his eyebrows. "Why would the governor tell you all of this Camille?"

She hesitated, fearing what Robert might say next. "We have a special relationship. I'm his woman. We make an awesome power couple, Robert. We've smuggled over 114,000 pounds of cocaine. We're big time, baby."

Shaking his head. "You have helped smuggle over 114,000 pounds of cocaine? You're his lady, and you owe him $100,000? Do you know how crazy and delusional that sounds? Do you know that amount of cocaine is worth over a billion dollars? The only thing that's logical is the fact that the cocaine you shoved up your nose has eaten up your brain cells. I'm so disappointed. I've always liked you Camille, but you can't stay her. You have to go. I will not let you endanger the lives of my family, friends, or me."

Slurring her words, she turns around pointing her finger in Robert's face. "You think you're so high and mighty? You, Mr.

Kelsey, just paid a $100,000 for a woman and brought her to your home against her will. You don't think human trafficking is a crime?" Laughing uncontrollably, she continued, "Your whole damn family is a bunch of crooks, and you're in bed with the biggest criminal in the Caribbean. So, what you got to say about that?"

Robert's efforts to keep his cool wasn't working. Yelling from the top of his lungs, "Get the hell off my island. I will deposit $150,000 in your bank account in the morning. You can pay the governor back the money you owe him, and use the remainder to either check yourself into rehab or buy yourself a ticket home, but you are no longer welcome in my life or my home."

Camille wasn't too high to understand the damage she had done. Her addiction had destroyed the most important friendship she had. But worse than that, she had destroyed her own life. Being void of self-respect, she looked up into Robert's face. "You want some of this don't you?"

Pacing back and forth across the garden, shaking his head in disbelief, Robert walked swiftly to the sparkling white beach adjacent to his villa and stared into the star-lit sky; hoping to regain a peaceful state of mind.

The rhythm and scent of the ocean slowly began to soothe him. As he sat quietly resonating over Camille's words, complete horror surfaced in the thought that she was correct. He had paid money for an unwilling participant. He had committed a crime. He felt horrible. His selfish desires had caused him to be totally unrealistic about his actions, and the effect it had on the lives of others. To add injury to insult, one of his family members was not only a mule for the governor, but was also a mole in his home and private enterprise. He felt betrayed. Each turn of events made it clearer that his desires to have Danielle in his life could no longer be greater than his desire to see her live a life of freedom and independence from everyone, including himself.

The fight between Camille and Robert had echoed fiercely throughout the entire property. Both Maria and Danielle were pacing around in their rooms wondering what had caused this eruption. Camille returned to her villa to pack and Robert sat alone on the beach full of anger and contempt for Camille. Maria walked to her door, with the intention of checking on Robert. At that moment, she saw Danielle emerge from her villa. She stepped back into her room, relieved that someone other than herself was concerned about Robert. But most important, she was happy it had brought sweet Danielle out of seclusion.

Moments later, Danielle found herself sitting beside Robert on the beach, offering a life-line to a man that seemed troubled.

"Robert, I have spent endless days in my villa trying to make sense of my life, wondering why and how this came to be. Then I heard your voice like I've never heard it before. Angry and hurt. It was then I realized that like me, you too need to make sense of your life. Consequently, I decided to come to you and extend the same friendship that you extended to me during my troubling and confusing times."

Robert was touched. "I don't really deserve it, Danielle. I have pointed the blame at your mother, without looking in the mirror at the man who made it all possible. I justified my actions by wanting to help you, but after some soul searching I realize I had carnal desires as well. Which could find that action unworthy of a man with strong moral fiber. Please know that your willingness to offer me friendship, after what I've done, is greatly appreciated. I also know that as beautiful and as intoxicating as I find you, it's your mind and your grace that draws me to you. I was just thinking how wonderful it would be to have my new friend to discuss things with. Talking with you always brings me clarity. I've missed your company, and I'm so terribly sorry for any pain I may have caused you."

The air was quiet and still as Danielle wiped an escaped tear from her eye. "Robert, I have been hurt beyond measure. I have been confused for days at a time, but through all of the insanity that I have found my life in the past few days, your compassion and your friendship has been my only constant. The days I remained in my room gave me an opportunity to look into your heart, pass your actions, during my abduction. Yes, you have displayed very selfish behavior, but you have glossed over your selfishness with kindness and respect. Did you have alterative motives, often times I'm sure you did. But never once have I felt scared or in fear of my life. I believe that deep down inside is a man you will one day be proud of."

Robert breathed a sigh of relief. "Thank you. Tonight, I was at the lowest point in my life. You, my beautiful lady, even though I deserved it, felt compelled not to dehumanize me. You are the most beautiful woman I have ever known, inside and out."

Chapter 8

Between the fierce waves dancing around the shoreline, and the dark of night, Danielle accepted Robert's apology. She was taken by surprise when she found herself sharing parts of her life that she'd never shared with Jon. To take the edge off the evening, she told Robert how terrified she was of the massive waves that stretched across the turbulent Atlantic Ocean. Involuntarily, she cringed. "They remind me of Aunt Lucy, having the power to both heal and destroy."

Robert, perplexed, pointed to an approaching wave. "How do the waves remind you of your Aunt Lucy?"

"It's going to sound really crazy," she replied. "Aunt Lucy is my mother's older sister. She was Grandma Sally's first born. She is a direct descendant of her father, Lucifer, the Haitian voodoo priest of fire. She was given the name Lucinda, after her father, of course. As children, we weren't able to pronounce her name, so we started calling her Aunt Lucy. All I know is Aunt Lucy is scarier than Lucifer himself."

Robert listened intently, reflecting back on his previous conversation with Dasheen. His facial expression changed as

Danielle continued to disclose what he hoped was idle chit-chat.

"It's a little-known fact that Aunt Lucy has clients from different parts of the world, including America. It's been said that her powers have crossed many oceans, reaching victims of all nationalities. Trust me, she is a wicked Obeah woman. Our family limits their rituals to only medical healing and counseling, because of her demonic practices."

It may sound crazy to you, Robert, but once I was very sick and Mother thought I was dying. My body was full of pain and my temperature was hot as boiling water. Mother carried me to several doctors, and no one could help me. Mother decided to take me to Aunt Lucy, so she could fix me. I didn't want to go. I cried and cried, but Mother didn't care. I was afraid of Aunt Lucy, and I wanted no parts of her. I was screaming from the top of my lungs, no…no…no, that's obeah…that's obeah! Mother grabbed me by my shoulders and shook me until I stopped screaming. She looked straight into my eyes and said, 'Listen to me. One day when you love someone as much as you love yourself, you will do anything to save their life, including obeah. Now wipe your eyes and let's go. You are a very sick girl, and I have no intention of losing you."

Mother wrapped a blanket around me and marched me right out the door, straight to Aunt Lucy's house. "I tell you, from the moment I saw Aunt Lucy I was as scared as a pig on its way to the slaughterhouse."

Robert laughed, but fear was beginning to creep in. "What were you scared of, Danielle?"

"Oh, you're laughing at me, Robert Kelsey?"

"No," Robert replied. "However, it's not normal for a person to be scared of their aunt, Danielle."

She tossed her head, as her long silky hair danced from side-to-side. "You don't have an Aunt Lucy, so until you do, or until you come face-to face-with her, reserve your comments and count your blessings." Flashing her infectious smile. "Now, may I finish my story?"

Robert chuckled and replied, "Of course, by all means, finish your story."

Carefully watching each movement of the waves, Danielle continued, "Mother dragged me to Aunt Lucy's house, the same way she dragged me to meet you, against my will."

Feeling uncomfortable with Danielle's remarks, Robert's smile slowly disappeared.

She noticed the change in Robert's facial expression. "I'm sorry, Robert, my intention wasn't to make you feel bad." She hesitated. "Hmm, but then again, maybe it was."

"I tell you what, Robert. Let's make a promise never to speak about the night we met until we can right the wrong. Ok?"

He smiled and gave off a little chuckle. "Ok. I can live with that."

It became clear as the conversation continued, the changes in Robert's facial expression was due, in part, to the unnatural topic of their conversation. Danielle adamantly explained her fear of Aunt Lucy merely by saying, "She's an evil obeah witch."

Robert laughed again, but this time with a look of concern. "Your aunt is a witch, Danielle?"

"Yes, Robert. My aunt is a full-fledged scary obeah witch, with a haunting reputation. However, it's acceptable in our culture to have wise obeah priestess, who protect their families throughout their lives. But, Aunt Lucy has endless powers and no normal boundaries. I repeat, no normal boundaries. I grew up watching and hearing about a lot of spooky stuff.

"The day my mother carried me to Aunt Lucy's I was standing in her dirt-filled courtyard admiring the beautiful red bougainvillea's growing along the broken rusty iron fence, when I saw old doll parts and jars filled with colored oils, eyes, fingers and vegetation that took my breath away. Before I knew it, Aunt Lucy and two old mangy dogs came up behind me. She grabbed my right hand, pulled me close to her left side and started chanting loudly, to the right...to the right...your path in life must turn to the right...heal her father of fire...prince of darkness...mother of death...king of life...boom shaka la... boom shaka la...boom shaka la...boom. Some children have memories of sweet lullabies, I have memories of old witchcraft rituals and chanting. As I was saying, I felt sharp sparks of electricity pulsating throughout my entire body, as if I was being electrocuted. She dropped my hands. My limp body fell to the ground. I saw my mother kneeling, eyes rolling around in circles, wiping my forehead with an old rag that smelled like the scent of death. Aunt Lucy removed another rag from the large coal pot that was filled with hot oils, snake eyes and bush leaves. As I lifted my head, I saw Aunt Lucy strolling slowly through the court yard, eyes piercing red, breathing fire, as if nothing had happened. I felt the presence of evil and visions of huge swelling waves. When I opened my eyes again, I was lying in my bed free of all aches and pain, and my body was cold as ice."

"Wow!" Robert replied. "What does that mean?"

"It means, every time I see swelling waves rushing to the shore, I remember that awful encounter. I see sickness, fire, life, and I smell death. They all remind me of Aunt Lucy. You need to stop laughing at me and start being concerned about your role in holding me captive in your private world of privilege. Aunt Lucy and the governor could be cooking up a big pot of satanic ritual roots for your handsome backside."

Robert appeared nervous. "Are you trying to scare me?"

"No, I wouldn't say that. I'm trying to warn you, Robert. I believe you're being set up. For what, I don't know. I'm not a Luciferin. I don't flirt with the devil. Common sense is the only powers I can count on. I'm relying on what I know to be true. Life and death lie in the hands of both Aunt Lucy and Governor Gunn."

"What does Governor Gunn have to do with your Aunt Lucy?"

"Robert, have you ever met the governor's wife?"

"No, I haven't," Robert replied. "I didn't know he was married. Every time I see him, he's with a different woman. I figured he was a single womanizing man."

Danielle laughed and said, "He is a womanizer, a married one. He hides his wife from public view."

With a puzzled look on his face. "Why would he do that?"

Danielle gave Robert a silly look. "Because he's ashamed of her, the governor is married to Aunt Lucy."

Shocked beyond belief, Robert shouted, "Good God, Danielle. The governor is married to a witch?"

Glancing at Robert. "Yes, the governor is married to Aunt Lucy. They've been married for over twenty years."

Confused and scrambling for the right words, "How could that be? I mean, how could that be? How would I not know?"

Now Danielle was amused and laughing at Robert's behavior. Jokingly she replied, "Because you're not a belonger, Robert."

Standing with a confused look and open palms he replied, "What the heck is a belonger?"

Laughing uncontrollably. "A belonger is a native Virgin Islander. You would have known the governor was married to the obeah priestess of the Caribbean, if you were born here. That information is very important. West Indians don't scare easy, but even the dumbest of man is smart enough to be afraid of dirty hands. The governor has been able to instill fear into our people through his connections with witchcraft. It's the number one reason he's always reelected. I have always prayed that the people of the Virgin Islands would go to the polls with vengeance in their hearts, and cast their votes for a reputable and qualified governor. There's an old West Indian proverb you should acquaint yourself with."

"Oh, really. What would be that proverb?"

Danielle hesitated. "Smoke yo cigar but min yo spit."

Robert was baffled. "I have no idea what that means."

"Sure, you do. It means be careful you don't get in water too deep for you. Which I think you've already done."

Slightly nodding his head. "I think you're right, that's an interesting proverb. Where do these proverbs come from, Danielle?"

Pleased to see Robert's interest, she explained, "West Indian proverbs are the philosophy of our people. They are significant to our cultural history. It identifies our heritage, like fingerprints identify a person. During slavery it was our language of choice, because it enabled us to communicate with each other without the slave owners understanding what was being said."

"Really, now that's interesting."

Danielle placed her hand under her chin and said, "You know what I find interesting?"

"No," Robert replied.

With a slight smile on her face. "I find it interesting that you're in business with a man you don't know very well."

For the second time that night, Robert was engaged in conversation that unmasked the governor as being a willing participant in activities that appeared to turn the bright lights of life lived into a dark place of criminal enterprise.

He rubbed his forehead at a slow, but steady pace. "He's the governor of the Virgin Islands, for God's sake. I consider you an intelligent person, so I'm baffled that you don't understand the advantage of having a relationship with the governor."

"Oh, I understand, but there are many reputable businessmen you could have chosen to do business with on the island. The governor is such a despicable man. I may be wrong, but the more time I spend with you, it doesn't appear the governor would be the type of man you would associate with."

"I didn't select the governor, I inherited him."

"How does one inherit a governor?"

"It's a long story," he mumbled under his breath.

Danielle crossed her legs, and leaned forward. "I've got all the time in the world, and tonight I'm all ears."

"Alright, you asked for it. I remember like it was yesterday. It was August 21, 1999. On a beautiful Tuesday morning, I stepped out on the terrace at the Mandarin Hotel in New York City. I was calm and in a relatively good mood, when the telephone rang. When I picked up the receiver, I heard a hysterical female voice on the line. I immediately knew something was wrong with my father. I closed my eyes and held my breath as Maria informed me of my father's death. I still have no idea how I got to the airport. All I remember is getting off the plan in St. Thomas. I loved my father and I knew he loved me, in his own way. We never really saw eye to eye. My father thought I was soft and not man enough to run his empire. I guess he was right."

Danielle rubbed his hand. "Don't be so hard on yourself. Your father probably wasn't as great as you thought he was, especially if Governor Gunn was his business partner."

Robert chuckled and continued. "I spent my whole life seeking his approval. When he died, I was angry. I felt cheated because he died without me having the chance to tell him how much I loved him. Both my mother and my brother refused to attend the services, and my little sister Debra was traveling to God knows where. By the time I located her, he was cremated and his ashes scattered out to sea.

"My parents hated each other. After the divorce; it got worst. My mother traveled in the upper echelons of high society. She was only concerned about not losing her social status and friendships with the upper registry of New York. She always says that where she resides is the most lusted after address in the world. She loves the thought of having others looking up to her, while she looks down on them. My brother, Randall, never bonded with dad. It was all mother's fault. One night during one of their drunken episodes, we were walking in the door when Mother shouted, 'Randall is not your child, you drunken fool.' Everything went downhill from there. Dad never spoke to Randall again, and Randall never spoke to Dad."

"You don't share any of your inheritance with Randall?"

"No, Randall's biological father was Dominick. He was a wealthy political powerbroker, and Dad's best friend; which made matters worse. After Mother spilled the beans that evening, Dominick stepped up and provided for both Mother and Randall. Being his only son, Randall inherited his entire estate. Therefore, I guess you could say that Mother hit the jackpot twice. As for me, I was left to handle the funeral arrangements and conduct his business affairs. The one thing that amazed me through the whole process, was Dad's request to be cremated."

"Why did his request amaze you?"

"Well, Dad was in a fire when he was a young boy and received third degree burns over 40 percent of his body. It was a hard time for him. He stayed in the hospital for almost a year undergoing numerous skin graft surgeries. He said he never wanted to be touched by fire again, not even when he was dead. I guess he changed his mind, because he had a prepaid cremation policy and a document stating where he wanted his ashes to be scattered. My father had a life insurance policy worth $20 million, and a $400 million estate. The total cost for his cremation was only $1,800. I knew he had money, but I didn't know he had that much. I truly have no idea how he accumulated so much wealth. All I ever saw him do was sit on the island, snort cocaine, and give money to every hooker he had on speed dial. You know what I mean?"

"Yes, I know exactly what you mean. Like father, like son."

"There you go, again."

Laughing with pure delight. "Again, I'm sorry. It's just hard for me not to throw shade when the window of opportunity is left wide open."

"Seriously? May I finish my story?"

"Please do."

"Thank you. To shock me even more, he left me everything. He left Debra a trust fund that should last her a lifetime. Plus, as she gets older, the amount gets unbelievably larger. I just hope she finds the right person to love her for her, and not her bank account. Okay, I'm getting off track. It was at that moment that I decided to run the business. I figured I didn't know what I was doing, but I had enough money to keep the business operational, until I learned the ropes. Today, I can honestly say I've caught on pretty darn good.

Laughing simultaneously, Danielle and Robert fell back on the sand and said, "Thank God for that."

"My father's attorney, Tom Taylor, informed me that running my father's business would be a breeze. He said it was a cookie cutter business, and all I had to do was follow the governor's lead. At the time it seemed okay, but tonight, not so much. Tom scheduled a meeting between the governor and me to discuss a new project he and my father had just started. I returned to James Island. Later that evening, while sitting on the veranda watching the water taxis make their runs to St. John, Maria announced I had a call from Governor Gunn. I will never forget the chilling sound of his voice and the insensitive remarks he made. He said, 'Good night, Mr. Kelsey. This is your business partner and your governor. I'm sorry for the loss of your father, but at least you didn't lose your money.' Laughing in an obnoxiously loud voice."

"I said to myself, what kind of insensitive person is this. I can't recount his conversation, all I remember is agreeing to meet him at 2:00 p.m. the next day at Government House. My concerns about my ability to run the business jumped to an all- time high. I spent endless hours living life to the fullest without having to earn one red cent, and now I was left to run a legitimate business I knew nothing about. I knew I needed the governor's assistance."

"When I arrived at Red Hook, I took the bright colored safari bus into town. The driver dropped me in front of Emancipation Garden and told me I had to walk up Government Hill, because his bus was too large for the narrow road. Everyone but me was moving at a snail's pace. As I passed a food truck the smell of fried fish lingered in the air. I rushed passed it to avoid the scent, when I heard an elderly lady shout, 'Take it easy, mon, take it easy. You're on island time now.' I gave her a quick smile and continued up Government Hill. I was totally captivated with the old historical buildings and massive cruise ships that framed the harbor from one end to the other. I had vacationed on St. Thomas numerous times, but today I looked at the island with different eyes. I looked at it as my future home. At that moment, I felt like a man with a purpose.

"When I arrived at Government House, I was greeted by a small petite lady that had the longest dread locks I had ever seen. I couldn't take my eyes off of her hair. I had always been fascinated by the whole Rasta thing, but as soon as I got up enough nerve to inquire about the upkeep of her hair, a tall robust man, extended his hand and gave a firm handshake that caused the veins to appear on his shiny bald head. The same boisterous voice I heard over the telephone was standing right in front of me. I looked at him from head to toe. He was built like a prize fighter, which was obstructed; however, by a large protruding belly. His voice was deep and his laugh was loud. I was intimidated by his presence. I wasn't impressed, but I was intrigued. He escorted me to his office, and after speaking with him I realized he had a cold heart, a brilliant mind, and a determined spirit. He appeared to have the traits of many men—some good, and some bad. He was surprised when he discovered I knew nothing about my father's business. He assured me, out of respect for my late father, he would take me under his wing and teach me everything I needed to know. It didn't take long for me to discover that he broke all the rules. I occasionally watched him wreak havoc and never look back. He was ruthless, and I realized I was in trouble. I just did not know how much. I had nowhere to turn. After all, he was the Governor of the U. S. Virgin Islands. I attempted to dissolve the relationship, but he reminded me how important it was to be alive and well in the Caribbean. I remained on my little island out of his way, and continued taking my money to the bank."

"Oh my God, Robert, that's awful. What kind of business are you in?"

"Well let's see, I have three check cashing and loan centers. The main office is in the West End Center, and the two satellite offices are located in Red Hook and Havensight."

Danielle smiled. "Oh, you're the cash and carry man. You have the island covered, mon. I've been to your west end location several times. It's a nice place."

"It's okay."

"You're being modest, Robert. You make a ton of money. Your stores are busy day and night. The Santos stand in line for hours sending money to the Dominican Republic. Between the Arabs, the down islanders, and the Americans, I'm positive more money leaves the island of St. Thomas than remains."

Robert laughed. "I never thought about it like that, but you're probably right."

"I know I'm right. With all the money you're making, Robert, you don't seem to be happy."

He nodded his head in agreement. "Was that another Danielle observation?"

"I guess you could say that. I don't get it. You are white, handsome, and wealthy living on a beautiful private island in the Caribbean. I don't believe you have to resort to buying and kidnapping a woman to share your life with. There has to be more to the story. This is far too much to comprehend. Why did you go to these lengths? It just doesn't add up. As a matter of fact, it makes absolutely no sense at all."

He lowered his head and voice simultaneously, "It wouldn't make sense to you, but if you were raised as a Kelsey knowing you could have anything you wanted, you find yourself taking and buying everything your heart desires. This time my heart desired to help you. You were the chosen one. I admired you from the first moment I laid eyes on you. You didn't strike me as a woman I could sweep off her feet. When I learned of your mother's plan for you, I knew I had to get involved—so I did."

"Until tonight, I thought my life was messed up, but I see that your life appears to be in worse shambles than mine." Danielle laid her head on Robert's shoulder. "How can I help?"

81

"It's late. As much as I enjoy your company, I think we both need to get some sleep. You will need it more than I will."

Looking surprised. "Why do you think that?"

"Well, let's see. Because tomorrow you will need time to start preparing for your houseguest."

Danielle playfully punched Robert in the arm. "Houseguest, what houseguest?"

Robert was eager to let the cat out of the bag. "I will be traveling for business on Wednesday. I wanted you to accompany me, but you've had such a stressful couple of weeks. I thought you would enjoy relaxing at home catching up on island melee with your friend, Robyn."

Jumping up and down like a rubber ball. "Are you serious? Robyn is coming to visit?"

"Yes, she will be here bright and early Wednesday morning and will stay here with you on the island until I return. Bill will provide transportation for you ladies, so whatever you would like to do, he's at your beck and call."

"Oh, Robert. This is the best surprise ever. Thank you, thank you. I will not be able to sleep a wink. The excitement is sure to steal my ability to sleep."

Robert was relieved to see a smile on her beautiful face. Her sadness had haunted him for days. That alone was enough to bring him to a peaceful place.

"One more thing. Camille will be leaving the island in the morning, never to return. Debra will be departing for Aruba. You, my fair lady, are in charge. Feel free to do whatever you want. You don't need permission from me or anyone."

"Wow! I'm in charge?" Danielle leaned over and asked, "Did you say Camille was leaving in the morning never to return?"

"Yes, that's correct."

"Am I the reason for her leaving?"

"No, she's the reason."

"Okay, do you want to talk about it?"

"Yes, I do. But not tonight."

Robert was extremely inquisitiveness about the governor. He realized Danielle was the only person he could trust. He needed to fully understand what he was dealing with. Slowly and deliberately he said, "Danielle, you are the only person in the world I can count on. Will you help me find my way out of this black hole with the governor?"

"Yes, Robert. You can count on me."

They both stood up, knocking the fine granules of sand from their clothes. With smiles on their faces, each went their separate way to their private villas; where they would spend the balance of the night reflecting on their budding friendship.

Chapter 9

The Caribbean air was damp and heavy as Captain Bill steered The Wanderer to the pier. He arrived early just as Robert requested. Standing on the dock was Camille wrapped neatly in a camel colored shawl, white linen shirt and navy slacks. Her eyes were covered in a pair of Chanel tortoise-shell sunglasses. Her stylish attire didn't reflect the appearance of a woman with a serious drug addiction. She held her head high as Captain Bill helped her on the vessel.

Polite as always, Bill extended a warm greeting, "Good morning, Camille."

"Good morning, Bill," she replied. "Is Robert joining us?"

"No, he'll be in town later this morning."

Disappointed to learn that she wouldn't have the opportunity to speak with Robert again, she pulled her sunglasses down over her perfectly appointed nose and caught a glimpse of Robert standing on the terrace. As she raised her right hand to wave goodbye, Robert turned his back and walked away.

Camille's heart sank. She was hoping for the opportunity to apologize to Robert for the senseless incident last night, but it was obvious that the hateful words spoken to him had destroyed their friendship forever. Free of drugs and alcohol, she was able to see things from a different perspective. Last night, however, was the straw that broke the camel's back. After such a devastating loss, she was ready to come face to face with her demons. Her first course of action would be to end her relationship with the governor and pay him the $100,000, then take the balance and check into rehab like Robert suggested. Maybe then she would be able to face Robert and restore their friendship. Robert had been the perfect brother-in-law, even after her and Randall's divorce. He had never turned his back on her, until she turned her back on him.

When Camille arrived at Red Hook Marina, she stopped at Willy's for breakfast. As she was waiting for her food to arrive, she made a call to the governor, hoping to meet with him later in the day. Her plans changed when she discovered that the governor was off island and wouldn't be returning until the following day. After breakfast, she hailed a taxi into town and got a room at the Iguana Inn, a locally run guesthouse she frequented with the governor.

As she was unpacking, she received a message from Robert confirming a $200,000 deposit was made to her bank account. Once again, he reiterated his hopes of her using the balance of the money to get herself some help. The call really hit home. Heartfelt, she fell to the bed sobbing, feeling sad and alone. She spent the night in complete darkness crying herself into a deep sleep.

She was awakened by a crowing rooster. After taking a long cold shower, she dressed herself fashionably in a light blue sundress, decorated with crystal flowers along the scalloped hemline. She pulled her beautiful blond hair into a ponytail, adorned her ears with diamond studs, slid on her Chanel sunglasses, and walked to the bank in grand style. When she arrived at Tri-Island Bank, she approached the teller and requested a withdrawal. The teller called for the branch manager. She escorted Camille to a private office adjacent to the window, where she privately withdrew $180,000 in cash, then purchased $2,000 in travelers' checks. She opened her tan oversized Hermes bag and inconspicuously placed the money in the bag.

As she stepped outside the bank she ran into Baller, one of the governor's body guards. During their brief conversation, she asked him to inform the governor she was staying at the Iguana Inn and needed to desperately speak with him before she left island. Surprised to learn of her leaving, Baller teased her. "Oh, the island too hot for yo' mama?"

"I guess you can say that," she replied.

"The governor will be sorry to hear that."

"Bullshit, the governor doesn't give a shit about me. All he cares about is getting his girls and boys on and off the island."

"Wait, wait a minute, mama. You don't sound like yourself. What's going on with you?"

"Nothing's going on with me. I'm just sick of messing up my life, and I want out of this hell hole. I'm going home and get clean."

Baller laughed hysterically. "You get clean? As much shit as you push up your nose? Now that's a joke."

"Yeah, I know it may sound like a joke, but I'm dead serious."

"Look, Camille. I've always liked you, but you talking some shit that just might cause you to be dead, seriously. You just need a drink or two to take the edge off, and maybe a little something to get you back to yourself."

Shaking uncontrollably, Camille snapped, "I don't want anything to drink and I don't want any stuff. Just tell the governor I have his package and I'm getting the hell off this island."

"Okay, baby, take it easy. I will make sure he gets the message."

Camille walked down the narrow street to the Iguana Inn and remained there waiting for Governor Gunn.

As day fell into night, Camille sat in room 6B waiting for the governor to arrive. Just as she picked up her phone to call him, there was a knock on the door. She stumbled to the door and asked, "Who is it?"

"It's me, baby. Open the door."

She unlocked the door. "What took you so long? I've been waiting for you all day."

The governor, irritated with the message he received from Baller, walked in the room closing the door behind him, but neglected to lock it. "So, what is this I hear about you wanting to leave your man?"

"Man, you're not my man. I don't mean anything to you."

"Now listen to how crazy that sounds. You mean everything to me. We're a power couple, baby."

"Power couple? You don't help run a billion dollars in drugs with your man and end up owing him $100,000.

The governor grabbed her roughly by the arm. "What are you talking about?"

"Stop, you're hurting me."

"I'm going to hurt you more than that if you don't tell me what you're talking about?"

"Robert said I was a fool when I told him how much drugs we were running. He became angry and kicked me off the island when I told him I was indebted to you for $100,000 because he didn't pay you for the other woman."

"You stupid bitch! You just had to open your damn mouth. I've lost my mule, my mole, and my access to cash. You're not worth your weight in bubble gum."

Camille scrambled for her purse. "No, you didn't lose your money. I have it right here." She reached into her purse and gave him the $100,000. "See, I didn't let you down."

"$100.000 is chump change compared to what you just threw out the damn window. No, baby, you didn't let me down. We need to celebrate our good fortune. I brought you something special. You go freshen up and then we'll have a little fun together and talk about our future."

Camille looked at him and asked, "You're going to kill me, aren't you?"

Standing behind her, he takes her face into his hands. "No baby, I'm not going to kill you. You're going to kill yourself." Placing his left hand over her mouth, he reached into his pants pocket with his right hand, pulled out a white cheese cloth and placed it over her nose and watched her fall gently on the bed. He placed the cheese cloth back in his pocket and walked out the door. As he left the inn, he passed two large males dressed in black from head to toe.

"Good night, boys. She, and whatever you find in her purse, belongs to you. Handle your business."

It was business as usual for the governor and his buffoons. Although he had deviated from his original plans the night before, he knew it would be necessary to start setting the wheels in motion for the problems he knew he would incur down the road.

The next morning the governor arrived at his office at 7:00 a.m., just in time to have breakfast with the one woman he truly had genuine affection, his office manager, Audrey. Everyone, including Audrey's husband, Chief of Police Monroe Hart, knew of their affair. Afraid of losing her completely, Hart kept his problems to himself and worked diligently behind the scenes to hopefully discredit the governor. During their morning meeting, he advised Audrey to cancel his appointment with Robert and instruct him to proceed without him.

Robert spent the morning sitting on the terrace, awaiting a call from the governor. When the telephone rang, he answered, "Good morning, Governor."

"Good morning, Mr. Kelsey. This is Audrey."

"Audrey, how may I help you?"

"I'm sorry to inform you that the governor will not be able to meet you as planned. He suggested that you proceed without him."

"Not a problem, Audrey. Tell the governor I will contact him later in the week with an update."

"Very well, sir, and do have a pleasant day. Goodbye."

"Goodbye."

Danielle observed a weird expression on Robert's face. "Hmm…The governor will not be joining us today."

From the moment Robert told the governor he had decided not to bring another young lady to join him and Danielle on James Island, the governor had cancelled two appointments and kept his distance from him. Robert knew when the governor sensed you weren't being loyal to him he would chew you up and spit you out. Having no concern about what condition you were in afterwards. No one or nothing mattered, but him. Although he required loyalty, he gave none in return. His egotistical, self-serving brutal and bullish behavior intimidated men, women and children. It was hard to imagine that the governor was made from the image of any normal human being.

However, Danielle was delighted she didn't have to spend another minute in the governor's company. It was a beautiful day in paradise. The ambiance was quiet and serene and the crystal blue waters were breathtaking. Governor Gunn's presence would only bring gloom and doom. He had a way of sucking the oxygen right out of you.

The morning passed swiftly as Robert and Danielle continued enjoying their delicious breakfast of spinach and bacon quiche, butter croissants, and lemongrass tea. Robert appeared preoccupied. Danielle knew the signs, and could easily tell he had something on his mind. She sat quietly for a moment. "Is there something you want to talk about, Robert?"

Looking into his teacup. "I was wondering if the governor cancelling our appointment had anything to do with Camille."

"What does Camille have to do with the governor?"

"I'm going to give you a quick, adult version of the insanity Camille shared with me the other night."

"I was wondering what happened between you two. You guys have been family and friends for a long time, then boom! Everything goes to hell in one night. I was baffled."

"That makes two of us. Camille has a cocaine addiction. Turns out she was dodging bullets for a $100,000 drug debt she owes to your favorite person, Governor Gunn. Fearing for her life, she sought safety here, where she put all of our lives in danger; including yours. I gave her money to pay off the debt, along with a little extra for her to check into a rehab facility. I may have been too hard on her, but she said some pretty nasty stuff, so I asked her to leave the Island, and never return."

Danielle took a minute to process all of this. "Okay. What does Governor Gunn have to do with her addiction?"

"She's running cocaine for him. She said they've run over a billion dollars worth of cocaine. From the Caribbean to Georgia, Florida, and New York."

"What did you say?"

"You heard me. You know I saw a strange boat circling around the island a few days ago. First, I thought someone had gotten lost. Now, I can't help but wonder if it had something to do with Camille."

"That sounds serious, Robert."

"Yes, I know."

"I'll be leaving on business tomorrow for several days. Although Robin will be here with you, I was going to ask the governor to have someone keep an eye on you ladies."

"We'll be fine. Robyn and Maria will keep me engaged and entertained while you're away."

"Can you guarantee that?"

"Yes, sir. Handle your business. I truly appreciate the concern. However, I would feel safer knowing that the governor wasn't involved. I don't trust that man, and when you return we need to get busy and figure out what he has up his sleeve. Besides his old musty arm."

Robert shook his head and smiled. "You are too chilly for the hot dog."

"What's does that mean?"

"Aye! Now, I've said something you don't understand."

"You're not going to tell me?"

"Yes, I'll tell you. It's an old White proverb from my Irish ancestors."

Danielle shook her head, laughing and pointed her finger. "You're an idiot."

The mood was light and airy, and Maria was humming quietly in the kitchen. She was happy to see both Robert and Danielle enjoying each other's company. She didn't want things to end so she appeared on the terrace with a big wicker basket on her arm. "Mr. Robert, it's a beautiful day for a picnic, and since you're leaving in the morning I thought you two might enjoy a day at the beach. I made a lovely lunch for you."

"That's a wonderful idea, Maria. What do you say, Danielle? Are you up for it?"

"You bet I'm up for it. I'll get my suit and meet you back here in thirty minutes." Danielle sat her teacup down and headed for the villa.

Robert walked over to Maria, and put his arms around her. "Do you know how much I love and appreciate you?"

Maria blushed. "Yes, Mr. Robert, I do, and I love and appreciate you too."

Robert walked over to the pool where his trunks were resting on the back of the chair. He pulled the dressing room curtain together and jumped right into his red Speedos. Maria handed him the picnic basket and two large beach towels. When Danielle returned, Robert couldn't keep his eyes off her gorgeous body. The two-piece LeTare white thigh-high bikini gave her legs greater length, and Robert more to admire. But Robert wasn't alone. Danielle couldn't keep her eyes off of him either. He was handsome, charming, and his tan body was carved to perfection. His sexy blond ponytail was just what the doctor ordered.

When Robert locked eyes with Danielle, it was apparent he was falling in love. And it had nothing to do with her beauty. He saw in Danielle something he had never seen in any other woman. She had accepted his apology, and now he wanted to protect her at all cost. Although he was excited to share the day with Danielle, thoughts of the governor were turning over and over in his head. He knew the governor was no one to play with. For years he had walked around willing to be totally oblivious to the governor's activities, but it now appeared the majority of his activities could possibly cause him death or imprisonment. If the information Camille shared with him was correct, then the governor was clearly one of the most corrupt officials he had ever encountered. Regardless of Robert's financial status, he knew he would always be an outsider and could easily be subjected to the governor's disgusting behavior. Robert knew his trip would put some needed distance between him and the governor. Things between the two had taken a new turn, and he had no idea what direction it was headed.

But for now, he was heading to the beach to spend quality time with Danielle. He rested the picnic basket on a large boulder to get a bottle of water. When he turned around, she was stretched out across the beautiful white sand. Lowering his head to hers, he whispered, "I could stay here with you forever." They both smiled and watched day turn into night.

Chapter 10

The morning came fast. Maria was running around making breakfast, Robert was packing, and Danielle was singing, "Oh what a beautiful morning." She was excited about the arrival of her friend Robyn. It was difficult for her to imagine that six weeks ago she had been sold into slavery by her own mother to a man she now called her friend. How could that be? It would appear that having been sold to a man 14 years her senior, and expected to satisfy his needs, would be a reality no one woman would want to face. But she was one of the lucky ones. She was purchased by a man whose morals had not lost its way through the abundant excess of wealth and power, and whose association with a greedy, deplorable governor pulled him into a criminal enterprise he had little knowledge of.

Danielle was eager to help Robert gather what information he needed to fully understand the activities of the governor, but today her time was reserved for Robyn. She couldn't wait to see her face and laugh into the midnight hours. Robyn was the complete opposite of Danielle. Although her features were thicker, fuller and broader, she was a beautiful woman. She was street wise, comical, strong and fiery. People found it surprising that the two girls had cultivated such a strong and lasting friendship. Everyone called them yin and yang. One thing for sure, both girls knew they had a friend in each other, and that provided them with a support that some women only dream of.

Starring out the window, Maria saw Captain Bill arriving. "Danielle, Danielle, she's here." Maria and Danielle had formed a genuine bond, and the two ladies would sit for hours sharing stories about their families and friends. It was easily understood why Maria was as excited as Danielle for Robyn's arrival.

Danielle slid across the shiny marble corridor with a bouquet of flowers in her right hand, while brushing her hair back with her left. As the yacht docked, Danielle and Maria both ran down the steps to greet her. Robyn was wearing a blue and white floral jumper and a big bright smile. The two ladies embraced as if they had been separated for years.

"Oh, my goodness, Robyn, it's so good to touch you, to see you, to hear your voice."

Laughing with pure delight, Robyn replied, "Girl, you look fabulous. I'm so happy to see your old skinny behind. When are you going to pick up some weight? You look magga. I told you nobody want a bone but a dog."

Everyone broke out in laughter. "There you go again. Don't worry about my skinny backside. You're just jealous."

"You are doggone right I'm jealous, but I'm walking around with enough meat on my behind to survive three major illnesses, and poor you wouldn't be able to survive a head cold."

"Arm-in-arm, the ladies climbed the stairs to the estate. Danielle looked back, "Captain Bill, will you please bring your wife's bags up?"

"I most certainly will." Bill stood there laughing. Neither Maria nor Danielle even bothered to say good morning. They were so excited to see Robyn.

Maria reached out to give Bill a hand. "Oh, Captain Bill, I'm so thoughtless. Let me give you a hand with the bags."

"No, Maria. You go ahead. I got this. Where's Robert?"

"He's on the terrace having coffee, why don't you join him? He's packed and ready to go."

When Robyn stepped on the grounds of the estate, her eyes were in total disbelief. "Girl, now this is a come up!" The ocean surrounded the small island, and appointed it a private sandy white beach. The stately villa looked like a fortress, where sloping hills stood stately on solid rocks. It was beautiful, and the large luxury yacht was the perfect accessory.

Danielle, was excited to introduce Robert to Robyn. He stood up and gave her a big warm hug. "Thank you so much for coming to spend time with Danielle. I can't tell you how many wonderful things I've heard about you."

Beaming with pride Robyn whispered in Robert's ear, "Don't believe anything she said. You know she got the liar of the year award, and you are fine."

Laughing, Robert said, "I'm so jealous that I have to leave and can't be here to enjoy your delightful company, but please know that you and Bill are welcome at any time."

"Thank you, Mr. Kelsey.'

"Please call me Robert. A friend of Danielle's, and the wife of Captain Bill, is a friend of mine."

Robert grabbed his bag, gave Maria, Danielle, and Robyn a big farewell hug. "I expect you ladies to behave yourselves while I'm away. Please enjoy yourselves, and know that anything or anyplace you wish to go Bill will be here to make sure it happens."

All three ladies stood at the front of the terrace watching Robert and Bill board the yacht. Robert looked up, waved goodbye, and blew a kiss to Danielle. "That kiss is for you beautiful. See you soon."

Danielle waved and shouted out, "Be safe my friend."

"I will."

Robyn turned to Danielle. "Bill said you needed us to help you escape from the island. Okay, now tell me again why we are planning your escape from this beautiful private island? Girl, Jon have neither calabash no' gold chain. He's a cutie, but in 40 years you will not even recognize him. Then you'll be looking at an ugly broke man without a yacht or an island."

Danielle smiled, "Robyn, I love your sense of humor, but this is a serious situation. Do you understand that my own mother sold me to Robert Kelsey like a slave? That's called human trafficking."

In a sad and low monotone voice Robyn replied, "Yes, I know honey, and it's sickening, painful, and disgusting. But on a positive note you're living on a private island with a rich and very handsome man who is infatuated with you. You're not being kept at the bottom of a slave ship in chains. From where I'm sitting all I see around your ankles are diamond encrusted shackles without a lock. Maybe it's me, but if you want to trade places, I will gladly leave Bill's old broke behind and move my happy ass over here today."

"Girl, Ebr'body t'ink ah dallar is ah dallar, but ah dallar ain ah dallar."

Robyn, scratching her head repeatedly replied, "Who told you that, your crazy Aunt Lucy?"

Laughing uncontrollably Danielle fumbled for words. "So, you think, my Aunt Lucy is crazy?"

Robyn jumped up, eyes bulging, waving her hands in the air, high above her head and bellowed, "Hell yeah! I think your Aunt Lucy is bat shit crazy. I will never forget the day I first met her. We were walking to your house and she appeared in the yard out of nowhere. In a stern and aggressive voice, she asked, 'Who is she?' I reached out my hand casually to introduce myself, and she threw a nasty old rag over my hand and started chanting in a jarring and intense voice. 'I know not where your hands have been, or where they are going, cleanse...cleanse...cleanse... the spirit of the heartless intruder.' She stood there looking in my face. Her eyes were turning from green to red to yellow. She looked like the broken traffic light at the corner of Mandela Circle. I knew that day, I would kill myself before I would come face to face with Aunt Lucy and her nasty rag again. You know I love you, but your Aunt Lucy has some serious issues. There are two things I learned as a child not to play with, matches and Aunt Lucy."

Danielle, laughed herself into a fetal position. "Robyn, I don't remember her eyes changing colors. "You are so dramatic. You're as crazy as Loco Larry." Danielle still laughing, "Stop it, you're insane."

"Did you ever wonder what happened to Loco Larry? His cousin Jerry said he drank a bottle of joy juice from Aunt Lucy, and his head hasn't been good sense. You can call me anything you want, but trust me it will be snowing in the Caribbean before I cross her path again. If yo don't hear yo feel. I'm not feeling her. "You know it's something wrong with that woman. She's evil.

"Do you remember poor little Jettie? She and Joyce were playing in the street and their ball rolled into your aunt's yard. The girls asked for their ball back and she refused to give it to them. As they were walking away, Jettie started mumbling things about your Aunt Lucy. Joyce said the old lady started shouting at Jettie. 'I heard what you said. Yo' betta watch wha' come out yo' mouth.' Joyce said seconds later black worms were crawling out of poor little Jetties' mouth, and not a single word has come out of her mouth since that day. You're lucky I'm still your friend. You might have some of that hocus pocus crap in you, it's all in the DNA, they say. Girl if I were you, I would think twice about having children. It would be bad enough if the little fellow came out waving a magic wand, but what if he came out looking like her ugly behind."

"Robyn, you need to take that show on the road. You're hilarious."

"Oh, I'm the crazy one? You are sitting over here mad at your mother because she sold you to a rich white man. She did you a favor by getting you away from Aunt Lucy and her evil husband. Girl, wild horses couldn't drag me off this island. I would sit over here nice and quiet and play like I didn't know the rest of the world existed. It's so peaceful. No killings, no drugs, no robberies, this is as perfect as it gets. Where the heck you going back to, Eastside Bay?"

"Excuse me please, ladies," said Maria, admiring the closeness of the two friends. "Would you ladies like something to eat?"

"That would be wonderful, Maria. I'm going to take crazy old Robyn by the pool and drown her."

"Crazy Robyn knows how to swim, Boo Boo!"

While relaxing by the pool, drinking Pina coladas and reading Patti Callahan Henry's book, *Becoming Mrs. Lewis*, Robyn spotted a mysterious black speed boat circling around the island. She raised her head slowly. Her eyes signaling concern to Danielle. She motioned for Danielle to take a look, only to discover that she too had spotted it a few days ago. "I mentioned it to Robert, and he said he saw the same boat circling the island a couple of weeks ago, but when he reached for his gun, the boat had turned around. He figured it was someone lost at sea."

Being street wise, Robyn inquired who or what they used for protection while Robert was away. The fact that Robert traveled for days at a time left Robyn concerned for the safety of her friend. Robyn felt it was time to have a serious discussion about living on the island with a false sense of security. She scurried to Maria's villa, where she was napping, and insisted she join them on the terrace to talk about their safety. In her comedic nature Robyn said, "I love living on this beautiful island, but I sure wouldn't want to die here."

Still half asleep, Danielle said tonelessly, "What crazy idea do you have in your head now, Robyn?"

Robyn looked seriously at Danielle and said, "Don't you watch the ID channel? If you need help when Robert is away, who is here to assist you?"

Glancing at her finger, she pondered and pointed to Maria.

"Honey," Robyn said with conviction, "if someone gets on this island while Robert is away, you and Maria are going to need some arsenal and a guardian angel to survive."

Danielle set upright. This time with a trembling voice, 'Robyn you're scaring me. What on earth triggered this conversation, besides the boat."

In a comforting voice Robyn replied, "The boat, in itself, is enough. I'm not trying to scare you, I just think we need to be smart. Hell, Robert isn't the only man with a boat. Shit, I just saw a strange boat circling the island and I realized we need to set up a little security. Do you know how to fire a gun, Danielle?"

"Of course not," Danielle replied. "Do you?"

"Does a mongoose eat snakes?"

Robyn looked at Maria and Danielle. "I suggest we install a security system on the property, and buy some guns. I can teach you and Maria how to load, aim, shoot, and fire. You ladies have to take this seriously, because the life you save could be your own."

Robyn succeeded in convincing Danielle. They both agreed to install surveillance cameras around the property. Robyn was surprised to discover Robert didn't have surveillance already installed living in such a remote and private island.

Robyn grabbed her laptop and began researching the smallest and best motion-activated video audio recorders available. She sent an email to her friend Puffy, with Mad Dog Electronics, to help them configure the perfect system. Robyn explained, "We need to make sure the system has automatic pause and a time and date stamp. We also want pin hole lens and automatic focus. We're not playing with these clowns. They can try some funny stuff, if they want to."

"Danielle, we need to go into town with Bill in the morning and pick up the equipment."

"You need to go. I really have no desire to go into town right now. I'm still processing my life."

"No problem, sister, you know I got you!"

"Thank you, my friend. You're the best."

Danielle paused for a minute and in a concerned voice inquired, "How will we get someone over here to install it?"

In a condescending voice Robyn replied, "Duh! Bill. He'll transport Sticky to the island to install the equipment. Remember my cousin Sticky? He got 5 years in the slammer for uninstalling surveillance equipment." All three ladies were laughing and crying at the same time. "He can get us a couple of guns too. All we need is the money."

Danielle knew money wasn't an issue. Robert was very generous and had already given her access to the cash on the property, if and when she needed it.

In a confident tone, Danielle said, "Don't worry about the money, just let me know how much we need. When we decide which day, I'll tell Robert your cousin will be coming out to help design your website. I'll also tell him we'll be doing target practice so he won't be alarmed when he finds shells everywhere."

"That's a good idea."

Making a joke, Danielle said, "Now, who will we get to watch Sticky?"

Laughing collectively, Robyn replied, "Sticky's not a problem. He doesn't have a boat and he can't swim. Plus, he knows I will kill him if he tries anything."

Danielle wondered if she should tell Robert that she was installing surveillance on the property, but decided she would keep it to herself. It was meant for her safety and she wasn't sure if Robert didn't need watching as well.

Danielle knew she would need to locate the perfect place to conceal the monitoring equipment. She began exploring every nook and cranny of the estate, when Maria interrupted, "I have the perfect place, Danielle. We can put it in the pantry closet. That would be the perfect hiding space. Mr. Robert was planning to install a safe there and decided against it. No one ever goes in the pantry, but me. Plus, it has an electrical outlet and ventilation."

Danielle pondered for a moment. "Robyn, do you think Bill and Maria will tell Robert I installed the cameras on the property?"

Robyn rolled her eyes at Danielle. "My husband is not a snitch."

Maria placed her hands on her little hips. "Maria no snitch either."

Both fell on the sofa and cheered. "We hear you, Maria."

Danielle left the ladies and went to the east side of the estate. She entered Robert's villa and was able to smell the sweet scent of his cologne. He wore the same Pitbull cologne every day, and it smelled sexy, just like Pitbull. She removed $5,000 from the safe and divided the money into separate envelopes. She placed $3,000 in one envelop for the equipment, $500 for the guns, $500 for Sticky, and $1,000 for her best friend.

Everything was back to normal; the ladies were able to relax again. They had a plan, the money, and the installer. Maria joined the ladies on the terrace where they snacked on tortilla chips, salsa and cream cheese, while listening to Santana's "Black Magic Woman."

Robyn left the ladies sitting outside and returned a few moments later with three virgin Pina coladas. Sighing with relief, Robin remarked, "This is the life. Let's make a toast."

The ladies raised their crystal goblets and toasted to their safety and everlasting friendship.

The ocean breeze made it easy to relax. All three ladies stayed together on the terrace to keep an eye out for the mysterious boat.

The next morning, Danielle and Robyn remained sleeping on the terrace. Maria was up preparing a breakfast fit for three queens. Corn beef hash, eggs over easy, fried potatoes, and toast served with fresh mimosas. Both ladies ran to the shower to make sure the heat didn't evaporate from the food. It was going to be another fun day on James Island. As the ladies returned to the terrace, Captain Bill was just arriving. He tied The Wanderer to the pier and jogged up the steps to join the ladies in laughter and breakfast.

Captain Bill grabbed Maria's hands, "Good morning, little lady, you are the best chef around." Then he made a quick spin and embraced Robyn, sealing it with a kiss.

"Amen to that," replied Danielle.

Maria smiled. "You are the best captain, and, ladies, you are the best friends."

The love was flowing and the tropical breeze added the beautiful scent of bougainvillea as the sun graced its presence on the lawn of James Island.

"What do you beautiful ladies have planned for today?"

Robyn turned looking to Bill. "I need you to take me into town to pick up some much-needed equipment and Sticky."

"Sticky? What do you need with Sticky?"

Glancing downward, she responded, "Sweetheart, we keep seeing the same mysterious boat circling the island, so we feel we need to add a little security; just to be on the safe side."

Bill wiped his mouth. "I think that's a great idea. I don't want to mess up your vibe, but I would feel better if I stayed out here with you ladies for a while. I'll stay out of your way."

They looked at each other. "That's a great idea, honey. Sticky is getting us a couple of guns, and I'm going to show Danielle and Maria how to use them."

Bill shook his head. "That's a horrible idea."

"Excuse me. Why is that a horrible idea?"

"First of all, you have no idea how many people have already been killed with the guns Sticky will sell you. Secondly, if you are going to carry a firearm, it needs to be legal. There's no reason to invite trouble when your intention is merely to protect yourself and your property."

Robyn was easy to convince. "You're right, but we need a gun."

Bill Rose to his feet. Robert has two legal M1 Enforcer pistols, and a Bushmaster. As for myself, I have a 357 magnum. We're good."

"Well I guess that says it all, Danielle."

"I guess so, girlfriend, Thank you, Bill."

"Anytime."

Robyn returned to the villa to finish dressing. Maria returned to the kitchen, and Danielle and Bill sat quietly on the veranda watching the water taxi sail to and from St. John.

Robyn returned with her cheeks glowing, and her eyes glaring from the intense sun rays. "I'm ready."

Captain Bill grabbed his hat, and his adorable wife, and headed towards the yacht. "See you guys shortly."

"Wait for me," shouted Maria. "I need to grocery shop. Why don't you come along with us, Danielle?"

Danielle smiled. "Not today sweetie, not today. Ai put mi name in de mout' of de public." She stood high on the mountain looking down on her friends as they sailed away.

Watching everyone leave, Danielle exhaled and took time to reflect on the events of the previous days. For the first time in months, she was totally alone. There were no interruptions, no demands, and no expectations. She had the freedom to look beyond yesterday and focus entirely on the present. The present, however, was unbelievable—unlike the life she had known, dreamt, or even wanted. Her current life was filled with lies, betrayal, loss, and confusion. A recipe for complete and unadulterated disaster. Her body became limp as she gazed lovingly at the climatic influence of the Atlantic Ocean.

Hypnotized by the rippling of the waves, her present state of mind floated away into memories of Jon, only to be replaced with visions of Robert Kelsey. He had departed only days ago, but the time seemed far greater than the true hours of his absence. She was beginning to miss the safety and security she felt in his presence. Even though he didn't display a visual appearance of a strong and fearless warrior, his calm demeanor and methodical thinking gave her a sense of security she now missed. The wealthy American, who purchased her freedom weeks ago from her mother, had now stolen her mind.

Lying quietly in the lap of luxury had now become the normal way of life for the impoverished West Indian beauty. Under his control, Robert Kelsey had treated her no less than royalty and with complete respect; unlike most victims of human trafficking. Then again, Robert Kelsey wasn't like most men. At no time did he ever think he was committing the hideous crime. In his own self-serving mind, his actions equated to buying Danielle's freedom. Purely on the strength that he could, even though his intentions were honorable. He would learn from the woman he found so intriguing, that he had been a willing participate in a crime against humanity… modern day slavery.

Chapter 11

Danielle was pulled from her hypnotic state of mind by the sounds of engines as Captain Bill and the gang returned to James Island. The hours had passed quickly and now it was time to begin the installation of their surveillance equipment. Robyn and Maria headed up the stairs with bags of groceries, and bright smiles, anticipating Danielle's excitement for their return. "Did you miss us," shouted Robyn?

"Well, of course. How could you not miss a hurricane?"

Robyn laughed. "I got your hurricane, missy."

Danielle took two bags from Robyn's hands, allowing her the freedom to embrace her friend. "I missed you too, sweetie. I hope you were able to relax a bit. You didn't spot that boat again, did you?"

"No, everything's been pretty normal."

"That's good to hear. I was hoping I didn't have to run up here guns a blazing."

"Girl, you sound like you just want to shoot somebody, anybody."

"Yes, that would be a fact if they came up here with some bullshit! It's on..."

At that moment, Captain Bill and Sticky entered the main villa. Danielle walked over to Sticky. "Hello, it's been a long time. I'm glad to see you."

Sticky turned around and around in total disbelief of their surroundings. "Man, this is some real serious living. How in the hell did your broke asses get up here on this mountain?"

Robyn replied, "It's a long story, but what matters now, is that we made it. Now your job is to sew up yoh mout and start installing the eyes."

"As you wish, Cuz!"

Sticky began to open up the boxes, separating the components and placing them in sections." We have a total of eight eyes. I'm going to look around the property and find the best place to set each one of these babies."

Taking his hat off, Bill said, "I'll go with you man."

Together both men walked around the grounds to determine the best locations for the eyes. Sticky paused. "Man, this is a crazy set up. Why the little houses all over?"

Bill laughed. "These little houses are called villas, man. It gives everyone a real sense of privacy. The residents and their guests come together in the common area of the estate, if they choose."

"That's some wild shit!"

Sticky observed the layout of the property and said, "If I were a thief, I would look for pivotal eyes in each direction, and the main entrance on the property."

Bill, bending over in laughter. "Sticky, you have vastly underrated yourself. You are a thief."

Laughing, Sticky agreed, "Yea, I guess you could say that. But I have other skills too."

"Of course, you do. That's exactly why you're here."

"Look man, if you want to catch a thief, use a thief. The police do it all the time. Some of them are the biggest thieves around."

"That's sad, but true man. However, we also have some real stand up cops."

"Yea, but they don't stand very long. The bad cops shoot them down for not playing the game. They become just like everyone else, a victim of our society."

"Wow! Sticky, I didn't know you were so deep man."

"When you sit in prison for five years you do a lot of reflecting, and life becomes very clear."

Bill shook his head. "Okay man, let's get these eyes installed."

The ladies were sitting on the sofa leisurely sipping passion fruit from monogrammed glasses. They looked up when Bill and Sticky entered the room. Robyn asked, "You guys figure out where the eyes are going?"

"We sure did," Sticky replied. "If you ladies will just get in the kitchen and do what ladies do, I will get these eyes installed. You can feed me and take me back home to my peeps, and you can sleep well under the security of eight watchful eyes."

Maria chuckled. "I can handle the kitchen; you ladies can stay as you are."

"You know," Robyn shaking her head, "That's not a problem for me. I find it a pleasure to be in the company of someone who takes pleasure in making my life carefree and enjoyable. I love…love…love…you, Maria."

Danielle nodded, "That goes for both of us."

Maria, being aware of Sticky's reputation, turned to him and pointed her two fingers forming a "V" from her eyes to his. "My eyes will be watching you too."

"I'm sorry to hear that, I had planned to carry that big jar of salsa home.

Everyone laughed as Sticky went about the business of installing the eyes. Robyn and Danielle continued talking, but were interrupted by the ringing telephone. A few seconds later Maria, walked into the room. "Danielle, Mr. Robert is on the line and wish to speak with you." Taken by surprise, Danielle accepted the call.

"Hello, Robert, how are things?

"Things are good, Danielle. How is your visit with Robyn going?"

"Everything is great. Robyn's cousin Sticky is here helping her install new software on the computer."

"Alright. Is Bill there?"

"Yes, do you wish to speak with him?"

Robert spoke with hesitation. "No, that's not necessary. I just wanted to make sure he was around to protect my girls."

For the first time, Danielle realized the infatuation she felt when speaking with Robert on the phone. Robert was slowly, but surely, navigating himself straight into her life. "Do you miss your friend?"

Danielle seemed to echo the very thoughts that were in Robert's mind. "Yes, I miss my friend very much, and can't wait to see her beautiful face again."

Blushing, she sat quietly and chatted with Robert about things of little importance, realizing once the conversation ended his voice would be gone again. The only thing left behind was the lingering smell of his cologne.

Clearing his throat, "I don't wish to be the bearer of bad news, but I have an important meeting to attend, so I've got to run. You guys stay safe and don't forget you're in charge."

"Well in that case. I think I'll go shopping."

Robert chuckled. "Shop away, you know where the money is. Buy whatever your heart desires."

Both Robert and Danielle ended their call with a heartfelt goodbye.

It was evident to Robyn that Danielle was beginning to fall for Robert, but why not, he was caring, attentive, handsome and very rich. "How do you feel about him?" she inquired.

"I don't know."

"What the hell do you mean, you don't know?" staring into Danielle's eyes. "You can't see you're falling for this man?"

"That's one of the most ridiculous things I've known you to say."

"Well in case you didn't know, that's one of the biggest lies I've ever heard you tell yourself."

Robyn placed her arms around Danielle's shoulders. "I hate to tell you this, but besides the obvious fact that you are falling for Robert, I stopped by to visit your Mother while I was in town, just to let her know you were okay."

"She doesn't deserve to know. Tis wha' yoh hole deh in yoh eye."

"Of course, she does. Minus the crazy stuff she did to you, she's still your mother and loves you in her own wicked twisted way. Anyway, I was attempting to tell you that Dior overheard your mother telling your Aunt Lucy about what she had done to you. She and Dior got into a big argument and she hasn't seen her since."

"What do you mean, she hasn't seen her since. Where is she?"

"She was staying with her friend, Phyllis. I passed by there, only to find out that she had gone to Babylon, in fear of her mother selling her as she did you."

"Oh, no! Where in Babylon? She doesn't know anyone there."

"I don't know. But we will find out."

It appeared Danielle was unable to catch a break. Every day she was tossed into the hole of darkness and despair. She began to beat her hand convulsively on the glass table; demonstrating her frustration, while trying to hide her tears of emotions. But they fell like ripe mangoes in rain. The past had continuously brought her great pain, and today the future for her little sister, Dior, threatened to hamper any ray of hope for a brighter future for them both. It became increasingly clear that Robert Kelsey would be the key to locating her sister. Days ago, it was he that had asked for her help, now it was she who needed his help in finding Dior. Danielle realized the alliance they needed to form would bring them closer than ever. The conditions of her life didn't change. Even the storybook life of the rich and famous came with seedy infractions of life disrupted.

Robyn tapped her foot repeatedly, "Okay! Enough of this woe is me. Girl, we have to put our big girl panties on and figure this stuff out. We're strong, smart, and thanks to Robert Kelsey, got some dead presidents to work with. It is really important that we lay out a plan that will be a win-win situation for everyone. I know you're concerned about Dior, but we have to trust and pray that she will be just fine until we can find her. Right now, our best partner is the heavenly Father. I need you to focus on your mental health, and for goodness' sake, girl, eat something other than carrot sticks and mangoes. If things continue at this pace, you're going to need your strength. I feel a category five hurricane in the making."

"Very well," agreed Danielle. "I must take these things seriously, but I can't allow them to take over my life. When do you leave?"

"I was planning to leave next week when Robert returned. Why, do you need me to stay longer?"

"No. When yoh hear de shout."

"Yoh know how ah stay."

It occurred to Robyn she should check on Sticky. "How are things coming along?"

"Everything's good, mon! I'll be finished in a few more minutes. I'm just doing a little finessing before we go live."

"Ok! Danielle and I were getting a little worried."

"Ah know whe' yoh comin' from. I got this." Turning his cap around backwards, lifting his eyebrows, he said, "Okay ladies, the eyes are open."

"Great! Show us how it works."

"No problem! I need to make sure the monitor is on point."

Danielle sprang from the sofa and took Sticky by the hand to the kitchen pantry.

Sticky's nose was pointed toward the ceiling. "Wow! It smells almost as good in here as you do, Maria."

"Oh! Dear God!" said Maria, with a surprise look on her face. "What am I going to do with you?"

Sticky laughed. "I've got a couple of suggestions."

Danielle said, with a little sense of humor, "Sticky have more tricks than damn monkey."

In the middle of the conversation Maria laughed, nodding her head. "Don't worry, 'e head too close to 'e tail."

Sticky pushed up his lips. "Don't you worry about my head or my tail, just get my food ready, little lady. I'm ready to mash up the pot."

Robyn and Danielle stood close by as Sticky showed them how to operate the surveillance equipment. Captain Bill remained outside, running around the yard to give everyone an idea how the eyes would record any intruders on the property.

"It looks great," Danielle remarked. "Now that should be enough."

Sticky stuck his chest out. "It may not keep someone from killing you, but it sure will help identify the murderer."

Rolling her eyes to the back of her head, Robyn replied, "Thanks, Cuz. I can always count on you to keep our spirits up."

The sun was beginning to set as Maria called everyone to the terrace for dinner. One by one everyone took a seat. It was a meal everyone was looking forward to eating. The table was covered with a delicious pot of stew beef, peas and rice, plantains, broccoli, and Johnny cakes. Between the installation of a new security system, a gathering of dear friends, and a delicious West Indian meal, James Island was looking like paradise. Before parting from James Island, Robyn paid Sticky for his services. Maria and Danielle cleaned up the kitchen, while Captain Bill and Robyn journeyed once more across the Atlantic Ocean to carry Sticky back home.

Ten o' clock that evening, Captain Bill and Robyn returned to James Island. Danielle had just dragged herself to the edge of the sofa, when she saw Bill securing the yacht to the dock. She was relieved to see them back safely, and even more excited to know that he would be there to keep watchful eyes on everyone. Robyn popped up. "When you're tired of me, let me know."

Danielle smiled. "I could never tire of you, my friend. Your company is refreshing and so pure and honest. I feel so blessed to have had a friend like you all these years. I never want our friendship to end."

"Now you're going to make me cry. Seriously, I feel the same way, Danielle. You're the sister I never had, and the friend every girl wants. I just wanted to let you know that I'm sleeping on the yacht with Bill. He's all serious about being our security guard. He's down there loading guns and drinking rum."

Danielle shook her head from side to side. "Now that sounds like a dangerous combination. I think he needs to either put down the rum or the guns. You may need to supervise him tonight. I'm fine sweetheart' we can talk in the morning."

The two friends embraced and both retired for the evening. Danielle returned to her villa and prayed for her sister's safety. Even though she was the eldest, Dior was always more aware. She knew that if anyone could survive the cruelty of Babylon, it would be Dior. Even though the night was upon her, Danielle wasn't sleepy. Her thoughts were running around in her head like a scared rabbit. If only she could will her mind into a state of calm. She laid still trying to envision the moving waves and the beautiful white beach of Magen's Bay, and the quiet grassy lawn of Emancipation Garden. She missed the beauty of St. Thomas. The island would forever remain in her heart. Still feeling like a lost ship at sea, she took pen to paper. This time the letter was addressed to Robert Kelsey.

My dearest Robert,

I lie awake in the middle of the night, thinking of you in a way I didn't think possible. To my surprise the smell of your cologne lingered inside my memories like my first ice cream cone. Deliciously satisfying and completely addictive. So much has happened in the past few weeks. I feel like I'm on reality TV, with the world watching as my life spirals out of control. I lost everything I cherished in one night. It seemed impossible that I could ever be happy again. That was until I found peace and solace in the sanctuary of your home and the tenderness of your voice.

There are many people who leave a lasting impression on you as you travel through life. I must say that today, I add your name to that list. Even in the mist of this insane situation, you have been gracious, respectful and kind. I thank God, every day, that deep inside of you is a man of strong moral character. A man, even though others would say you owned me, never tried to force himself upon me.

A man that listens to my pain with ears of sensitivity, and offered me friendship through truth. This is not the manner I would expect a person that engaged in this form of criminal activity to behave.

I chased the words around in my head that I wanted to convey to you. However, they allude me at this time, so I will try and rest myself and leave you with the thought that I look forward to your return, and to spending time with a man who has taken up residence in my mind. I certainly hope that your trip is going as planned, and your return will be safe and speedy.

Highest regards,

Danielle

After sharing her intimate feelings in her letter to Robert, Danielle drifted into a peaceful state of rest.

Chapter 12

As the smell of bacon replaced the morning breeze, Captain Bill and Robyn emerged to have breakfast and discuss their plan of action. They greeted each other in their normal fashion: a hug, a kiss, and a strong supportive embrace. Danielle found it ironic that God had surrounded her with the support of her loyal friends. It was exactly what she required to remain resilient, and persevering against all odds. Danielle assigned each person a task. Robyn's assignment was to learn as much as she could about the death of Robert's father, and Captain Bill's was to identify and locate the only witness present during the demise of Robert's father. She urged them to take extreme precautions and report all information in person. After breakfast, Danielle gave Captain Bill the letter she had written Robert to include in his weekly shipments to Robert.

With everything that was happening, days on the island swept by in rapid succession. The dynamics of the household had shifted since Robert's departure. Danielle was now chief executive officer, Captain Bill had assumed the role as chief security officer, and Robyn was the administrative assistant and confidant. Everyone was from the island of St. Thomas, except Robert, so everyone involved understood the behavior of the culprit with which they were confronting. Danielle wasn't sure if the governor had a hand in the disappearance of Dior, or if she actually did go to Babylon in search of freedom from her mother's unorthodox way of arranging marriages for her daughters. The wheels were being set in motion.

New moles would be recruited to provide information on the ins and outs of newsworthy criminal activities on the island of St. Thomas. Only trusted friends and family would be allowed in their inner circle. It was too risky to seek information from someone who hadn't been vetted through years of dedicated friendship and loyalty.

The news of Dior had given Danielle a new sense of purpose. It was obvious she would require Robert's complete support. She began to work diligently to secure information on his father's death before his return. Captain Bill and Robyn made their way to the yacht and Danielle set up a temporary office on the terrace. Her first course of action was to identify all questionable crimes and deaths that had gone unsolved over the past five years. She set up individual clusters to identify commonality of events and suspects. She was determined to provide Robert with the information needed to bring closure, and end his association with the despicable Governor Gunn. Danielle was completely aware of the risk she was taking, but it didn't matter. She knew Gunn was responsible for disrupting her life. What she didn't know was how many other people's lives had been disrupted by his wicked and evil behavior.

She spent the morning searching through archives of police arrest records, drug raids, and suspicious deaths. For such a small island, the body count and number of missing women and girls were staggering. It was hard to fathom so many people were unable to be located. Where did they go? A series of questions would reside in her head as she pieced together story after story. She ran several missing person searches. There was a slight chance her investigation might alert someone, but she didn't care. Even if she had to take a forbidden trip into cyberspace, she was determined to shed light on the criminal enterprise of the governor. She hesitated as her slender fingers stroked the keyboard, nothing populated. She closed and opened her eyes; this time with fingers crossed. Within seconds the computer screen lit up displaying pages and pages of mysterious deaths in the Caribbean.

Maria noticed Danielle working hard without taking a break. She joined her on the terrace with a light snack and a beverage. She rubbed her shoulders and offered her assistance. "Is there anything I can help you with Danielle?"

Gazing up, Danielle smiled. "No, thank you, Maria. I have everything under control right now, but if I need you I will let you know. Why don't you take a nap, you've been working so hard?"

Maria kissed Danielle lightly on the forehead. "I think I will take a little nap." Maria retreated to the villa and Danielle continued analyzing the reports. She noticed a recent news article citing the discovery of the body of an unidentified white female. She had been so focused on her research, she didn't realize that Captain Bill and Robyn had returned. As the two walked in the door, Danielle greeted them, "Hey you guys, listen to this. The St. Thomas Coast Guard retrieved the decomposed body of a white female at Victory Beach on Tuesday morning. The results of an autopsy concluded she had been deceased for approximately seven days. It is currently being ruled as an accident, as there were no obvious signs of foul play. The unidentified woman was found wearing a light blue sun dress. Officials are focused on finding out the identity of the woman, asking anyone to come forward with any information."

Robyn paused. "Okay, what are you saying?"

"I don't know, it just seems so weird that bodies of young women or either coming up missing or found floating in the ocean. I believe it's all connected somehow."

Robyn turned to Danielle. "I'm confused. I thought we were focused on finding information relative to the death of Robert's father."

"We are, but as I was doing my research I kept seeing numerous stories of unidentified women's deaths and missing persons on every page. It's too many to be considered a coincidence. I believe it's all part of something bigger. I would bet my life on it."

"Well hold up on betting life and stuff. I'm spooked just looking under rocks for information on Robert Kelsey Sr.'s death. Let's just see where this takes us, Sherlock Holmes."

Nodding her head in agreement. "Fair enough, partner."

Robyn headed towards the kitchen. "Where's Maria? My belly is lonely for some of her good old cooking."

"Maria is napping. She was a little tired, but she prepared chicken salad. It's in the refrigerator, and there's chips in the pantry."

"That's sounds like a winner to me. What about you, honey. Care to join me for a little something to eat."

Bill scooted straight to the kitchen. "Count me in, I could eat an elephant."

Robyn laughed. "If you don't get back in the gym, you're going to start looking like an elephant."

"Ha! Ha! Ha! Real funny."

Danielle looked at them both with a quirky smile. "Ok, hungry people. When you finish eating. I would like an update on what you were able to find."

"We didn't find much, but I found something very interesting Robert can follow up on."

Danielle waited patiently for Robyn and Captain Bill to finish eating. She was excited to hear what Robyn had to say.

Robyn sat beside Danielle on the sofa, "Are you ready for this?'

Looking suspicious, "I don't know, you tell me. Am I?"

"Okay." I went down to Jimmy's Chicken Fry. Jimmy was there, so I sat down next to him and we starting talking. He had one too many, and you know how he is when he's had a few. Since he's a regular at Club Lacey I thought it was a good time to ask him about the girl they found with the dead rich white guy on the private island. He said, 'Come on Robyn, you know I can't talk about that. I love drinking, but I love living better.' So, I said, come on, this is me. Your girl, Robyn. You know I love a good piece of melee.

"Jimmy told me that it's not good to know everything. Some shit can get you killed. I told him it was safe to share with me because I wasn't going to tell anyone. He said one of Molinda's girls, Suzi Rose, was with the old man when he died, but she wasn't alone. She disappeared shortly thereafter. Everyone thought she was dead, but she appeared back on island six months ago. He doesn't know how true it is, but what happened to Robert Sr. was not natural. They said he got next to the governor. 'E buy it. Now you know why you have to sew up yoh mout."

"Wow!" Danielle pondered for a moment. "Are you serious? The governor had something to do with Robert Sr.'s death? I knew he was dirty, but I wasn't expecting to hear that. When Robert returns I'll tell him, but I'm not sure how he's going to deal with this revelation. God forbid, it's hard for me to even swallow. When I read the obituary section of the paper it said that he was found unable to breathe by his girlfriend, and later died from an apparent heart attack."

Raising her left brow. "Well, we know that part of the story isn't true. I know we all want to help Robert find out what happened to his father, but we must ask ourselves if we are willing to put out lives in jeopardy. After all, the man has been dead for almost five years, and he damn sure is not coming back. I never met him, and I sure don't want our first meeting to be in the damn cemetery. Danielle, your friendship is toxic; teetering on the edge of death. I survived your crazy Aunt Lucy, now we have entangled ourselves with her old corrupt murdering husband. Bill fix me a drink, and please, no virgin Pina colada. I need some serious rum here."

Danielle laid her head in Robyn's lap, laughing like a hyena. "I wish you could hear yourself."

"Hell, I'm not deaf. I hear myself very well. I'm crazy as hell over here attempting to uncover a murder at the risk of losing my life for what, two weeks' pay at three times my normal pay and a million-dollar view at the Atlantic Ocean. Girl, if we're not careful, they'll find all three of our asses in the Atlantic Ocean swimming with the sharks."

Sitting up with a serious expression on her face. "Don't worry, sweetheart, Robert's got plenty of money and he's not going to let anything happen to us."

With a quirky look on her face. "News flash! Robert's daddy had the money first, and it sure as hell didn't save his ass. You have to come up with something better than that to settle my nerves."

Standing in the middle of the room, Captain Bill exhaled. "Ladies, ladies, calm down. I will be the first to admit this is some scary, crazy shit! I don't think there is anything else we need to do. We have all the information Robert needs to proceed. He can hire a private investigator to get to the bottom of things. You, my dear, can return home with your handsome husband and get back to the life you love so much. Then you and Danielle can get together as your schedules permit, and things will be back to normal in no time."

Both Robyn and Danielle were looking at each other grinning like two clowns. "Bill is right," replied Danielle. "I will give Robert everything he needs to move forward. Thank you, my friends. I really appreciate you both sticking your heads out for me and making be laugh at the same time. I truly can't tell you how much having you here has meant to me. Robyn, I promise you one thing, I will never ask you to spend time with Aunt Lucy again, unless it's a matter of life and death."

With her hands in the air and eyes rolling. "I promise you, Ms. Danielle Harrigan, that I will never spend time with that crackpot. She's just too friggin evil!"

Nodding in agreement. "Yes, she is. But she is my aunt."

Robyn cries out, "You have my deepest sympathy."

The full moon was in clear view as the two ladies wished each other a goodnight. "Goodnight, Sherlock."

"Goodnight, my friends"

Captain Bill and Robyn descended down the steps to the yacht, where they would relax under the moonlight while providing security for their beloved friend.

Danielle stopped by Maria's villa to check on how she was doing, only to find her lying on the floor. Kneeling down beside her she cried out in panic, "Maria, Maria, talk to me."

She was terrified. Danielle ran down the steps screaming for Captain Bill. "Help, help, it's Maria." Bill and Robyn joined Danielle as she ran swiftly up the stairs. Captain Bill immediately performed CPR on Maria, while Robyn signaled the Coast Guard for assistance. After several minutes of Bill trying to resuscitate Maria, she began coughing. When she opened her eyes, she saw a frightened Danielle with tears streaming down her face. "Ms. Danielle, what happened?"

Wiping her eyes. "I don't know, Maria. I came in to check on you and found you lying on the floor unresponsive. Thank God, you're okay."

The Coast Guard entered the villa, checked Maria's vitals, and gave her oxygen to stabilize her breathing. Captain Bill walked over to the guard. "Do we need to take her to the hospital to be examined?"

The men placed Maria on her bed and continued examining and asking her questions. Within minutes the guard replied, "She'll be fine. Her vitals are stable. She's breathing on her own. It appears that she went to sleep without taking her blood pressure medication. When she stood up, she felt dizzy and you know the rest. She's lucky that the cold tiles helped to keep her body temperature normal. I will advise her to be sure and take her medication."

Danielle was relieved. She wanted to call Robert, but Maria asked her not to. "I don't want him to worry about me. I will be fine." Danielle agreed, but made the executive decision to give Maria some time off. She decided to take over preparing the food and managing the other household responsibilities.

Captain Bill and Robyn returned to the yacht, and Danielle laid at the foot of Maria's bed to watch over her as she had so graciously done for her since her arrival on James Island.

When the sun opened its eyes, Danielle was standing in the kitchen preparing breakfast for her extended family. She carefully prepared a lovely breakfast tray for Maria, to make sure she remained in bed. Captain Bill and Robyn entered the kitchen. "Wow, it smells good in here. What's for breakfast?"

"Well, let me see," lifting the top of the pots. "It looks like we have saltfish pate, a pot of hot cereal with a cinnamon stick (from Grenada), Johnny cakes, cheese, and hot lemongrass tea."

Bill glanced at Robyn. "Looks like this Island girl knows her way around the kitchen. I can't wait to see what we have for dinner."

Danielle leaned back with her hands placed on her hips. "This is dinner too! I can't stay tied to the stove all day. I suggest you don't get too ravenous." She tucked her hair behind her ears, picked up Maria's tray and off she went. Leaving Robyn and Bill standing in the kitchen with their mouths agape.

131

Chapter 13

The next morning when the mail arrived, Robert's Mother immediately delivered it to him in the dining room, where he was having breakfast. He opened the express mail package with a jewel tone encrusted letter opener. As he dumped the contents on the table, he noticed a small envelope accompanied by the scent of lavender.

He smiled when he saw it was a letter from Danielle. He ignored everything on the table and immediately opened the letter, eager to read the contents. He smiled with pure delight as he read each line. He had no idea Danielle would be prompted to write such loving and eloquent words. He leaned back in the chair with his hands folded behind his head and carefully envisioned her beautiful face into his memories. He was more than smitten; he was a man in love. He opened his case, took out a sheet of monogrammed letterhead, and penned a note.

My dearest Danielle,

When I think of you, my imagination carries me to a place where the pleasure of your company is witnessed. The sweetness of your kiss, which I have yet to taste, will never be erased from my mind. Only the removal of miles traveled will reveal what is already known.

You are loved and missed,

R. Kelsey

Robert placed the note into an envelope, placing a drop of his cologne on the inside of the envelope and around the edges of the note, and slid it into his case. It would be only minutes before he would give the letter to the doorman with a $100 tip, to ensure an express mail delivery to St. Thomas. He then journeyed by taxi from the bustling traffic of Manhattan to the upper eastside to meet with his brother. Even though the two were caught up in the insane dysfunctional behavior of their family, the brothers remained close. Robert had decided to reach out to his brother to express his concern about Camille's current behavior.

When Randall appeared at the Lacroix Restaurant, he was dressed in a casual, but striking ensemble of navy slacks, a stripe shirt, and alligator loafers. His Rolex watch and initialed gold cuff links added another layer of sophistication and class. He embraced his brother passionately, then remarked, "I'm surprised you're not wearing a pair of khaki shorts and topsiders." They both broke out in laughter.

"You know, Randall, I thought about it, but I just couldn't bear to hear Mother's mouth."

"I know what you mean. But, of course, you were always on point with, 'When in Rome do as the Romans do' rhetoric."

Randall gazed at an attractive waitress passing by, "Man, look at what you're missing living like a hermit in the jungle of the Caribbean. That place is meant to visit and come back home. But you, my brother, has turned living there into an art form. Be careful. That place will eat you up and spit you out if you're not careful."

Robert shook his head. "The island is cool, plus I've met someone special and I really want to make a life with her."

"You, lover boy, are narrowing down to one woman? She must be an extraordinary lady."

"Now that's the first sensible thing you've said yet."

The expression on Robert's face changed. "Randall, I really wanted to talk with you about Camille."

"What about Camille?" Watching the waitress parade in and out of the kitchen door. "The last time I saw Camille, she looked like she had been rode hard and put away wet."

Robert gritted his teeth." Come on man, she was your wife for goodness sake. Have some compassion for her."

The veins were popping in Randall's forehead. "Compassion! That bitch stole my money and gave it to some punk-ass junkie. I'm sorry, but she made her bed, now she has to lie in it."

"I understand your anger, but you have so much money, you couldn't possibly be crying over that little chump change she took from you. I think you're still in love with her."

"Look, Robert, you may be right, but it doesn't matter. Mother was right. You can't make a whore a wife. I learned my lesson well. I'm not reaching out to Camille for any reason. Now can we change the subject? Your conversation is making me sick to my stomach, and I need to eat."

"Okay, brother, call the waitress you've been looking at for the last ten minutes."

Randall lifted his finger to gain the attention of the waitress. She appeared within seconds. "Yes, gentlemen, are you ready to order?"

Gazing into her eyes. "Yes, sweetheart, I'd like a double kiss of the luscious lips you're wearing on your beautiful face."

Robert lowered his head, then gazed up at the waitress. "Pay him no attention. He's like an old dog chasing a car. Once you stop for him, he doesn't know what to do."

Both men laughed. "Try me."

She stiffened. "Why do you feel the need to deliberately embarrass me?"

Chuckling, while reaching for her hand, Randall responded, "Because you left me this morning without kissing me goodbye."

Robert looked puzzled. "Do you two know each other?"

"No, not really," Randall replied, "we've just being living together for the past 12 months. Joy, this is my baby brother, Robert. Robert, this is your new sister-in-law, Joy."

Robert looked up at the ceiling. "Well, I just be damn." He leaned over to Randall. "Why is your girl working as a waitress, when you have so much damn money?"

Randall laughed. "She doesn't know I have money. I want to be sure she loves me for me, then I'll buy her the whole damn restaurant, if she wants it. If not, she can just sit at home and have a house full of babies. I don't care. I just know I care a lot about her, and I don't want to make the same mistake twice."

The two brothers enjoyed their meal and their conversation, making plans to have dinner on Friday so Robert and Joy could become better acquainted.

Robert left the restaurant feeling happy for his brother. It appeared the brothers had hit pay dirt. They both found women they wanted to settle down with. Even though he was truly happy for Randall, he was still concerned about Camille. He took a taxi to her apartment building, only to find that she wasn't home. Her doorman, Larry, was acquainted with Robert and, in confidence, told him about the upcoming foreclosure on Camille's unit. Robert had made several mortgage payments for Camille over the years, so he was aware of the financial institution preparing to foreclose on the unit. He gave Larry a $100 tip and took a taxi to the Third Bank of Manhattan.

Upon his arrival, he requested to speak with the bank manager. A short round man with a receding hair line and a black tailored suit emerged from the rear office of the bank. He introduced himself as Mr. Kincaid and escorted Robert to his office. With a serious expression, Robert explained his sister-in-law, Camille Kelsey, is under doctor's care unable to travel. She asked him to make the mortgage payments, which are currently in arrears.

Mr. Kincaid paused. "Do you have a letter authorizing you to complete this transaction for Ms. Kelsey?"

Robert was perplexed, "Why would I need a letter to make a payment?" Looking agitated. "I'm making a payment, not withdrawing funds."

"I understand your concerns, sir. However, I'm not at liberty to discuss the monies owed on Ms. Kelsey's account."

Robert was really getting unnerved. "I don't need you to discuss her business, just tell me how much I need to pay,

$2, 000, $5, 000, or just give me a hypothetical number that will bring the account current."

The bank manager wrote the amount on a piece of paper and slid it over to Robert—$20,000 was the amount required. Robert removed his checkbook from his jacket pocket, wrote the check for $60,000, and handed it to Mr. Kincaid. He knew if Camille had checked herself into rehab, the chances of her being out to make her payments were slim, and he didn't want her to lose her home. He was disappointed in her behavior, but he still considered her his sister-in-law and his friend.

Robert left the bank feeling exasperated. He knew exactly what he needed to put him back in a peaceful state of mind. Without hesitation he called home. The sounds of the busy New York streets were too noisy, so he jumped into a taxi. When the driver asked for his destination, he replied, "Just turn the meter on, man. I just need a little piece and quiet."

The telephone rang. Danielle answered, "Kelsey residence, may I help you."

With a smile on his face. "Yes, you may. I would like to speak with the most beautiful woman in the world. Is she available?"

"I believe she is, sir. Who may I say is calling?"

"Tell her it's her secret admirer. Hello, beautiful. I received your wonderful letter, and I just had to call and hear your voice."

Blushing with great reserve. "You always say the sweetest things, Robert."

"It's easy to do with you, young lady."

"Robert, when are you coming home?"

"Oh! Does somebody miss me?"

Danielle giggled like a little girl. "Just a little."

Robert now had no misgivings. "I'll be home in a week. Do you think you can hold out that long?"

"Well, of course, I can. The question is can you?"

Both laughing and feeling the comforting exchange of their words, ended their conversation with a soft goodbye.

Robert tapped the taxi driver on the shoulder. "Nine seventeen Park Place, sir. And please take the long route."

The day had been filled with a multitude of surprises: Danielle's early morning letter, Randall's new love interest, and Camille's banking ordeal. He was happy to close the blinds on another day in New York, especially since his last conversation was with his alluring West Indian queen.

Robert's mother was anxiously awaiting his arrival. The minute the door opened she called out, "Robert, dear, do come and join me for a little chat."

Robert knew exactly what was coming. His mother always wanted to chat when she wanted to meddle in one's personal affairs. He took a deep breath and joined his mother in the parlor. "Good evening, Mother, how was your day?"

"My day was wonderful as always. I spent the day telephoning friends, being massaged, and shopping for a new wardrobe. What on earth did you do with your day son?"

Robert, stood there smiling to himself. "Well, Mother, compared to your list of accomplishments, I did very little."

"Of course, you did dear. Now Randall tells me you have a lady friend. Why haven't you shared the wonderful news with me?"

Robert ignored the question for a minute. "Let's put it like this way, my feelings for her are stronger than her feelings for me."

"Nonsense, any woman should consider herself lucky to have a wealthy man like you interested in her. She must be pretty special not to be impressed with your wealth and power, darling."

"She is, Mother. I have found that many people with little or no money are happier than people with money."

"Son, I hate to contradict you, but that my dear is a bold face lie. People without money always say that, but if they were so happy without it, why are they always trying to steal it from those who have it? It's true you can't buy love, but you can rent it."

"Mother, everyone who knows you, know you're about your fascination with money."

"If you think I'm going to apologize for my love of money, you're delusional."

He nodded, "Yes, I know. Mother, there is something I would like to share with you. I'm pretty sure I know how you will respond. However, I want to make it absolutely clear your response will not alter my plans."

Glancing up with a look of suspicion, "Oh, dear, whatever are you planning to do?"

"I'm planning to get married, Mother."

"Is that it? Well, that's wonderful news, darling. Who is the lucky lady, and when will I meet her?"

Robert paused and cleared his throat. "Danielle is her name, and she's a beautiful West Indian lady."

Without hesitation. "Good God, Robert, are you saying she's black?" His mother gasped for air. "Are you serious?"

He nodded. "Yes, I am. I know this comes as a surprise to you."

"No, it's not a surprise, it's a shock." Still reeling from Robert's news. "How on earth could you do this to me?"

His face flashed signs of anger. "Do what to you? This isn't about you and your social registry, this is about my life and my happiness."

Rising from her cashmere, houndstooth chair. "It damn well is about my social registry, and my ancestry. I will be the laughing stock of Park Ave. Our pedigree is superior to most, and you want to breed with some poor black island girl. Do you understand that you don't breed a Tibetan Mastiff with a Dalmatian? I knew it was a bad idea for you to take up residency in that jungle of a country. Always remember son...a fish and a bird can marry, but where would they live? Certainly not on Park Avenue."

Robert was steaming around the collar. He wanted to be respectful; however, he was appalled at the remarks made by his mother. It was the exact attitudes of her social circle that compelled him to stay as far away as he could. He understood the position his mother was taking, and he was hoping that she would one day understand the position he was choosing to take. It didn't matter to him whether or not she approved of his marriage to Danielle. He did know if his mother knew the entire story that she would have him committed to the nearest mental institution in New York City.

The silence between the two was deafening. His mother left the room, and Robert soon followed. He had intended to spend a few more days in the city, but after their disruptive conversation, he thought it best to return to the island. The city wasn't really his style any longer. He felt like a fish out of water. The bustling noises of the city invaded his peace each time he took to the streets of Manhattan. He found himself longing for the quiet walks on the beach, the breathtaking sunsets and Maria's smiling face greeting him with his first cup of morning coffee. Robert sat down at the small mahogany desk in the corner of the room and penned a note to his mother.

Dear Mother,

It pains me to leave without your well wishes. Please understand that your view of the world and the people who reside in it isn't the same as mine. I see people loving each without prejudice. I decided to spend the night preparing for my departure in the morning. As my mother you are forever loved. You know where to find me if you should ever change your mind.

Love,

R. Kelsey

In the morning he placed the note at the table where his mother had her breakfast and quietly exited the apartment. When he reached the lobby, the doorman hailed a taxi and Robert was once again in motion. He reached in his jacket and pulled out the letter Danielle had written to him earlier. A smile etched across his face. "Driver, I would like to make a stop by Tiffany's on the way to the airport."

"As you wish, sir."

As the city came alive, Robert was feeling good about himself and his new life. He was connecting with himself, in a way he'd never imagined. For the first time in years, his heart was as full as his bank account. He harbored no fear and felt no guilt. The ridiculous path he embarked on had brought him full circle to a place he'd always wanted to be; full of pride, determination, and self-respect.

The taxi stopped. "Tiffany's, sir."

Robert opened the door. "Keep the meter running. I will only be a minute."

"Take your time."

A tall distinguished man greeted him at the door, "Good morning, sir, welcome to Tiffany's."

Robert nodded and headed straight to an attractive well-dressed woman. "Good morning, I'm in search of a special ring for a special woman." The sales professional carefully displayed three beautiful rings. Robert examined each one with a discerning eye. He glanced up with a smile on his face. "This is the one." He had chosen a forty-carat yellow diamond ring, surrounded by smaller stones.

The woman smiled. "Can I make a suggestion, sir?"

"By all means," he replied.

In his hands she placed a pair of yellow diamond earrings. "I assure you the lady will love these as well."

Nodding his head in agreement. 'I will take them." He handed her his card.

The woman stepped away and returned with each gift beautifully wrapped.

With a beaming smile, he took his purchase and walked out the door and into the taxi. "LaGuardia Airport, please."

Chapter 14

Much to Captain Bill's surprise, he received a call from Robert. "Good morning, Bill, a little change in plans. I will be returning to the island today and need you to meet me in Red Hook at 2:00 p.m."

"'No problem, sir, I will let everyone know."

Robert hesitated. "Bill, I'd rather you didn't. I would like to surprise Danielle."

"Very well, sir, I look forward to seeing you."

Captain Bill and Robyn had been living on the vessel since Robert departed, so he needed Robyn to spruce things up without revealing why. He joined the ladies on the terrace.

"Robyn, sweetheart, I need you to spruce up the yacht this morning. I have a few errands to run and I will be picking up a friend of Mr. Kelsey's this afternoon. Can you take care of that for me?"

"Sure, honey, no problem!"

Captain Bill turned to Danielle. "What do you have planned for today, Ms. Detective?"

"Well, I don't really have a lot to do today. I thought I would wash my hair and spend quality time with my girls."

"Well, that sounds kind of boring."

"Boy, please. Maybe to you, but not to me. I think we could all use a little rest and relaxation."

Raising her glass. "I'll drink to that." Robyn sprung up. "I'd better get started on the boat. Bill, you finish your breakfast, and Danielle you should get better acquainted with your laptop. I need to make sure your communication tools are in working order before I leave you again."

Danielle smiled. "You've got it, my friend."

While Bill was eating breakfast, he was thumbing through the mail and spotted a letter to Danielle from Robert. "Well, what do we have here? It's a letter to you, Ms. Sherlock Holmes, from Mr. Robert Kelsey."

Danielle broke out in a big smile. "You're joking, right?"

"No, seriously. How much will you give me for it?"

"Give you for it? It's mine. Give it to me."

Bill laughed and held the letter in the air above his head to keep Danielle from reaching it. "You don't even like the guy, why would you want his silly old letter?"

Danielle thought to herself, why did she want his letter? It was strange that she thought less and less bout Jon, and more and more about Robert Kelsey. Jon was her first love and she had hoped to marry him and have a family together. What she didn't realize was there was a part deep inside of her that enjoyed the gentleness and maturity of a man who knew what to say and when to say it. She felt like a woman inside of her was struggling to emerge. It was a feeling she'd never experienced before and the fear of being captured by the unknown was becoming more intriguing every day.

Bill handed the letter to her. She quietly curled up in the corner of the sofa and read his brief but intoxicating message. The few words written on the paper was an invitation she wanted to grant. The scent of his cologne that lingered in the air was a confirmation that she would.

The remainder of the day was spent with each lady doing as they pleased. Robyn relaxed by the pool reading her Patti Callahan Henry novel. Maria relaxed in her villa, and Danielle sought solace in complete meditation. The day was filled with tropical breezes and mindless activities. As the time ticked swiftly away, Robyn decided she would prepare a special dinner to let everyone know just how much she appreciated their friendship. As she prepared to enter the kitchen, she saw Bill heading to shore. She stood waiting to extend a loving greeting to him, and to her surprise she saw the handsome Robert Kelsey step off the yacht. She was standing there in shock when she heard Danielle's voice, "Robyn is that Bill returning?"

"Yes, it's Bill, and boy does he have a surprise for you."

Danielle jumped to her feet. "A surprise for me?"

At that moment, Robert walked in the door. "Yes, beautiful, he has a surprise for you."

Robert walked directly to Danielle and looked in her beautiful eyes. "I've missed you."

Ecstatic, Danielle replied, "And I missed you too, Robert Kelsey."

"Where's Maria," he asked?

"She's in her villa. Maria gave us a little scare the other night so she has been resting and we've been taking care of her for a change."

Robert and Danielle stood outside the villa, knocking on Maria's door. When Robert entered the room, Maria cried tears of joy. "Mr. Kelsey, you're back."

"Yes, Maria, I'm back. What is this I hear about you not taking your medication? That's a no-no! You have to take good care of yourself. We love you and need you around."

Maria smiled. "Okay, Mr. Kelsey."

The Kelsey household was happy as they all gathered around the beautiful glass table on the terrace where they broke bread, laughed, and shared dreams. Robert had a calm and happy expression on his face as he looked at everyone sitting around the table. When he got to Danielle, he gave a relaxing sigh. "Danielle, care to join me for a walk on the beach?"

With an alluring glance. "I thought you'd never ask."

He pulled her chair away from the table, took her hand, and together they walked down the path to the beach that was lit by a beautiful full moon. The night was filled with magical silence as they strolled hand-in-hand on the sparkling white sand. There were no words spoken between them as her foot made its last impression. She placed her arms lovingly around Robert's waist and laid her head upon his chest. There was no denying the moment of complete intimacy. He looked down into her almond-shaped eyes and there was nothing for him to do but gently place his lips onto hers. He kissed her and kissed her until her body gave way to gravity, both falling lightly on the moist granules of sands. Together they had arrived in a place she had feared and he had desired. As he watched her body quiver from the cold of the water. He saw a vision of beauty as the flow of water fell slowly across her long slender torso and full formed breast. Their intimate encounter had Danielle craving for more. She laid there silently gazing into Robert's melting blue eyes. Without a moment's hesitation she whispered, "I feel the power of your love and the sweetness of your touch. Tonight, I give you all of me. Take me, Robert. Take me now." When he touched her breast, her lips surrendered into a kiss of unforgettable pleasure.

There was nothing for him to do but ravish the beautiful body he craved night after night. Gathering her succulent lips into a kiss, he pressed his body gently against hers. "Love me...love me," she cried. Releasing herself from his clutches, then thrusting her velvety smooth body back to center stage. The tender sounds of intense passion would linger in the air on the private island until the break of dawn. Without notice, Danielle surrendered herself to Robert Kelsey at will, with intense passion and no guilt.

Never before had either of them experienced such intense passion. Gazing into the vast blue sky, they both knew he needed her fire and she desired his love. In a passionate and sincere voice Robert spoke, "I will respectfully honor your decision to return home, Danielle."

Still feeling slightly hypnotized from their intense moment of lovemaking, Danielle replied, "Return home and leave you, Robert Kelsey? Thank you, but no thank you. I wish never to leave your side."

Robert gave out a sigh of relief as he gently pulled her body into a fetal position and held her close in his arms. He took her hands in his and whispered, "I have spent hours upon hours exploring your mind. Visiting each curve of your body.

Watching each tear that fell from your beautiful eyes, and I knew that God made you just for me. I was a man without a purpose, a man willing to live without true love or meaning. Then you, beautiful lady, came into my life and traveled into the spirit of my soul. Through you I found the remnants of a man I was able to piece back together. Because of you I am whole again. You have no idea what having you in my life means to me. I promise you that I will never disappoint you. I will provide a life for you which you deserve. I will honor you as my wife, if you will have me."

Rubbing her hands along his arms. "Was that a proposal?"

Nodding his head. "Yes, it was a proposal. Will you do me the honor of being my wife?"

"Yes, Robert, I will marry you."

Giggling, about the sun coming up, Robert and Danielle, made a b-line back to the villa. Robert walked Danielle to her villa, which she slipped into quietly. She took a quick shower and slid into bed, where she relaxed and reflected on the beautiful night she and Robert had spent together.

Robert retreated to his villa, where he showered and slid into bed, only to find himself unable to be separated from Danielle. He grabbed his gifts from Tiffany's, a bottle of wine and two glasses from the kitchen, and walked quietly to Danielle's villa and into her bed. Danielle was surprised to see Robert, but she was even more surprised to see the beautiful forty-carat yellow diamond engagement ring. Danielle eagerly accepted the ring and his proposal. It was perfect, and she was loving every minute she spent with him.

The two slept longer than usual. Everyone in the house was wondering when they would emerge. When they did come out,

Danielle was wearing her beautiful engagement ring, which she flaunted in Robyn's face.

Robyn couldn't stop screaming, "Oh my gosh, it's beautiful. Congratulations!"

Smiling. "Thank you my, my friend."

Captain Bill stood up. "I think we need to make a toast to the happy couple."

Maria was smiling as she took five glasses and a bottle of champagne from the cooler.

Robert opened the champagne and filled each glass. With his arms around Danielle's waist, he raised his glass. "To the light of my life, my angel, and my future wife."

Everyone was in good spirits and happy for both Robert and Danielle.

Robyn announced that since Robert had returned home and love was in the air, she would be returning home and touch base once the couple had enough of each other.

Danielle embraced her with a big hug, whispering in her ear, "I love you so much. Please don't be a stranger, you are welcome here anytime you want to get away or just see my ugly face."

Robyn agreed. "I promise I will do just that. I'm okay now that I know you can each me, and I can reach you. Robert, you better take care of my girl. "Otherwise, I'll have to kill you."

Robert gave Robyn a big hug. "You can count on me doing that. Thank you so much for your love and support, and remember, we're family."

Captain Bill and Robyn headed to the yacht. Robert and Danielle returned to the villa, where they hibernated for two days, wanting nothing but to be wrapped up in each other's arms. Robert made himself more real to Danielle. Every morning she didn't have the strength to resist him. She hungered for his love and she could tell from the movements of his body that he was weeping for joy just as she was. Neither had any idea the explosive feeling they would experience when they surrendered to their desires.

Maria finally got enough nerve to knock on the door. "Mr. Kelsey, I'm sorry to disturb you, but the governor has been calling you for days. This morning he said he must speak to you."

Maria slowly walked away from the door mumbling in Spanish.

Danielle and Robert were so caught up with each other, they never spoke about the governor or the information she needed to share with Robert. She had planned to speak with him once they cooled down a bit, but cooling down didn't seem to be an option. She knew they needed to have a serious conversation, which she imagined would put a damper on things.

While Robert reached for the phone to call the governor, Danielle grabbed it from his hands. "I'm here with you, who else do you need?"

Smiling mischievously. "No one, baby. I don't need anyone but you."

She leaned over and gave him a big kiss. "That was the perfect answer, sweetheart. Now, make your call."

"Thank you, baby."

Before Robert could place the call, his phone rang. When he answered, an angry loud voice replied, "I've been trying to reach you for two days."

"I've been busy," Robert replied.

"Busy, my ass. You've been lying around sucking up to Danielle. Have you lost your damn mind? That woman's going to be the death of your weak ass."

"I'm warning you, don't you ever speak to me like that again. I don't give a damn about who you think you are. I will not accept that level of disrespect from you. You're talking to me like I'm one of your boys. I'm a business partner and that's all. I don't work for you. I work with you."

The silence stole the moment. "You're right, Robert. Please accept my apology. I got a little carried away, that's all. I understand the roles we both play in each other's life. A few things have come up that require your attention and I was frustrated that I was unable to reach you. You know you can't turn your phone off when we have so much going on. Work is too important to let a little piece of ass get in the way."

"Give me the details."

"It isn't that simple. We need to meet. How soon can you get into town?"

"How about two hours."

"That'll work. I'll meet you at Fortuna Mills."

"Fortuna Mills it is."

Danielle shrugged her shoulders and looked at Robert, and in a seductive voice, "Are you going to leave me lying here exposed with no one to protect me?"

"No, baby, I'm going to wrap you up in this beautiful white bath robe and tie you to the bed, so you will be here waiting for me when I return."

While Robert was dressing to leave, Danielle felt she had to tell Robert about her findings regarding his father's death. She knew it was going to be a touchy subject, but she didn't feel right allowing Robert to meet with the governor without knowing.

Without giving any real thought on how she would begin, she took a deep breath and uttered, "Robert there's something I need to tell you before you meet with the governor. While you were away I started looking for information on your father's death, as you requested, and quite frankly, I don't feel good about what I discovered."

Robert sat attentively on the side of the bed. "Go ahead, I'm listening."

"Rumor has it that the governor may have had something to do with your father's death. The woman, Suzi Rose, who was with your father at the time of his death, was missing for several months. The Santos thought she was dead, but she resurfaced six months ago and is currently working at Club Lacey. It was said that your father and the governor had a disagreement about a business deal. There are a lot of suspicious activities that I personally believe are connected, but it will take some more research to determine all of that."

Robert was stunned. "I never once thought the governor was involved in any way with the death of my father. This is serious, Danielle."

"I know, more serious that you realize."

Robert was speechless, seemingly shocked by Danielle's report. He knew it would be impossible to cultivate another business deal with the governor until he was able to determine if he was involved in his father's death.

Danielle handed him the phone. "Governor, I won't be meeting with you today."

"Alright, if today isn't good for you, what about 9:00 a.m. in the morning?"

Robert paused. "No that won't work either. I've been looking over some things, and I'm not sure I want to expand my business to Puerto Rico. I'm going to put on the brakes for a minute and evaluate everything. I'll give you a call once I make my decision."

The Governor fired back. "Look, man, we have been working on this for a while and the Governor of Puerto Rico has already bought into the project, now you're looking to back out. What the hell is going on? I think we need to talk."

Robert, reiterated, "As I said previously, I'm not sure if that is something I wish to do. As for backing out of the deal, I'm sure you can find someone else to partner with. I really have my hands tied at the moment, so we'll have to have this conversation later in the week."

Robert terminated the call and climbed back in bed with Danielle.

The governor was steaming. He didn't know if his brash comments had irritated Robert to pulling out of the deal, or if something more sinister was going on. One thing he knew for sure was Robert Kelsey was beginning to affect his bottom line and that was something he couldn't afford. All the governor could think about was how much Robert had changed. He was positive Danielle's presence in his life was making a difference. The only way he could find out if he was wrong about Robert, was to put a tail on him.

Things were beginning to heat up. Robert was investigating the governor, and the governor was investigating Robert. The governor immediately put the word out to observe and advise him of any suspicious activity by Robert Kelsey. At the same time, Robert Kelsey was making plans to locate Suzi Rose and determine if she would be forthcoming with additional information surrounding his father's death.

That night Robert met Captain Bill at the yacht dock and traveled to St. Thomas to speak with Suzi Rose. Captain Bill tipped Robert off that she was currently at Club Lacey. When Robert arrived at Red Hook, he took his car into town. Club Lacey was located in a seedy part of town, where the bravest of locals feared to tread. The idea of a white man sneaking around in this particular part of town was considered more than bravery. It teetered along the lines of temporary insanity. When Robert arrived at the club, he remained in the car checking out the area. He hid completely out of view, watching the movements of all the colorful characters going in and out of the club. He observed several police cars picking up girls from the side of the building. All which he thought was unusual behavior. He filed it in the back of his mind. Tonight, he was here for one reason and one reason alone, to speak with Suzi Rose.

Chapter 15

Robert saw House Cat come out of the club heading his way. He called him over to the car. "Hey man, long time no see."

Flashing all thirty-two teeth. "Hey there, rich boy, what you doing in my neck of the woods, looking for some action?"

Robert smiled, "I guess you can say that. I'm actually looking for Suzi Rose."

"You'll find her across the street at Club Lacey."

"Thanks, man."

"No problem. Be sure and watch your money, the ladies are really treacherous in there."

Robert chuckled. "Thanks, I'll do that."

Robert didn't feel entirely safe. It was dark and late and he could barely see his hands in front of his face. He strolled briskly across the street with both hands in his pockets and eyes focused on the two bouncers at the door.

Club Lacey was bursting with noise. Through the window Robert noticed a dancer sitting at a table alone. He decided to go in. When he entered through the door, he spotted Old

Smiley, one of the governor's goons. Dammit, he thought to himself. He knew it would only be a matter of minutes before the governor would know he was there, but he had to risk it.

"Hey Smiley, I'm looking for Suzi Rose."

Smiley never looked up, instead he pointed to the table directly in front of him.

Robert approached the table. There she was, the only witness to his father's death. She was tipsy, reeling side to side. There was an empty rum bottle sitting right in front of her.

"Excuse me, I've been looking for you, Suzi Rose. I understand you were with my father, Robert Kelsey, when he died."

"Oh him," she snickered. "I got nothing to do with that."

"Wait a minute", said Robert. "I don't like your attitude, and it's not funny."

"Listen here," said Suzi Rose. "Maybe not to you. He got some bad shit, and that's all I know."

"What drug was he using, Suzi Rose?"

"Ask me something harder, the substance doesn't matter," she said with a glare in her eyes. "It's like everybody and everything was there. When I woke up everybody and everything was gone."

"I don't understand what you're saying. You're speaking in riddles."

Robert could see she was out of it; a drunken look had settled on her face. Clearly, he wouldn't get any significant information until she sobered up. He decided to take her to James Island and keep her there until she could speak with clarity.

Robert hobbled to the door with Suzi Rose attached to his right side. The bouncers were blocking the door.

"Wait a minute" said the bouncer. "Where are you going with the lady?"

Robert hesitated, and replied, "I had planned on spending a little time with her, but she was more into the bottle than she was into me. I thought I would be a gentleman and make sure she made it home safely."

"Listen," said the bouncer. "I'm trying to see what's in this little arrangement for me."

"Of course, man, why not?" Robert reached in his pocket pulled out two crisp one hundred-dollar bills and placed it in the palm of the bouncer's hand.

Lowering his voice, he said, "That's all, man, she's only worth two hundred dollars?"

Robert shook his head. "No, man, but that's all I have with me right now."

The two men stared at each other, stepped aside and allowed Robert and Suzi Rose to leave the club.

Frantically, Robert hurried to his car. Just as he got Suzi Rose into the car, he saw a black Lincoln Town Car pull up. He was sure it belonged to the governor. He didn't waste another minute. Knowing the governor would expect him to depart from Red Hook Marina, he called Bill and directed him to meet him at Havensight.

Robert parked the car in a dark isolated spot on the parking lot. When Robert spotted the yacht, he pushed open the car door and signaled Bill for help.

Perplexed, Bill glared suspiciously at Robert. "Is she alive?"

Robert whispered, "Of course, she's alive."

Bill gave a sigh of relief, breaking out in jarring laughter and said," Thank, God, for that. I need my job, but I don't need a murder rap."

The two men got Suzi Rose settled on the yacht and headed to James Island, as swiftly as they could.

Robert walked to the front of the yacht to speak with Bill. "I'm sorry this looked so suspicious, but I assure you I have a good reason."

Bill shifted his eyes towards Robert and responded in a respectful manner, "Boss, as long as she's alive and we haven't kidnapped nobody, that's your business. But the minute something crazy goes down that jeopardizes my freedom and my life –it's a wrap."

Robert slapped Bill on the back and said affectionately, "I understand, man. I wouldn't do anything to jeopardize your life or mine. The only thing I'm concerned about tonight is explaining to Danielle why I'm bringing another woman to James Island."

Bill laughed and replied sheepishly, "A drunk woman on top of that."

They fell into laughter as Bill steered the yacht safely to James Island. When they reached the dock, Robert knew it was late and suggested, after getting Suzi Rose settled, Bill call Robyn to tell her he was spending the night on James Island, and would be home in the morning.

As they were entering the main villa, Danielle was walking down the corridor of the estate. Looking at both Robert and Captain Bill with an inquisitive glance, she asked, "What's going on here, gentlemen?'

Robert, determined to get Suzi Rose into bed said, "Give me a minute to lay her down and I'll explain."

Danielle's ears perked up. In a sarcastic voice she replied, "I can't wait."

Robert and Captain Bill returned to the terrace, joining Danielle at the table.

"Well, honey, I went to speak to Suzi Rose and she was so drunk I wasn't able to get any useful information. I was afraid she would disappear again, so I brought her here to sleep it off until I could question her about my father's death."

Danielle remained calm. "Oh, I see. You couldn't get any information from her, so you kidnapped her and brought her home with you?" Shaking her head. "Robert, you have to stop abducting women and bringing them to the island. That's a crime. You're playing with fire, honey. Did anyone see you with her?"

Stumbling over his words. "Well, the two bouncers at the club and Smiley."

"Smiley, are you serious? That's the governor's pit bull. I'm surprised he let you leave with her. This isn't good, Robert. Did you happen to think pass the first leg of your plan?"

"Honey, I know this seems a little out there, but I just couldn't chance her disappearing again. I really need your help. In the morning when she wakes up, if you and Maria will sober her up and assure her I mean her no harm, maybe she will talk with me. Then I can take her back to St. Thomas."

Nodding her head in agreement. "Okay, but you have got to discuss your bird brain ideas with me before you execute them. This isn't New York. This is the Caribbean, and things are a tad bit different here. The island is too short to run, and too small to hide. Let's get some sleep, morning will be here before you know it."

The next morning Suzi Rose woke up screaming, "ayúdame ... ayúdame ... que alguien me ayude por favor."

Her loud cry for help echoed throughout the estate. Danielle was the first to reach her door. As she was about to enter, Maria appeared. "Who is crying for help, Danielle?"

With a disgusted expression on her face. "I will explain later, Maria, but for now I just need you to follow my lead."

Nodding in agreement, Maria opened the door and saw a disheveled Hispanic woman scantily dressed standing in the middle of the floor, tears streaming down her face. "Porque' estoy aqui'?"

Looking directly at Maria, Danielle asked. "What did she say?"

Maria responded, "She wants to know why she is here."

Danielle paused. "Tell her we just want to ask her a few questions."

Maria took her hands in hers. "Solo queremos hacerle unas preguntas."

"Quie'n?"

"Señor Roberto Kelsey."

"No, señor Roberto Kelsey esta muertos."

Maria spoke softly. "Hijo del señor Kelsey."

Danielle was standing there looking confused. "What are you two saying?"

"I told her Robert Kelsey brought her. She said he was dead, and I told her it was Robert Kelsey's son."

162

"Seriously," Danielle, responded. "I'm tired of this translated conversation. Ask if she speaks English?"

Before Maria could open her mouth, Suzi Rose turned to Danielle. "Si."

Danielle shook her head. "Then why on earth are you speaking Spanish?"

Maria responded, "It easier."

"For you two, maybe, but not for me. Please let's just go to the kitchen, find something to eat, and have a good old come to Jesus meeting."

The ladies filed in a line of three and marched straight to the kitchen where Maria cut slices of spinach quiche and placed it on the table, along with hot tea and fresh fruit. The women were sitting comfortably at the table when Robert entered the room.

He walked over to Suzi Rose. "I'm terribly sorry about last night, but I wanted to ask you a few questions about my father's death. You were completely out of it and I couldn't take the chance of you disappearing again. Please forgive me, and know that I will take you home anytime you desire."

Suzi Rose gazed at Robert. "I understand, señor, but what you don't know is I disappeared for my safety, and now that you have taken me, I am a dead woman. My life will be over as soon as I return to St. Thomas."

Robert was shocked at her response. "Why? Better yet, who would want to kill you?"

With a lowered head. "The same people who killed your father."

Robert jumped to his feet. "Who killed my father?"

"I'm not certain. They said that I did, but I know I didn't. I was told they were sending me away to protect me."

"Who sent you away?"

"Molinda sent me away."

Perplexed, Robert inquired, "Who is Molinda?"

"Molinda Gonzales is the owner of Club Lacey, and the business partner of the governor, who she loathes."

Rubbing his forehead back and forth with his left hand. "How does the governor fit in to this picture? Tell me Suzi, how did they say you killed my father?"

"They said I gave him an overdose of drugs."

"The medical report said my father died of a heart attack."

"Yes, I know."

"There's something very strange about my father's death. What you're saying doesn't add up. If the police thought you were responsible for my father's death, they would have arrested you for murder. Instead Molinda sent you away for your protection. No way...that dog don't hunt. Tell me everything you remember about that night."

Suzi Rose exhaled. "Mr. Robert, your father was a very nice man. I was one of his favorite girls. Many times, when he sent for me, I would do my drugs and sit and listen to him talk for hours. He seemed sad and lonely. That night, when I arrived, he told me he wouldn't be around much longer, that his eyes had caused him to see things he shouldn't have seen. I didn't know what he was talking about. He kept talking and I kept doing drugs."

"I remember the phone ringing, and I heard him say, 'No, not tonight. I have company.' I was really wasted. I remember opening my eyes lying next to your father in the bed. Both of us were naked. There were three men. Two were standing in the dark hall and one standing over me pushing a phone in my face telling me to say I needed help, my friend had a heart attack. When the coast guard came, the men were gone and Molinda was there. She said I called her for help, saying I had given Robert six tablets of Viagra. She told me if I wanted to stay alive I need to go back home to Santo Domingo until things cooled off. She gave me some money, put me on the plane, and I went home and stayed until six months ago."

Thinking of his father's last moments on earth, Robert's expression turned to a sympathetic frown. "Man, oh man, that doesn't seem fair."

"It isn't fair, Robert. Your father was murdered and his killers have gotten away with it for over three years, while stealing the life from another person through fear and intimidation."

In a soft whispery voice Danielle asked, "Suzi Rose, why did you return?"

"My country is very poor. I was hungry and homeless. When the men came to bring more girls to Molinda, I knew it was my chance to get a free ride back to America. I cleaned myself up and hid in the trailer of girls leaving Santo Domingo. When we got to the club, Molinda changed my hair color and told me to work inside the club. We were hoping no one would recognize me. Smiley remembered me, and a few days later I got a visit from the governor. He threatened my life if I told anyone anything about James Island. I knew for sure, then, that I hadn't killed your father. I'm telling you this because you need to know. I, like your father, will not be here long. My life is over."

Robert felt bad that he had created a life and death situation for Suzi Rose. She seemed like a nice girl who got caught up in a life she didn't like, just to survive. He knew she was right; her days were numbered. Smiley was at the club last night and watched him leave with her. He didn't know how this was going to play out. What he did know was the longer he kept Suzi Rose on the Island, the better chance she had of staying alive. If he could get her to the airport and on a plane with enough money to live a comfortable life, his conscious would be relieved of a great deal of personal anguish.

Robert signaled for Danielle to join him in the kitchen. He was emotionally devastated by Suzi Rose's confession. It was at that moment Robert told Danielle of his plan to keep Suzi Rose on James Island until he could get her back safely to Santo Domingo. She smiled, then laid her head softly on his shoulder. As powerful as he was, she swelled with pride watching his humanity for others lead the way.

Suzi Rose remained on James Island. Her self-esteem and image soared under the loving care of Maria and Danielle. Each day plans were being made for her departure. New clothes and personal items were being purchase and carefully packed, waiting for the perfect time to escape. Even though Suzi Rose felt like she was a world away from St. Thomas, she was really only a few distant miles.

Robert had no idea how he would get justice for the death of his father. He knew it wouldn't be possible to depend on Suzi Rose to testify. After all, the courts probably wouldn't even consider her to be a credible witness. She was a prostitute, a drug user, and an illegal immigrant. His faced burned with rage. Just thinking about the fact that he had been doing business with a man he didn't really like, but trusted to some degree, only to discover that he was behind the death of his father. Robert couldn't help but remember his brother's last words to him, 'This island will eat you up and spite you out.'

This couldn't be the cost of doing business in the Caribbean. If so, the price was much too high. He placed his hands over his face and gazed at Danielle. "I need a proverb, give me a proverb sweetheart."

"I have no idea what you're talking about, Robert."

"Can and will you, give me a West Indian proverb that will express what I'm feeling about my current situation."

"Just a minute," clearing her throat. "Yoh?"

"That's it, you?"

"Sometimes less is more, Robert. That one word carries a powerful message. It implies you will get yours. Your time will come."

Robert replied, "I see. It's a matter of principal. As long as I'm alive I will do whatever I can to make sure he gets what he deserves.

Danielle stroked Robert's arm. "I know baby, I know."

By the time it became crystal clear with that the despicable Governor Gunn was more of a criminal than they imagined, visions of murder, and cruelty resided in the minds of every person present. A few weeks ago, inquiring minds were looking for answers, and today the answers they were seeking could change everyone's life in a flash. This was a game of life. A game everyone, including the governor, wanted to survive. The road ahead was going to be even more challenging due to Robert's business dealings with him. It was going to take some serious acting and extensive planning to get usable information against the governor. He was a lot of awful things, but one thing he wasn't, was stupid.

Robert sat quietly pondering on what the governor's next move would be. He was already suspicious of him backing out of the Puerto Rico deal. He knew he left Club Lacey with Suzi Rose. From where Robert was sitting, he could see that the governor had already being playing him. He planted Camille as a mole in his home to spy on him. He set up his marriage to Danielle, the only plan he knew of thus far, which back fired on him. Robert had hired dozens of employees the governor recommended.

Paranoid and frustrated, Robert knew he had to take a tactical approach of determining exactly what he was up against and how he could get out of it alive and financially intact. Danielle was the only person he trusted. Each night was spent developing a strategic action plan to conduct background checks of all his employees. Robert hired a private investigator to find which rehabilitation center Camille had checked into. He wanted to know what else she knew about the governor's business activities.

A burning fire was now residing in the belly of Robert Kelsey. His laid-back way of life had been replaced with a fast thinking, hard hitting businessman. Naiveté was no longer a feature that attached itself to his being. He was in the major league now. He knew his life, and the lives of others were in his hands. Even though business was at the forefront of his mind, he never lost touch with fulfilling the needs of his woman. He took her on various trips to surrounding islands, where they would sail, swim, and make passionate love. Of all their trips, Danielle enjoyed traveling to Little Dix's Bay, so Robert made sure they sailed there weekly. They were friends, but behind closed doors they were lovers.

On July 31, the fresh smell of rain was seeping through the white wooden shutters, as the sweet aroma of bacon entered every nostril on the estate. Today was a special day. Maria and Suzi Rose were making their final breakfast together. Captain Bill was sitting patiently on The Wanderer, waiting for the light shower to wipe its eyes and sprinkle a glow of sunshine to this happily anticipated day.

In a matter of hours, Robert would stand guard at the Cyril King Airport and watch the plane carrying Suzi Rose descend into the beautiful blue sky. Things had been relatively quiet and everyone's confidence was soaring in the belief of a safe and successful journey for Suzi Rose was attainable. Captain Bill had already carried her bags aboard, and Robyn was sitting patiently at the Red Hook Marina to drive Robert and Suzi Rose to the airport. Danielle and Robert joined Maria and Suzi Rose on the terrace as they their last breakfast together.

Everyone was in good spirits as Suzi Rose said her final goodbyes, "I am so thankful for your kindness. I will always remember what you have done for me. I will miss you all and pray to see you soon, this time in Santo Domingo."

Everyone laughed and hugged Suzi Rose goodbye as Robert escorted her to the yacht. Danielle and Maria stood next to each other weeping for joy, as they watched them sail away.

Robert sat closely by Suzi Rose, giving her a sense of security as they skipped along the fierce waves. The ride was a little choppy, but it was worth every bounce. When they arrived at the Marina, Captain Bill anchored the yacht, extended his hand, and passed Suzi Rose's bags safely into Robert's care.

As they walked swiftly down the crowed pier, they caught a glimpse of Robyn. She was waving and flashing her signature smile. "Over here slow pokes. Let's get this iguana moving."

For safety purposes, Robyn decided to bypass the waterfront and drive over Crown Mountain to the airport. Hoping to avoid attention, everyone in the car was on pins and needles as silence became the fourth passenger in the car. Within fifteen minutes they were sitting in front of the airport. Robert removed Suzi Rose's bags and shuffled her swiftly to the Jet Blue Airways counter. Robert never left her side. He purposely purchased two tickets so he could be with her all the way to the plane. Both Suzi and Robert cleared customs and security. They took a seat at Gate 3, and waited for her flight to be called.

Robert took Suzi's hand. "Everything will be fine, Suzi Rose, and you're almost there."

She looked up and smiled. "Thank you, Mr. Robert. You are a nice man. Your father was right to be proud of you."

Robert laughed. "My father proud of me? No way."

"Oh, yes. Your father talked about you all the time. He said he wished he had a heart like yours, and you were the man he always wanted to be."

Robert fought back tears. "Oh, Wow! Suzi Rose, you have no idea how much that means to me. Thank you so much for sharing."

"It's true. He said it all the time. Now I know why."

Squeezing her hands, Robert replied, "I sure wish we had met under different circumstances, young lady."

She lowered her head. "Me too, sir. Me too."

Their conversation was interrupted by the calling of passengers for the flight to the Santo Domingo. "Well, that's us young lady."

Excited and nervous, Suzi Rose jumped up from her seat, hugged Robert, and hurried to the gate.

Robert watched as she handed her boarding pass to the agent. She looked back flashing a big smile and walked towards the plane. He never took his eyes off her as she walked up the stairs and into the door. His heart relaxed as he saw her waving at him from the window. He waved back, standing there until the plane rolled down the runway and into the sky.

Chapter 16

Robert walked out of Gate 3, passed the two travel agents who were conversing about a delayed flight. The taller slender agent waved Robert through pointing him in the direction of baggage claims. Robert cleared his throat and said, "Thank you."

The agent looked him squarely in the eyes. "No problem, Mr. Kelsey. You changed your mind about traveling today?"

Robert was puzzled, he had no idea who this man was and how he knew his name. He paused momentarily. "Yes, I had a change of plans."

The quick exchange with the travel agent made Robert uncomfortable. So much had been going on, and it seemed like everywhere he turned all eyes were on him. He walked to the parking lot, where Robyn was waiting. As he entered the car, Robyn gave a quick sigh of relief. "Thank God you're back. I was beginning to worry."

The anxiety of providing a safe haven for Suzi Rose, until she escaped the island was taking a toll on everyone. Turning to Robyn he asked, "An agent in the airport just called me by name, inquiring if I had changed my mind about traveling today. Do you think I'm being paranoid, Robyn?"

Glancing over at Robert, "No, I don't think you're being paranoid. This had been some real crazy shit, not to mention the unsavory characters we're fighting against. I say the more paranoid, the better. It may be the one thing that keeps us safe. As for me, I've traded in sleeping with one eye open to not sleeping at all."

Robert and Robyn laughed, slapping both their hands on the dash board. "Let's get out of here, our mission is accomplished."

When they arrived at Red Hook, Captain Bill was docked and waiting. Robert stepped out of the car and leaned in. "Thank you, sweetie."

Robyn smiled. "Anything for you my friend, and remember to take care of my girl."

He chuckled and strolled toward the yacht. Looking back at Robyn he waved and threw her a kiss. She flashed a big smile, caught the kiss, and threw it back. "Take care of my husband, Robert Kelsey."

Engulfed in happiness, Robert, stepped off the pier and onto the yacht Captain Bill nodded. "Welcome aboard, Sir. Just relax. I'll have you safely home in twenty minutes."

Captain Bill could see the tension in Robert's face. It was a beautiful day in paradise, so he refrained from talking; giving Robert time to enjoy the ride on the open sea. When they reached their destination, Maria and Danielle were waiting. As he walked into the room both ladies lunged at him. "Did Suzi Rose get off alright? Did you see her get on the plan? Did anyone see her leave? Do you think we will see her again?"

Robert took two steps back with his hands pushed out in front of him. "Ladies, ladies! One question at a time. Yes, she got off fine. I not only saw her get on the plane, she waved goodbye to me, and I waved back. I didn't see anyone else around, so I can't answer that one. As for seeing her again, I certainly hope so, but more importantly, I hope she's able to live without fear of retribution."

The past few weeks had been filled with fear and uncertainty. Each moment of the day was spent wondering what the governor's next move would be. Danielle had been the perfect trooper, providing Robert with the support he needed to move forward with the resolution of his relationship with the governor. It was because of her support they were able to spend quality time together. He had an idea and wanted to discuss it with her. He asked her to join him in the villa, where he was preparing to take a shower.

He wrapped a towel around his waist, leaving his muscular tan chest and legs exposed. Danielle's eyes were fixated on Robert. "Just what am I supposed to do while you're taking a shower?"

Robert photographed her with his baby blue eyes, peeling every piece of clothes off of her perfectly shaped body. "Your presence is what I request. You can just sit there and allow me the satisfaction of your company, sweetheart."

Smiling mischievously. "I don't think I'm capable of doing that, Robert Kelsey. Why don't I join you, and we both can enjoy the pleasure of each other's company?"

Robert stood behind her, carefully unbuttoning the two gold buttons which held her one-piece jumper securely on her body. As it fell to the floor, Robert smiled. "Commando, Danielle? You naughty girl."

"From what I appear to be feeling, it appears we're both a little naughty." Danielle held Robert's arms securely around her breasts, causing their bodies to stick together. As they entered the shower, Robert spoke slowly and clearly, "I just love touching your body. It feels incredible."

There was an intense explosion of passion as Danielle surrendered to sounds of Robert's breathing in her ear. Her arms stretched across the white slippery subway tile as shivers ran down her spine. She moaned, "Just like that baby, just like that!"

The water flowed over their bodies for hours as their love for each other was consummated through pure unadulterated passion. Neither had experienced such intimate and sexual pleasure before. It was clear that the two would find themselves in each other's arms every opportunity that presented itself. They stepped out of the shower. Robert wrapped Danielle in a large white sheet towel. She opened it and invited him in one more time.

Shaking his head, he gasped, "Are you trying to kill me?"

Danielle wrapped her long slender legs around his back. "No, I'm trying to love you to death."

The pair remained wrapped in each other's arms sharing conversation and laughter. Robert pulled Danielle gently to his chest and whispered in her ear, "I think it's time we get married sweetheart, what do you think?"

Still intoxicated from Robert's incredible performance, she exhaled and replied, "I'm ready whenever you are, baby."

As Robert moved his hands over Danielle's breasts, he asked, "Am I distracting you?"

"Yes, you're turning me on. Leave it to you to build sexual tension."

He squeezed her gently." I wish we could stay in bed all day, but we have a wedding to plan."

"Baby, I don't want a big wedding with lots of fake people around. I would like a small intimate wedding on the terrace with Maria, Bill, and Robyn."

"What about your mother, don't you want to invite her?"

"No, baby I don't."

"Sweetheart, I know you have issues with your mother, but she did bring us together."

"I know, but I'm just not there yet, Robert. I love her and always will. But she did an awful thing. What if she hadn't sold me to a man with compassion and a thread of moral fiber?"

"A thread? All I have is a thread?"

She tossed her head, rolled her eyes, and laughed uncontrollably. "No, you have more than a thread, but remember you too were a part of that hideous crime."

"I know. Every day I thank God that you were able to forgive me and see I did it all for you. Eventually, you saw a man who you could admire and love."

"I do admire you, and I love you more and more every day."

"Based upon that response, you can do whatever your heart desires regarding the wedding. I will just show up."

"Alright. Mark your calendar for Sunday, 4:00 p.m."

"This Sunday?"

"Yes, This Sunday. Is that too soon?"

"Heavens no. It's not too soon. I'm happily surprised."

"Okay, it's settled." She got up and kissed him gently on the lips. "So, when do you think I can get my new ring? My first one is beautiful, but I'm afraid someone will mug me for it. It's far too extravagant, Robert."

"No problem, sweetheart. I understand. I wouldn't want anyone to hurt my baby for a piece of jewelry. When I saw how beautiful it was, I wanted you to have it. We'll keep it in the safe as one of your investment pieces."

"That puts my mind at rest. Thank you, baby."

"Anything for you, sweetheart."

Danielle was ready to move forward with her marriage to Robert. She found happiness in his company, extreme pleasure in their lovemaking, and financial security with his wealth. Even though she never valued a man by what he possessed. She had to admit the life she was privileged to be living was a life she truly enjoyed. Her perception of people with money was slowly changing. She was determined to use her husband's money to make a difference in the lives of others. Through the greed of her mother and the blessings of God, she found in her future husband a man she knew would support her desire to improve the quality of life for those less fortunate.

Excited about their upcoming wedding, Danielle started making plans. Even though she was planning a small intimate wedding, she wanted to make it tropical and beautiful. She would decorate the terrace with yards and yards of white tulle. A beautifully decorated Vienna two-tier wedding cake, steel pan music, and bird of paradise floral bouquets. She got dressed and hurried to the kitchen to share the news with Maria, who was just as excited as she was. It was her intention to call Robyn later that evening. However, to her surprise, both Captain Bill and Robyn were walking up the steps. When Robyn entered the kitchen, she found Danielle arranging white lilac and pink roses in a large crystal vase.

"What's the occasion?"

"What makes you think there is an occasion?"

"Well, you're arranging white lilac and pink roses in that beautiful vase. It looks like you're decorating for a wedding."

Danielle laughed. "You have such an imagination."

"Look girl, I didn't come way over here to be lied to. When is the damn wedding?"

Robert walked in and stated, "Sweetheart, tell her how you plan to make an honest man out of me on Sunday afternoon."

Danielle, sucked her teeth and glanced up at Robert. "Did you spill the beans, Robert Kelsey?"

With a muffled laugh, Robert replied, "You were so excited, I called Bill and asked him to bring Robyn over for dinner, so we could celebrate together."

"You are impossible."

Captain Bill and Robyn both rushed over to hug Danielle." Congratulations my friend, now what can we do to make your wedding as beautiful as you?"

"Really? Will you be my maid of honor Robyn, and Captain Bill will you be Robert's best man?"

"We'd love to. Let's leave the guys to themselves while we make wedding plans."

Robyn and Danielle giggled all the way to the terrace. Robyn hadn't seen Danielle this happy in a long time. It was easy to see that she was good for Robert, and he was good for her. She was happy for her friend, and was delighted Danielle finally saw the blessings being bestowed upon her life. Now, if only she could get her to understand the importance of forgiving her mother for her despicable act. Robyn felt she at least deserved credit for selling her to a man that not only loved her, but could give her a life she could only dream of. As the two ladies exchanged ideas about the wedding, Robyn gave Danielle a serious look. "If you do something crazy and give this man up, I will be the first one to move in."

Danielle was laughing, but Robyn stopped her. "You're laughing, but I'm more serious than cancer, and we both know how serious that is. By the way, where's your ring? The last time I saw it I was blinded by the sparkle. That's an insane piece of jewelry."

"I know, and that's why it's not on my finger. It's not practical. Some fool will cut my finger off for that ring. I've already told Robert he has to buy me another one."

Robyn blinked. "Now look who's getting comfortable spending money. Oh! She needs two rings now. Is this the same friend who told me money doesn't make the man, the man makes the money?"

"Smart ass."

The two ladies fell back in the chair and laughed until tears formed in their eyes. Maria passed by, flashing her infectious grin. The dynamics between the three ladies were like magic. They were not only friends, they were family. Danielle's presence on James Island had brought a new sense of purpose to their lives. She was beautiful, intelligent, gracious and charming, which made it difficult to dislike her.

Maria prepared the table beautifully, making sure to acknowledge the special occasion they were celebrating. To make sure Maria was included, Robyn and Danielle both helped bring the food out and placed an additional place setting for Maria. Everyone was excited to be dining together. Maria served ginger marinated pork chops, corn meal fungi, roasted plantains, and steamed asparagus. The incredible aroma lingered in the air until every bite had disappeared.

Danielle was completely smitten as she sat directly across from Robert. As everyone relaxed in the quiet of the evening, Maria excused herself from the table, returning with a bottle of champagne. After filling everyone's glass, Robert turned to Danielle, lifting his glass. "To you, Danielle, my wonderful friend and my future wife. You are simply the wind beneath my wings." Everyone lifted their glasses smiled and took a sip.

Danielle lifted her glass to Robert. "To you my knight in shining armor, you are every woman's dream and my reality."

Robyn commented, "We have to stop all this toasting and sipping. My husband told me not to get drunk and embarrass him."

Everyone laughed. There was nothing they didn't share with each other. The men took a stroll around the grounds, and the ladies cleared the table, placed the dishes in the dishwasher, and opened another bottle of champagne. Danielle reminded Robyn she had promised Bill she wouldn't get drunk. While taking another sip of champagne, Robyn replied, "It's too late for the drunk part. He has to worry about me embarrassing him now."

Laughter filled the air and tears fell from every eye. The ladies came together in a small circle, embracing each other as if they were seeing each other for the last time.

Danielle asked Robyn to join her in her villa. When they entered the room, Danielle stepped into the closet and returned placing three thousand dollars in her hands. "I want you to pick up my wedding cake from Grandma Sandy's, then find yourself the prettiest dress and accessories for my wedding. After all, my maid of honor has to look stunning. It doesn't matter how much you spend, it's up to you. Just remember whatever you have left is yours, so you might want to be cheap like you always are."

"That's an insult."

"But did I lie?"

"No, Skinny Minnie, you didn't lie."

Robin laughed and poked Robyn in the side. "I would really appreciate it if you would meet with Maria on Friday, when she does her shopping, and help her pick out a dress. She's not that familiar with the boutiques on island. I want her to feel special. I'll make sure she has her own money."

"What about your dress?"

"Oh, I have my dress. I found it on line and had it shipped to me two weeks ago."

"Two weeks ago? You little stinker. Can I see it?"

"No, you can't. I want it to be a surprise. And Robyn get a dress you can wear again. I hate to see people waste money on dresses they can only wear once."

"You are so damn controlling. I might buy one of those ugly bridesmaid dresses."

"I don't think so. You like to talk about other people, you don't like other people talking about you. I promise you, if you come over here with some ugly butt dress. I'm going to laugh my ass off."

"That will only take a minute."

"Don't hate, appreciate."

They chatted a little longer about their plans, then joined the others on the terrace. It was getting late and Captain Bill wanted to get back to St. Thomas. Everyone said their good-byes as Robyn and Bill made their way to the yacht. Danielle stood in the yard with her arms wrapped around Robert, gazing passionately at the constellations. "Robert, I see the milky way and the big dipper."

Robert smiled looking into Danielle's amazing eyes. "I see, love. Speaking of love, where do you want to go on our honeymoon?"

"Anywhere we don't have to take a yacht to get there."

"If that's the case, we'll have to remain on James Island."

"Exactly, I wish to remain on island with you. We can give Maria a two-week vacation. She can visit her family, and take a break from caring for us."

"Okay, who would cook for us and run the household?"

"Your wife, silly. That would give me a chance to show you what an awesome wife I will be."

Robert kissed her softly on the forehead. "I don't need Maria to take a vacation to find that out. I just spent the day in bed with you, remember."

Danielle flashed her beautiful amber eyes up at Robert. "Tell me more."

"Don't look at me like that, you know it turns me on."

Smiling, they walked hand- in-hand to their villa and retired for the night.

For the next few days Danielle and Maria was busy organizing the caterers, and florist in St. Thomas. Even though she elected to have a small ceremony. She still wanted it to be beautiful. She decided to have steel pan music; there was something alluring about the sound of steel pan. It represented her, a West Indian woman, proud of her heritage and culture.

Robert didn't know Danielle had been planning her wedding for weeks. She already had her wedding dress, her decorations, and her menu selected. All she required was the judge, photographer, and servers. She could have everything completed before Sunday with the help of Maria and Robyn.

She joined Maria in the kitchen for a cup of coffee, and was joined shortly by Robert.

"Someone left me alone in the bed this morning."

Danielle winked her eye. "If I had remained in bed, you would still be there."

Maria placed her hands over her ears. "You too jump around like rabbits, you better be careful."

Robert laughed. "Oh! You can't scare us, Maria. We're fully protected."

Danielle look at Robert strangely. "Maria's right, I need to exercise some caution."

"Don't worry about it baby. I'm not."

Danielle kissed him on the cheek, thinking to herself, how wonderful it was that Robert didn't care if she got pregnant. That was the one thing they had not discussed, and it was the one thing she was passionate about. Having children was always something she looked forward to.

Robert requested Danielle accompany him on his trip to St. Thomas. He knew it was a big step for her. She had not returned to St. Thomas since that dreadful night she was brought to James Island. To his surprise she agreed.

"I'll get my purse."

"You sure you'll be okay, sweetheart?"

"Yes, baby, I will be fine. People will have my name in their mouths regardless. I might as well get prepared for it."

Robert was delighted Danielle was coming. He wanted to purchase her wedding ring and thought it might be better if she selected it. Danielle consented to go so she could buy Robert's wedding band, and felt it better if he selected it himself. The two always seemed to be in sync with each other. Their union was solid. Filling the day with small talk and laughter; ending the night with passionate lovemaking. The only thing that cast a shadow over their lives was the despicable Alex Gunn. Together they would soon be able to eradicate him from their lives.

Captain Bill arrived on James Island and was surprised to see Danielle running down the steps in front of Robert. "Well, well," he said, "look who is venturing out today."

"Yes, Captain Bill, I'm going St. Thomas today."

"I think that's marvelous, my friend."

Robert helped Danielle on the yacht, and quickly jumped aboard in case she changed her mind. He looked to the back of the vessel and saw Danielle sitting in the same seat where she sat on her original journey to James Island. He didn't like thinking about that night. It always reminded him of how pathetic the event was. The only redeeming factor was the woman he took captive, was by his side without force. She had fallen in love with him, just as he had fallen in love with her. Their friendship had blossomed into a full-fledged romance, and everyday his desires for her presence in his life continued to grow.

To minimize Danielle's exposure, Robert had Captain Bill dock at the Havensight Marina. The boutiques were high end, the locals were far and in between, and the restaurants were top notch. He planned to protect Danielle at all cost, wanting her first trip back to St. Thomas to be filled with joy and contentment. When they docked, everyone got off the vessel and strolled up and down the sidewalk, looking for the perfect jewelry store to shop. The shopkeepers were waving to tourist, trying hard to sell their merchandise. Robert took Danielle by the hand and said, "Let's try this one. It looks like they have a nice collection."

Robert began looking in one jewelry case as Danielle was looked in another. The sales clerk wasn't aware they were together. It wasn't often you would see a white man with a West Indian woman, and certainly not in a jewelry shop. Danielle saw a ring that caught her eye, and asked the clerk if try it on. The clerk hesitated.

"That ring is very expensive. I'll show you rings in your price range from the back of the store."

Robert overheard the woman's remarks, and immediately rushed to Danielle's side.

"Excuse me, what did you say to my fiancé? Get the manager, please."

The woman stuttered, "You don't need to speak with the manager. I can show her the ring, sir."

Robert repeated himself, "Get the manager, dammit. You can't show her anything."

The lady walked to the opposite side of the store and returned with the manager, a large East Indian man with shiny black hair brushed backwards, revealing his large forehead, and wearing a pair of wire rimmed glasses.

"How may I help you, sir?'

Robert exhaled as he explained how the sales clerk had disrespected and embarrassed his fiancé by telling her she couldn't show her the ring she selected because it was too expensive. He held his breath and counted to ten. "Sir, I can buy your entire inventory and still have money left. Which means my fiancée has the ability to do the same. We came to your store to purchase our wedding rings, now this imbecile of a sales clerk has placed a damper on what should have been one of the happiest days of my fiancée's life."

The manger was floored." I'm so sorry, sir, I assure you it is not our practice to discriminate against anyone. Please accept my apology. I assure you I will speak with the young lady about her treatment of my customers. Please allow me to help you with your purchase."

Robert placed his business card on the glass jewelry case, took Danielle by the hand and said, "Thank you, but no thank you. My money spends everywhere, and it will not be spent in this store today or any other day."

"Are you serious?" the manager replied in a stern voice. "Linda, in my office now."

Danielle passed by the sales clerk as she walked out. "You're not smart enough to judge a book by its cover."

Robert gave Danielle a big hug. "I'm sorry, baby. Let's try Cardow's. This time I'm not leaving your side."

As soon as Danielle entered the store, she was greeted by a beautiful young African American woman, "Hello, beautiful lady, I'm Brenda. Are you looking for something in particular today?"

Danielle replied, "Yes I am. I am looking for my wedding ring and a wedding band for my fiancée."

"So, I don't waste your time showing you items that don't interest you, do you have a particular cut, setting, or budget you wish to make select?"

Robert replied, "Yes, she would like a platinum setting, 10 or 15 carats, diamond and emerald in a round and baguette cuts. As for me, a medium width platinum band with three diamonds. You may show the lady her rings first, but let me warn you, she doesn't want it too big. I purchased her a forty-carat yellow diamond, and she gave it back."

Danielle hit Robert on the arm. "Stop talking about me like I'm not present."

Brenda leaned towards Danielle. "I'm only allowed to take two rings out of the case at a time so I will show you a few pieces that fit your specifications, and you tell me which ones you wish to see first. Do you know your ring size?"

"Yes, I wear a size six."

"That's a great size. We always have plenty of inventory in your size, which means you don't have to pay for sizing."

Robert was prepared to be in the store for a while, but when Brenda brought out the emerald cut diamond with perfectly appointed baguettes around it, Danielle fell in love. Robert placed the ring on her finger and it remained. The sales clerk understood exactly what Danielle wanted and she plucked the perfect ring from the showcase.

Within a matter of minutes, she showed Robert a wedding band they had just received. It was just what he wanted. He, however, had to have his sized. He paid for the rings and advised Brenda they would return in two hours to pick up his wedding band. Brenda was a happy camper walking away with a healthy commission.

Hand-in-hand the happy couple decided to dine at the Dockside Cafe. It was one of Robert's favorite places, because they served breakfast all day. They grabbed a seat and when the waitress appeared they placed an order for two corned beef hash, eggs, hash browns and toast. They sat quietly in the booth looking directly into each other's eyes. It was apparent to everyone in the cafe the handsome couple, who walked in the door, were deeply in love.

They both enjoyed the corned beef hash and vowed to return at least every two weeks. Robert left a $50 tip on the table, and escorted his Caribbean queen back to the stores to continue shopping. As they were walking pass the tall wrought iron fence, Danielle glimpsed a view of her mother. Dasheen walked fast trying to get Danielle's attention. Danielle gave her mother a disapproving look, turned her head, and kept walking. Holding back tears, Dasheen lowered her head and continued walking towards Mandela Circle. It had been months since she had seen her dutiful daughter. Every night she prayed Danielle would one day forgive her, but she realized today wasn't the day.

Danielle didn't want to chance seeing her mother again, so she asked Robert to walk her back to the yacht while he continued to wait for his ring to be sized. He agreed. As they were heading towards the yacht, they ran into Captain Bill. "Hey, where you guys going?"

"Danielle is going back to the yacht to rest a while."

"Okay, she can walk back with me."

"Great, I will see you both in about thirty to forty-five minutes."

"Sounds good to me."

Robert leaned in and gave Danielle a kiss. "See you in a few minutes, sweetheart."

"Okay, baby. Love you."

"I love you more."

Danielle climbed aboard the yacht, and began thinking about her mother. A part of her felt bad, but another part of her was still angry and resentful of the role her mother played in selling her and Dior. Even though things had worked out well for her, she still was unable to understand how a mother could sell her own children for money. Danielle didn't know if she could ever forgive her mother. One thing she knew for sure, she wouldn't even attempt to forgive her until she was able to locate her sister and make sure she was alive and well. This situation was much too fresh for her to even look her mother in the face.

When Robert returned to the yacht, Danielle was asleep. Robert leaned over and planted a kiss on her cheek, and laid down beside her. The trip back to James Island was uneventful. The ocean was quiet and the journey was swift.

Danielle jumped up from the bed and into Robert's arms. "Are we home yet?"

"Yes, sweetheart, we're home."

Robert and Danielle had spent so much time together they were beginning to read each other's mind. Even though the trip was enjoyable, Robert sensed something was wrong with Danielle. As he escorted her up the steps he asked, "Baby, I noticed a shift in your mood after we left the cafe. What happened?"

Danielle glanced up, "Robert Kelsey, don't act like you know me so well. Nothing really happened. I saw Mother today, and she just disturbed my spirit. I'm fine, baby."

"Look, sweetheart, when something bothers you please tell me. I was a willing participant in this situation with you and your mother, and I'm doing what I can to make it right. One day I pray you and Dasheen will have a chance to restore your relationship. As awful as what she did to you, I truly believe she loves you and thought she was doing the right thing."

The silence between them was interrupted as Maria joined them, rejoicing at their return. "I'm so happy you're home safely. I didn't prepare dinner, I thought we could eat sandwiches and chips tonight."

"That's fine, Maria. Sandwiches will be fine, but we're not hungry at the moment. I think we will retire early."

Danielle interrupted, smiling from ear to ear. "I'm not retiring until I show Maria my wedding ring," as she flung her hand in Maria's face.

Maria grabbed her chest. "Oh my, it's beautiful."

"Yes, it is, Maria. It was love at first sight. I really do need to retire early. I will be working with Eddie tomorrow on the wedding decorations for the garden. I think I have everything under control. You and I will finish coordinating everything tomorrow as well."

"That's fine. I will have all my information together."

Danielle hugged Maria, kissed Robert, then retreated to the villa to rest.

Morning came early for Danielle. For the next few days, she, Eddie, and Maria were extremely busy. Maria organized the florist and the caterers. Eddie set up the gazebo and groomed the lawn. Danielle spoke to the Rev. Turner, hired the musician, and ordered the wedding cake. Robert and Captain Bill traveled to St. Thomas to pick up Robert's tuxedo. There were a thousand details to attend to; yet Danielle remained as cool as the ocean breeze. It was the happiest she had been in years.

To Maria's surprise, Danielle informed her that she and Robert were giving her a two-weeks paid vacation to Puerto Rico to visit her family. "We have made the reservation for you to travel home. You will be taking the last flight right after the wedding ceremony. Robert and I decided to remain on island and behave like rabbits."

Blushing, Maria replied, "I'm glad I won't be here for that performance." She took a deep breath and exhaled. "You and Mr. Robert are so good to me. I love you both."

"And we love you. You are family, Maria. Please don't do any cooking for the rest of the week, we can eat sandwiches and fruit. We have way too many things demanding our focus."

Danielle turned to walk away, but stopped. "Maria, when you go into town to shop, be sure and pick up any items you wish to take home to your family. We want you to have a marvelous time."

"Thank you, Danielle, I will."

Maria was happy that Robert Kelsey had found the woman of his dreams. He had always been a wonderful man to work for, but with Danielle becoming his wife, the joy and laughter on the island made it a perfect place to work and live. She couldn't imagine things being any better. Both of them had made her feel like a member of the family. For that reason alone, she vowed to protect them both as long as she was alive.

The number of guests for the wedding had increased to ten, which included the bride, the groom, Maria, Robyn, Captain Bill, Eddie and his wife Anna, the photographer, the musician, and Rev. Turner. Exactly how Danielle envisioned it, close family and friends. Periodically, she would reflect on how wonderful it would be to have her father and Dior present, but never once did she think about her mother.

Finally, the big day arrived. Marie and Eddie carefully draped the gazebo with voluminous swags of white tulle and cascades of baby's breath and white roses. The white runner was laid in the center of the aisle between the silver Chiavari chairs, and the six beautiful tropical bouquets made of palm leaves, bird of paradise, white rose and baby's breath were arranged in large crystal urns.

Captain Bill and Robyn arrived early, bringing alone the entire wedding party. The caterer carefully carried the wedding cake and placed it on a beautiful cloud of overlapping layers of white scalloped chiffon tablecloths embellished with tiny Swarovski crystals. The two-layer Vienna wedding cake was perfectly accented with rhinestone ribbon embellished around the sides of each layer and two rhinestone encrusted doves decorated the first tier. White ribbon and baby's breath were woven around the cake knife and the silver champagne bucket was monogramed with the letter K. The garden was absolutely stunning; displaying Danielle's unique style and flair.

Everyone knew their places and their responsibilities. There was a quiet excitement in the air as Robert met Captain Bill, dressed in his white captain's uniform, at the podium. Robert was wearing a white tuxedo and ice blue bow tie and matching cumber band. Maria and Robyn both wore elegant ice blue chiffon dresses. The jewel neckline was accented with white pearls, and they wore light blue silk pumps covered in small white pearls. Maria walked over to Robert and kissed him on the cheek. In her hands was a white rose (removed from Danielle's bridal bouquet), that she pinned it to his lapel.

As the alluring sound of steel pan music filled the air, the bride entered the garden looking beautiful in a low cut, off-the-shoulder white chiffon ankle length gown, designed for her by Tasha's of Atlanta. She wore a pair of Christian Louboutin crystal-embellished pumps. Intertwined in her hair were baby's breath and miniature white roses, and long Swarovski crystal earrings, by Koconut Designs, adorned her ears.

Robert was nervous and excited as he watched his beautiful bride walk down the aisle as the band played, "One in a Million." Danielle took her place beside Robert. They both listened intently and repeated their vows spoken by Rev. Turner. They exchanged rings and were officially pronounced husband and wife. Robert kissed his bride and their faces were covered with smiles. It was apparent the two were happily in love. The ceremony was performed in fifteen minutes.

After the ceremony everyone gathered around the cake, where they did the traditional cutting of the cake. She fed him a piece as the photographer continued taking pictures. Everyone participating in the ceremony joined the bride and groom at the elegantly dressed dinner table.

The table was layered in white chiffon and accented with a cascade of tropical flowers which completely covered the center of the table. White candles, housed in crystal candle holders, were placed strategically with protective glass globes. The waiters served Lobster Newburg, roasted potatoes, fava beans and toasted almonds on silver rimmed bone china plates. Champagne was flowing like water and smiles were glistening as the steel pan created a perfect touch to a tropical wedding in paradise.

Robert raised his glass to make a toast. "I love this woman and I love this island, for it is a symbolic gesture of where our love began." Then he presented her with a pair of canary yellow diamond earrings and a blank check to start her not for profit organization.

After dinner everyone returned to the Garden and released dozens of white balloons into the sky.

By 7:00 p.m. the wedding was over and the guest were preparing to leave. Maria's bags were packed and in the yacht. The steel pan players, Rev. Turner, photographer, servers, and the gardener and his wife followed Captain Bill, Robyn, and Maria down the stairs. Everyone left the happy couple. They all turned around and yelled in unison, "Congratulations!

In love and exhausted, Robert and Danielle threw them a kiss and retreated to their villa. Danielle wiped her eyes, as Robert declared it was by far the happiest day of his adult life.

He took his bride in his arms. "Did I tell you how much I love you, Mrs. Kelsey?"

"Yes, you did, Mr. Kelsey, but you can tell me again."

"I love you, sweetheart."

"I love you too, baby."

"Really? Well, did I tell you that there was no one on the planet that I wanted to marry but you?"

"Yes, you did, Mr. Kelsey."

"Really?" Well, did I tell you I will honor and protect you until the day I die?"

Danielle smiled. Her affection for Robert had grown beyond her expectations. "No, you didn't tell me that." Looking deep into Robert eyes. "I'm going to be your little minx tonight."

Slowly unzipping her dress. He leaned down and kissed the nap of her neck. "I can't wait." There was no end to Robert's fascination with Danielle. Soon the sounds of the night, would be replaced with the sounds of passion.

After three days of intense love making, Danielle emerged from their private villa and sprang into action. Danielle was hungry. "Maybe we should eat something."

"Sounds good to me," Robert said. "Eat, don't eat, or keep making love?"

"What does that mean, baby?"

"It means I could just keep making love to you, that's enough food for me."

She poked him lovingly in his side. "You're, crazy. Man can't live on sex along."

"Speak for yourself, and give me another serving of love, baby."

"I hate to disappoint you, but you're going to need every drop of your energy to fight our old partner, Governor Gunn."

"As always, you're right again."

Danielle entered the kitchen where she prepared fresh fruit, scrambled eggs, and toast. She returned to the villa, only to find Robert on the phone with Governor Gunn. She stepped away, signaling for him to join her on the terrace.

When he arrived, she observed the look on his face. "Well, what did he say?"

"Not much. He was indifferent, but I agreed to travel to Puerto Rico with him in the morning to meet with Governor Torres. He said the least I could do was to tell the Governor in person that I had decided not to invest in his venture in Puerto Rico."

"He has a point. But is the Governor Torres a corrupt official too? I'm not liking all these shady characters, Robert. I don't feel safe with you traveling to Puerto Rico."

"Oh, Sweetheart, I'll be fine. What are they going to do kill me?"

Silence occupied the space momentarily. "That's a good possibility."

Danielle's reply shook Robert to the core. He never thought of being killed, maybe he was naive when he came to dealing with harden criminals. He found it disgusting that he not only knew these people, but he was in bed with them like a two-dollar whore. The life he was accustomed to living was slipping slowly out of his grasp, as he wrestled to relieve himself of the demonic behavior of the governor and his criminal enterprise.

Robert was truly over his head, and out of his element, but there was no turning back. After breakfast, he and his lovely wife spent the entire day laying the ground work for removing the governor out of their lives forever.

Chapter 17

The next morning, Robert joined Danielle on the terrace for breakfast. The mood was good, but quiet. Both had been up all night trying to draft a plan which would allow their freedom from the governor's horrible way of life. When Captain Bill arrived, Robert kissed Danielle goodbye, but not the long passionate kiss he always gave her. Danielle watched Robert run down the steps to the yacht. It didn't take long for Captain Bill to notice Robert was present in body, but absent in mind. He looked like a man with the weight of the world on his shoulders. As the yacht left James Island, Danielle called out, "Be careful, baby, and hurry home."

Robert smiled. "I will sweetheart."

The ride to St. Thomas was rough, the water was choppy, and the sky looked as if it wanted to cry. Robert couldn't help but wonder if Governor Gunn had also corrupted the beautiful weather of the Caribbean as well. It seemed whatever he put his hands on became vile and disrupted. Danielle was right, the governor was a despicable man. Just as Robert was preparing to depart from the yacht, he received a call from Audrey. She advised him the governor had taken an earlier flight to Puerto

Rico and would meet him at the airport. He was also told to take a private plane from Bushwhackers, due to the American Eagle flight being overbooked. Now Robert was even more suspicious. Where is all of this coming from, and why didn't he call himself. Instead of the usual glass of orange juice, Robert poured a shot of tequila and swallowed it down in one gulp.

Captain Bill, walked up to Robert, laying his hands on his shoulder. "Look, man, I can see you're a little tense, but everything is going be fine. You're a good man and the heavenly Father always looks out for good men. Be strong, my brother."

"Thanks, man. I needed that. I'll let you know what time to expect my return."

"I'll be waiting."

Robert took the safari to the airport. Having plenty of time, he requested the driver to take the scenic route. When he arrived at the airport, he saw a tall Hispanic pilot standing beside a beautiful Citation XLS Cessna. "Good Morning, Mr. Kelsey. I'm Roberto, your pilot, and I will be flying you to Puerto Rico this morning. You know I don't get the opportunity to come face to face with a celebrity every day."

Robert replied, "I'm not a celebrity, I'm just an average Joe Blow."

The pilot smiled. "Well buckle up, Joe Blow, we'll be taking off in a few minutes."

Robert couldn't help but wonder why it was so important to travel by private plan, after all he could have taken a later flight on American Eagle. The whole trip was beginning to clog his brain. He couldn't wait to land so he could see what was really going on. The pilot tried making small talk with his one and only passenger, but Robert was so distracted he didn't hear a word he was saying. When the plane landed, both men disembarked. The pilot headed straight to the office with his flight manifesto, and Robert walked into the waiting area to be picked up. He turned around after hearing a familiar voice. It was Governor Gunn, standing back on his heel and puffing his awful smelling cigar.

"Welcome to Puerto Rico, Robert. Let's get going. We have places to go and people to see. The governor tapped the driver on the shoulder. "Calle Fortaleza, please."

All of a sudden, things were in a rush mode as he was shuffled into the car like livestock. There was no time to ask the governor about the meeting, but to his surprise the governor broke into loud laughter. "I hear congratulations are in order. You finally own a piece of the rock, uh son?"

"How did you know Danielle and I were married?"

"Nothing happens on my island that I don't know about. You, young man, should be mindful of that."

"That's an interesting piece of information. If it's true, then you would know what really happened to my father and the unsolved murders that have taken place on the island."

"Careful boy, you're treading in water too deep for you to survive. You think you know me, and you don't. I have more fire in my eyes than you have in your entire body. If I were you, I would focus on how to weasel your way out of the venture with Governor Torres. You and I can discuss this matter when we return to the rock."

When they arrived at the home of Governor Juan Torres, Robert couldn't keep his eyes off of the beautiful blue cobblestone streets. Observing Robert's interest, the governor remarked, "I just love old San Juan. Did you know it's the oldest settlement within Puerto Rico? It's actually a national historic landmark." The men walked to the front door, where they were greeted by a beautiful Hispanic lady. She was dressed impeccably and spoke in perfect English. "Welcome gentlemen, I'm Gabriela Torres."

"Good morning Mrs. Torres, Governor Gunn from the Virgin Islands, and Robert Kelsey. I think your husband is expecting us."

"My husband will be right down, Governor. Please follow me to the study. He will join you there. May I get you something to drink while you're waiting?"

"No, thank you. It's kind of you to ask."

Robert was scanning the room looking for an exit in the event he needed it. The house was stunning, with crystal chandeliers hanging beautifully from the ceiling in every room.

Robert observed the governor as he entered the room. He had spoken to him on numerous occasions by phone, but had never met him in person. It didn't take long for him to realize that he looked nothing like he sounded over the phone. He stood about 5'7" and weighed every bit of 300 pounds. The suit he was wearing looked as if it would explode on his body if he gained one more pound. His entire head was covered with thick wavy hair and his top lip was protected by a large bushy mustache. "Gentlemen, so pleased you were able to make the trip."

Robert didn't know that Governor Gunn had been in Puerto Rico for the past two days meeting with Governor Torres. "Well, Robert, the governor tells me you've had a change of heart about opening a franchise in Puerto Rico. That's a huge disappointment. I'm always looking for ways to make our

beautiful island better, and truly felt your business would provide job opportunities and additional revenue for Puerto Rico.

"It's just not the right time, Governor. I'm still weighing
my options."

The governor crossed his legs. "I understand a man has to
be more practical with his decisions when he takes on a family.
How is your beautiful wife, by the way?'

"She's fine. I see news travels fast in Puerto Rico, as well."

"Good to hear. One must always do what's right for the
family. You know they depend on us men to protect them and
keep them safe. I tell you what, Robert, why don't you give
a little more thought to your decision, and get back with me.
Sometimes it just takes a little meeting like this to help one
understand that opening a franchise in Puerto Rico may be the
best thing for your family."

Robert set there shocked, but not unnerved, thinking to
himself. This Spanish-speaking bastard just threatened my and
Danielle's lives. He knew this trip was going to be different,
but he didn't expect that level of pressure would be applied.
There's no way his failing to open a franchise would generate
this type of dialogue. Robert knew he was involved in something that was very valuable to both governors. Nodding in
agreement. "You're right. I'll give it some thought and get
back with you."

"Perfect! Now gentlemen, you must excuse me I have a
very important meeting I must attend. My wife will see you
out."

Minutes later the governor's wife returned and showed
them to the door. The real challenge for Robert was riding
back to the airport with the governor. Being emotionally dev-

astated by Governor Torres's conversation. Robert concluded that whatever decision he made, he and his wife would suffer at the hands of the governor. So, he walked passed the governor heading in the opposite direction. Offended by Robert's action, the governor descended like bees on Robert. "Wait one damn minute. You may have enough money to buy a piece of black, but all the money in the world won't save you or your eye candy if you keep fucking with me. You're in the big league, white boy. You're playing on my field. I will always have the home court advantage, and you will always be a spectator. Remember that."

In a state of anger Robert screamed, "You fat evil bastard. The hour will come when the devil you serve today will devour you and have you begging for mercy tomorrow."

"It'll be a cold day in hell before that happens. Now get your ass in the car so we can get back to St. Thomas."

Robert looked at the governor in disgust. "I'd rather walk to St. Thomas than accompany you. Nah, I pass."

The governor stepped into the taxi. He began to twist his hands out of frustration. He was shocked with Roberts's behavior. He'd always thought of Robert as being weak. However, he stood up to the governor like David did Goliath. This was truly a problem in the making. The governor had lost control of his golden boy. He was positive Governor Torres's conversation would scare Robert, but it didn't. It only pushed him farther away."

When Robert arrived at the airport, he didn't see hide or hair of the governor. He was really quite relieved. The trip to Puerto Rico had placed additional stress on Robert. All he could think of were the threats they made against Danielle's life. It was bad enough he had disrupted her previous life, now it appears he had put her life in complete danger. He didn't know what to do. If he told her she would worry. If he didn't tell her, she would think he was being deceptive.

Deliberating on the emotional roller coaster of the day, he was approached by a young pilot. "Mr. Kelsey, we're ready to board now."

"Thank you." Once they boarded, Robert asked, "Where's the other pilot, Roberto?"

"I'm sorry, sir, maybe you have the name wrong. We don't have a pilot named Roberto."

Robert chalked that up as another unexplained coincidence.

A few minutes later a petite Hispanic woman, wearing a bright red skirt and yellow tank top, stepped on board. She pushed her oversized sunglasses down on her nose to see, then walked passed two empty seats and sat right beside Robert.

After takeoff the woman started a conversation with Robert. Being preoccupied, his interaction with the woman was very limited. By the time he decided to be social, the plane landed at Cyril King Airport. Being a gentleman, Robert extended his hand to help the lady down the steps; while the pilot looked on with great interest.

Robert walked pass baggage claims to the taxi stand and took a safari to Red Hook. As he got off the safari taxi, he noticed the Hispanic woman was on the same safari. She waved at him, and he nodded. He was looking back to see where she was headed, only to see her get back on the same safari she'd just gotten off. Robert was feeling so paranoid. The sight of Captain Bill on the dock with his baby, The Wanderer, gave him a sense of relief.

"Welcome back, boss."

"Man, you have no idea how happy I am to be back. This has been one fucked up day."

Bill laughed." It must have been. I have never heard you use that language before."

"Believe it or not, I have used a lot of language today I have never used before."

"Wow, I'm sorry to hear that. Well, I know something that will cheer you up. Your beautiful wife has prepared a wonderful dinner for you, and is waiting patiently for your return."

A huge smile stretched across Robert's face. "You're right. That cheered me up."

As Captain Bill was heading towards James Island, he spotted the black speed boat that had circled the island a month ago. "Did you see that boat, Robert?"

"Yes, I did. It's the same boat that was circling the island a month ago."

"What the hell is going on?"

"I don't know, Bill, but I've got to get to the bottom of it."

"For sure, man, for sure!"

Captain Bill secured the vessel to the dock and turned to give Robert a few words of wisdom. "Yoh kin expect trouble when marine butt up wid sailor."

Shaking his head from side to side. "You West Indians and your proverbs. What does that mean?"

Captain Bill laughed at Robert. "It means, 'No use in avoiding the inevitable. You have to fight until you get tired of fighting, then get up and fight some more.' It'll be alright, man. Let me know if I can help in any way."

"I will. Thanks, my friend."

"I'll see you in the morning."

"You know, Bill, why don't you take the day off. I'm going to stay home with Danielle. There's something I need to discuss with her."

"Okay I'll see you Wednesday."

"Great, give my love to Robyn."

Captain Bill waved his hands in the air, and headed back to Red Hook.

Danielle was busy planning a quiet dinner for her handsome husband. When he entered the main Villa, she was standing in the middle of the kitchen floor preparing dinner with only an apron and a pair of black pumps. Robert leaned in to her and kissed her on the right cheek, and the left cheek. Then he kissed her forehead, and made a mad dash for her sensuous red lips. "If you weren't in this kitchen, baby, I would be doing naughty things to you right now."

Smiling sheepishly. "Don't look at me like that, you know it turns me on."

"What about this turns you on?" whispering in her ear in his distinctively calming voice. "Forget about dinner, baby, it's you I'm hungry for." He placed his hands gently under her apron caressing her passionately. He loosened her apron and led her slowly to the bedroom by the apron strings—where day turned into night and a bad ugly day turned into heaven.

True to his promise to Danielle, Robert laid next to the love of his life, having no idea on where to start the conversation. He looked into her beautiful eyes. "Danielle, I find myself in a situation where I must seek your advice."

"Okay." A lump in her throat began to form. What is it, Robert?"

"It's about my meeting in Puerto Rico with Governors Gunn and Torres. They threatened our lives if I don't move forward with the franchise in Puerto Rico."

"What? I told you the governor was into some deep criminal activity. There must be something you know absolutely nothing about regarding their plans for your franchise. We can't go to the police, because we don't know who to trust. The governor has so many government officials on payroll. It's best we take things outside of the local jurisdiction. We have to fight this battle together. You don't need to get further involved with this creep. I'm not scared of him. We just have to fight fire with fire, baby. Did you pull the personnel files on the people the governor had you employ?"

"Yes, I have them in my office."

"Did you have a chance to look over their files?"

"Yes, and I found something a little disturbing. Three of the employees I hired in the accounting department all worked at The First Third Bank of the VI before coming on board with VI Cash and Loans. They were all very personable and knowledgeable. Of course, I was clueless about the operations at that time. I didn't have a chance to review the files any further."

"That's okay. Give me the files and I will go through them later."

Danielle cleared her throat. "I made a cluster board of all the unsolved homicides on the island. When I started connecting the dots, I found there have been fifteen unsolved homicides in the past four years, which are directly connected to the governor."

"How do you know that?"

"Because I'm a native Virgin Islander and know a lot about who's doing what, and with whom. Believe me, there's many local islanders who know and frown upon the criminal activities that plague the islands, but they are fearful of the consequences they or they families might have to endure if they turn against the governor. They could lose their jobs or worst, their lives. I mean, look at the fear he placed in our lives. The only advantage you have over them, is that you have the resources to pack up and leave this nonsense behind."

"Everything has completely changed. I'm positive the governor knows we are trying to build a case against him, before he can build one against us. We have a serious problem. We are fighting a corrupt governor with criminal ties to some really scary people. First thing in the morning, we need to get busy and stay focused. No more three-hour love making sessions. This is our life we're talking about. I know this may sound crazy, but we may need to contact the FBI."

"The FBI?" Danielle's words struck home. Robert sighed, then hesitated for a moment. Confused and dismayed, he slowly grasped the meaning of Danielle's words. "We are in over our heads. We must gather as much information as possible, so we're able to get the attention of the FBI. Like you said, we have a lot of work to do."

"It's not going to be easy, but as long as we stick together we'll survive. Based on your trip today, I feel that your business was probably used to launder money from the governor's criminal activities."

"Really, is that what you believe?"

"Yep! Think about it, who cares if someone opens up a loan and check cashing business in Puerto Rico? The business only employs five to seven people, so unless it used to launder money it's not solving a big labor issue. You've been sitting back collecting money, not really keeping a good eye on who and where the money is coming. I want you to understand that if we bring the FBI into the picture, we may find ourselves on the wrong side of the law. That's why it's important for us to find out all we can, so the authorities can see that we haven't been willing participants in this charade."

"My God! You're right, again. What would I do without you?"

The question is, "What would we do without each other?"

"I have no idea how much money you have made or lost through some of these dealings, and you, yourself, said you have no idea where or how your father acquired so much money. The answer to your father's death may be linked to the things we're discovering now, which could eventually result in our death, if we're not smart. We may not be living on James Island before it's all said and done. You know how the government likes to seize properties if they can prove it was money acquired from criminal activities."

"I know, but we don't need four-hundred-million dollars to live, Danielle. And, quite frankly, I'm getting a little tired of living on a private island."

"No, we don't, but we'll need something. If you don't have secret off shore accounts, I highly suggest you get a couple. If we live, we'll need money to survive. If we don't, it won't matter. As far as being tired of living on James Island, if they try and put a little orange jumpsuit on your sexy backside, you'll be happy to live on James Island with every iguana and mongoose in the Caribbean. Besides that, I'm just beginning to enjoy the life of the rich and famous."

They both laughed at each other. "How do you know all this stuff?"

"I watch American Greed, the ID channel, and CSI Miami."

"You are such a cute old soul. Are you sure you're only twenty-one?"

"I'm twenty-one going on forty-five."

"I know that's right!"

"Listen at you sounding all hip."

Robert stood up and said, "Well, young lady, your husband is getting a little hungry. I'm going to fix us a little snack before we turn in for the night."

"Aren't you a sweetheart? Do you need some help?"

"No, I got this. Let me wait on you for a change. You know what I've learned most from this experience?"

"What?"

"Never let Maria off for more than a week, unless we're off island too. It may be a long time before I eat another sandwich and chips."

"You wait a minute. It hasn't been that bad. I fixed you a great dinner last night, but you wanted me instead. So, don't cry on my shoulder."

"Yes, ma'am," he said jokingly, as he slipped out of the bed and into the kitchen.

Chapter 18

When the Kelsey's finally climbed out of bed the next morning, they showered and went straight to the kitchen where they nibbled on bagels and cream cheese and sipped hot lemongrass tea while reviewing the files of the unsolved homicides on the island. Robert sat down his teacup while looking at Danielle. "You're so beautiful."

"Thank you, baby. That's so sweet of you to say."

She picked up her bagel to take another bite and realized her husband was still staring at her. "Are you okay?"

"Yes, I'm fine. I was just thinking about what a lucky man I am to have a wife who is beautiful, sexy, smart, and supportive. Now that's a great combination."

"Robert, stop it. You're making me uncomfortable."

"I love it when you feel uncomfortable."

"There you go, again. Focus baby, focus!"

"Baby, I truly enjoy making love with you, any time of day. But, we have serious problems. I'm happier than I've ever been in my life, and I don't want anyone to try and take it away. It's up to us to take care of each other's needs, but we have to also think about other important issues, like being alive so we can continue to make passionate love together."

"See, that's why I love you. You even make being responsible sound sexy."

"Robert Kelsey, you're an idiot! Back to work." He reached for her hand and squeezed it gently.

At that moment the phone rang. "Another interruption? Oh, no!"

"It is okay, sweetheart. It's Richard, the private investigator in New York. He might have some news about Camille."

"Well, by all means take it, baby."

"Hello, Richard, you find out anything?"

"Yes and no."

"What does that mean?"

"Well, I found that Camille Kelsey hasn't check into any rehabilitation center in the Unites States or abroad. She hasn't traveled, used a credit card, and haven't flown on a plane since she flew to St. Thomas. It appears that Camille is still on island."

"That's impossible. There is no way she could be on island and no one has seen or heard from her."

"Mr. Kelsey, I've been in this business for twenty years. If a person doesn't want to be found, they will not be found or they are dead and can't be found. I didn't find any activity on her. I can keep taking your money, but I think it would be wise for you to start checking with the local authorities. If nothing turns up, give me a call and I'll see what else I can do."

"Ok, Richard. Thanks for letting me know."

"Danielle, Richard said there is no movement on Camille. He thinks she may still be here on island. He even alluded that she might be dead."

"Wow! I hope not. She was disgusting, but I wouldn't want anything bad to happen to her."

An alarm went off in Danielle's head. "Wait a minute! While you were away in New York, a tourist from Tennessee was snorkeling out near Victory Beach and discovered the body of a female floating in the water. It was published in the paper and broadcasted on the radio asking anyone to come forward with information that might help in identify the body."

"Oh my God, Danielle. I pray that wasn't Camille."

"Me too, baby. You should go into town tomorrow and she what you can find out."

"Wow, I gave Captain Bill the day off."

"Baby, you're stressing. Bill was off today, he'll be back in the morning. Why don't you go rest for an hour or two?"

"I think I will." He stood up, and before walking away kissed her softly on the lips.

It was the first time Danielle had seen Robert so beaten. His energy was always high and his attitude was always positive. However, the continuous drama with Governor Gunn, Suzi Rose, and now Camille was eating at his core. Danielle knew she would have to remain strong in the days ahead. She was a native Virgin Islander and understood the lay of the land. The battle Robert would be fighting ahead would be ten times harder than what he was currently experiencing. This was not the life he was accustomed to, and soon he would be challenged beyond his wildest imagination. He would need his wife and friends' continuous support.

Danielle never stopped working. She would occasionally glance over to check on Robert, but her main focus was finding out as much as she could on the governor. She didn't want Robert to know they had an ace in the hole with Aunt Lucy, since she had scared him to death telling him about her practicing witchcraft. Although she was afraid of her aunt, her mother and Aunt Lucy were closer than any sisters could be. She knew if her life was in danger, both her mother and Aunt Lucy would come to her defense.

As Robert slept, Danielle continued to create a personal profile on the governor; which she learned watching Criminal Minds. Dior always laughed at the programs she watched, but she was drawn into the tragedies people found themselves from the demonic behavior of morally void people. Little did she know that she would be using the same techniques she viewed to try and save her family. She realized, with every passing day, she and Robert were truly soul mates.

As the sunlight disappeared into the sunset, orange and yellow became the back drop for a quiet evening alone. Her mind was in constant movement. Wanting a little laughter, she took a break and called Robyn. The phone rang four times before Robyn picked up. "Goodnight, my friend. I thought you would never answer."

"Look, girl, I got more to do than stand by this damn phone and wait for you to call."

Danielle broke out in laughter. "That's exactly what I need. A good old laugh."

Robyn was happy to hear from Danielle. "So how is life in paradise?"

"Girl, it's been one thing after another."

"You damn rich folks are getting on my damn nerves. What the hell you complaining about now? The steak wasn't cooked properly."

"Shut up, silly, people with money have problems too."

"Yes, I know, but they can generally be solved with money, which they have. So, I'm confused. I tell you what, you deal with my crap for a week and I'll deal with yours. I promise you whatever you're dealing with will be solved the first day I get my hands on Robert's checkbook, or the day he gives me the combination to the safe."

"Oh, my friend, I can't imagine life without you."

"You're going to have to, if you don't stop worrying the shit out of me."

They laughed uncontrollably. "Seriously, Danielle, what's going on? Bill told me when he picked Robert up he looked like he was carrying the weight of the world."

"Yea, things have been a little rough on the old guy. It's the governor, Robyn. He's being really nasty and very scary."

"Just sic your crazy Aunt Lucy on his ass and she'll have him looking like soft peter in no time. You know she can do some wicked shit."

"Will you go by there and ask her to help me out?"

"Hell, to the double no! That's not going to happen. You know how I feel about that voodoo chanting, spell casting aunt of yours. I'll take my chances with her old evil ass husband."

"Oh, Robyn, I miss you. When are you coming to visit me?"

"Aren't you on your honeymoon?"

"Yes, but I'm getting bored."

"Girl, get a dog."

"That's a good idea."

"You see what I mean. A dog is not a good idea! You'll be calling me bitching about the dog pissing and shitting up the house and chewing on your $500 shoes."

"Girl, bye."

Danielle wiped the tears from her eyes. "Goodbye, psycho."

"Back at you."

Speaking with Robyn lifted her spirits. Danielle knew that she could count on Robyn to shake things up. As she stood up from the table, she noticed the black speed boat passing by heading towards St. John. Being concerned, she called Robyn again.

Robyn picked up on the first ring. "Is that better, your majesty?"

"Girl, quit playing. Look, I just saw that black boat again."

"Tell Robert."

"He's asleep."

"Wake his rich ass up. Oh no, that would be too sensible. Instead, you call me; who is at least a forty-five minute ride away."

"Yes, I called you, but not for that reason. I need you to ask Sticky to get me a pair of binoculars and a 35mm camera with the best zoom lens he can find. I need to get some pictures of this boat. Somebody's up to no good and I want to know who it is. I'll have Robert give Bill the money in the morning."

"Consider it done."

"Thank you, my friend."

"No problem."

Robert woke up, just as Danielle was leaving." Don't go baby, stay with me."

"I've been with you all evening, now it's time to go to bed, and one thing I know for sure is you, Robert Kelsey, are not sleepy."

"No, I'm not. Are you?"

"Not really, I just need to relax for a while."

"That sounds like a good idea. Would you like to take a stroll on the beach?"

"That sounds wonderful, baby. I'll get my sandals."

"Bring mine too, please."

Danielle returned with a big smile etched across her face. "You have got to be the most romantic man in the world."

"And you, my love, have to be the most magnificent woman in the world. You're right up there with Michelle Obama."

"Wow! Michelle, now that's the best compliment you could have ever given me. She's incredible."

"And so are you."

Robert took her hands into his as they walked down the narrow path to their private beach. The trade winds were singing as the moonlight was lighting their path. It was another evening of wordless conversation. The occasional glance they shared spoke volumes. Robert stopped suddenly, kneeled down and picked up a beautiful seashell that sparkled like diamonds. He placed it in Danielle's hand. "I want you to keep this seashell with you at all times to remind you that I'm always with you." He turned and kissed her passionately until his love she could no longer resist.

Intoxicated by the air of passion, they strolled slowly back to their villa and laid in each other's arms, sharing laughter and love. Danielle fell asleep immediately while Robert watched over her, as she had watched over him earlier in the day. The two of them were a perfect match. His strength was her weakness, his weakness was her strength. It was something they both understood, and embraced. They disagreed, but never argued. One was black and one was white, but both were in love.

The morning was full of sunlight, as the water taxi's zipped back and forth to the beautiful island of St. John. It was the activity of the waves that kept island living full of vigor and excitement. Danielle took note of Robert's little hint regarding her lack of cooking. She rose early and prepared a breakfast fit for a king. As he laid in the bed mentally preparing himself to venture into town to visit the morgue, his thoughts were replaced by the smell of bacon. He took a quick shower, put on a pair of shorts and a polo shirt, and made his way onto the terrace where he joined Danielle, Robyn, and Captain Bill. The table was far from ordinary with bacon, pancakes, scrambled eggs, sausage, biscuits, and grapefruit.

"Good morning, my friends. I didn't know you were here."

Bill replied, "We decided if we got an early start, we might get lucky and get a free breakfast."

"Well, it is your lucky day. Look what my beautiful wife prepared for breakfast this morning."

"I surprised you, didn't I? I wasn't going to have you talking smack about me not cooking for you like Maria."

"Baby, I was just having a little fun." Robert stood up, walked over to Danielle, and planted a long juicy kiss on her lips.

Rolling her eyes, Robyn sighed, "Oh, get a room."

Robert replied, "That's not a bad idea."

"Please don't get him started Robyn. His appetite is good in the kitchen and the bedroom."

"Telling trade secrets, are we?"

"Robyn, why are we blessed to have your company this bright sunny day?"

"I had to come check on my persecution."

Danielle smiled. "I don't care what you call me as long as you're here."

Captain Bill turned to Robert and said, "I hope you know it's a package deal when it comes to these two. I've been trying to figure them out for years."

"I love it! It brings me so much joy to see the type of friendship and support they give each other. To be honest, I'm a little jealous. I have never had that kind of friendship."

"Oh, it's definitely rare, my friend."

"I'm glad you came, Robyn. I didn't want Danielle to accompany me to the morgue."

Captain Bill looked surprised. "The morgue?"

"Yea, man, I got a call from Richard last night telling me there hasn't been any movement from Camille since she flew to St Thomas. He suggested I check with the local authorities. Then Danielle told me about the body they found floating in the ocean. I'm going to the morgue, in hopes that it isn't her."

"That's deep."

"As soon as we finish this wonderful breakfast, my wife so graciously prepared, we can head to town. I was hoping you would tag along for support."

"Sure, no problem."

The two men continued to talk as Danielle and Robyn cleared the table and put the food away. Both ladies were standing in the yard taking in the fresh air when their husbands walked over and kissed them goodbye. "You girls try to stay out of trouble while we're away."

They both laughed. "I think we can handle that."

As the yacht pulled away from the dock, the ladies headed straight to the pool to relax. So much had happened since the two ladies had seen each other. This was the perfect time to bring Robyn up to speed on the craziness she and Robert had been faced with.

When Robert and Captain Bill arrived at the morgue, he noticed Bonehead, one of the governor's body guards, was lingering in the corridor. He turned his back and watched him walk out the door and into the governor's car. All night he had prayed that the unidentified woman in the morgue wasn't Camille, but, after seeing Bonehead, he wasn't quite sure.

Robert walked over to the desk with a sorrowful look, and requested to view the body of Jane Doe, the woman they found floating in the ocean.

The young lady was very pleasant and professional. "Have a seat, gentlemen. The medical examiner will be with you in just a moment."

Robert and Bill took a seat and within seconds a tall distinguished looking gentleman, dressed in a white lab coat, came out and introduced himself.

"Hello, gentleman. I'm Dr. Dean Howard, VI Medical Examiner. I understand you're here to view the body of Jane Doe, Case #72349, for official identification."

"Yes, sir, we are."

"Follow me please." He escorted them through two large metal doors to a wall of twelve stainless steel refrigerated drawers. "An unidentified person may be somewhat decomposed or damaged. So, gentleman, prepare yourselves. Viewing a body can often cause discomfort."

Both Robert and Captain Bill took a deep breath and exhaled as Dr. Howard opened the door exposing a large manila toe tag hanging on the right big toe stamped with VI Government Office of the Medical Examiner. The case number, date, and sex were listed right above the name Jane Doe. As he pulled out the long metal tray, Robert recognized the letters CK tattooed within a heart on the outside of her right ankle. It was the tattoo she had engraved the day after she and Randall were married. His greatest fear was now his reality. He leaned over, his voice which was normally low became loud and abrasive. "I promise you, Camille, I'm going to make the bastard pay for this."

Robert stood awkwardly before the body, and cried. "Why, God, why? She had her own way of living, but she didn't deserve this." The sad expression on his face was frozen in place. Within minutes his silence began to speak as he dropped his head and wept.

"No, she didn't," Bill replied. He tried his best to comfort Robert, but the pain was too deep and the wound too fresh. Bill knew it would take time for Robert to come to grips with Camille's death, especially with the way in which they parted. Everything seemed so surreal. In a matter of a few months he watched his boss, now friend, ride a roller coaster of ups and downs that would paralyze most men. He was concerned, but he wasn't worried. He knew he would weather the storm, in time.

This was hard on Robert. He made the official identification and advised Dr. Howard he would make the necessary arrangements for the body. Upon leaving the hospital, Captain Bill suggested they stop by Grandma Sandy's to get a cup of coffee. Captain Bill was a friend of Grandma and knew the lunch crowd would be gone and the place would be relatively quiet. Grandma always had soothing music piping through the speakers which would provide an oasis of tranquility for the grief-stricken men.

As they entered, Grandma Sandy greeted them with a warm smile. Noticing a strained expression on their faces, Grandma Sandy asked, "Is there anything I can do for you?"

Bill replied, "We just need a little space and a cup of coffee. My friend just received some disturbing news."

"I'm sorry to hear. Grab that table in the back by the coffee bar and help yourself. It's on the house."

Robert looked as though he had been shot. He walked over to the table and sat in silence, staring into space, occasionally drinking his coffee. He tried hard to picture the face of his favorite sister-in-law, but he saw only her disappointed face as she sailed away from James Island and to her death. It was hard to believe her life had ended in the place she loved so much. The longer he sat, the angrier he got. He knew that Governor Gunn was the cause of her death. He now had one more reason to bring him down. The governor had gotten away with so much he thought he was invincible, but not this time he thought to himself. He's truly gone too far.

Robert glanced at the coffee cup, pushed it aside, rose, and walked out the door in a zombie-like state of mind with Bill close behind.

It was a long quiet ride back to Red Hook. Captain Bill parked the car and Robert walked to the yacht totally unaware of his surroundings. Captain Bill ran up behind him. "Hey man, you're going the wrong way. Come on, I got you." He helped Robert upon the yacht and to the master bedroom, where he rested until they arrived home.

Captain Bill didn't awake Robert, instead he went to the terrace to share the horrible news with the family. "This is a sad day for Robert, he's going to need our love and support. He's taking it really hard, Danielle. He might need a little space with this one."

"That's not a problem. Whatever he needs, I will provide."

A few minutes later Robert emerged. He walked over to his wife and wrapped his arms around her. "Sweetheart, if I act unloving and foster an attitude, I'm asking for your forgiveness in advance."

She whispered softly in his ear. "I understand, baby. Thank must have been really upsetting for you. I think it would be a good idea for you to retreat to your villa so you can try and wrap your head around this horrible situation."

"Thank you for being so understanding."

"You would do the same for me. I'll be right here if you need me."

Robert thanked Captain Bill, hugged Robyn goodbye, and retreated to his villa to spend time with himself, by himself.

Captain Bill and Robyn gave Danielle a group hug as they prepared to return home. Before leaving, Robyn turned and asked, "Do you still want Sticky to pick up that equipment for you?"

"Yes, by all means. I need to get the money from Robert, I will be right back. Please take some of that fruit home with you, it's just going to spoil."

Danielle made her way to Robert's villa. She knocked lightly on the door, then entered. "Baby, I need to get some money to give Robin. She is going to pick up a camera and a pair of binoculars. I'm determine to find out who owns that black speed boat that keeps popping around."

"That's a good idea, baby. You have the combination to the safe, get what you need. Give Robyn a little extra for keeping you company and picking the things up for you."

"Oh Robert, that's not necessary. We're family. I don't have to pay her anything, we look out for each other."

"I know, sweetheart, but we have more than enough to share with Robyn and Bill. They're our family and I want them to know how much we value their love and friendship. I don't want them to think one minute that we take it for granted."

"Okay. That's one of the reasons I love you so much." She leaned down and kissed him on the forehead, as he pulled her down and kissed her on her voluptuous lips.

Danielle pulled the door together gently. Robyn impatiently yelled, "Danielle, you better not be in their doing the nasty."

Shaking her head as she turned the corner. "You can rush me if you want to, but Robert wanted me to bring you a little lunch money for being such a great friend and sister."

"Well, get back in there and get my money."

"I got your money, knucklehead. Here is $1500 for the equipment. Let me know if you need more. If there's any left, give it to Sticky. Here is $5,000 for you and Bill."

"Bill who, are you shitting me?"

"Girl, if you ever try to leave that man I'm going to kick your behind all the way to St. Croix."

Danielle laughed. "Bill, take her home. And thank you for taking such good care of Robert. He really values your friendship."

"That's not a problem, Danielle. I value our friendship too."

Danielle watched her friends disappear into the night as she retreated to her private villa without the presence of the man she loved.

Robert found himself upon the veranda of his villa. He took out his phone and called the governor. The phone ranged once.

The raspy and cold-hearted voice of the governor came rushing into Robert's ear. "Mr. Kelsey, what a surprise. I was beginning to think you didn't like me anymore."

Robert took a deep breath. "A woman sacrificed her dignity for you, she suffered at your hands, and the animals you employ. And this is her reward?"

"You don't know what you're speaking about, son."

"Don't call me, son. You're not my fucking father. I will see you burn in hell for Camille's murder, you asshole." He hung up the phone, gathered his composure, then placed a call to Randall.

The phone rang repeatedly, then went to voicemail. As he started to leave a message, Randall picked. "Hey man, what's going on? You people don't sleep in paradise?"

"I'm sorry to call so late, but I've got some bad news. Camille is dead."

"What? Dead. When, who, how? Don't just tell me she's dead and leave it like that."

"Calm down man. I've been going through this shit all day. It's messed up. She was murdered. A tourist found her body floating in the water, it had washed up on shore. The autopsy report states she was unconscious at the time her body was placed in the ocean. There's a lot more to it than that, but I can't get into it right now. I need you to get in touch with Camille's attorney to find out if she had insurance. I'm arranging to have her cremated. Her body was decomposed and the fish had their way with her. I feel the cremation is the best option. You know how vain she was, so I'm going to honor her the best I can. I'm bringing her ashes home. I don't think I could live with myself if I left her here with the son of a bitch who killed her."

"Hey, you talk like you know who killed her."

"I do, but I can't prove it yet. But I will. Trust me."

"Little brother, hold on now, you're talking some scary shit. I don't intend on bringing your ashes to New York, so just bring it down a notch and we'll talk when you get here. Let me know if I can do anything else."

"Alright, man. I'll be in touch."

Amid all of the upheaval in their lives, Danielle was the eye in Robert's hurricane. She stood in the middle of the storm beside him, adjusting herself to bring power to him from the center of her calm. Knowing that she would open her eyes in the morning and find him beside her, just as he she always did.

Chapter 19

When Danielle opened her eyes, she found Robert lying next to her. She leaned over to kiss him and felt the presence of tears streaming down his face. She squeezed his hand tightly. "Baby, can I get you anything?"

Shaking his head. "No, sweetheart, please forgive me for being so emotional."

Danielle kissed the tears on his face. "Our tears are what happens when it rains deep inside our hearts and we're unable to hold the rain any longer. The governor has caused us to wallow in the blood of death and destruction which he created. However, we must be strong and rise above his evil ways, so we can find the strength to survive."

Robert pulled her into his arms. "That's another reason I love you so much. You have the courage to suffer."

Danielle knew Robert was harboring guilt about Camille's death, but she wanted him to accept her blood wasn't on his hands, it was on the hands of the deplorable Governor Gunn. As tragic as her death was, Danielle couldn't allow the tragedy to linger above their heads and in his mind. She gently placed her head on his shoulder and whispered softly in his ear, "You have to take the initiative to save yourself. You didn't force Camille to run or use drugs, spy on you, or jump into bed with the governor. She was a fully-grown woman, who made foolish choices, and her choices caused horrific consequences. You did the right thing, Robert, and if she had remained on James Island or left as she did, her death would have inevitably occurred. Camille is dead and there's nothing we can do about it but grieve and bring the people down who is responsible. I will help you with both, but right now I need you to be concerned about what we need to do in making sure we're not lying next to her in the morgue."

"I know, baby. It just hit me like a ton of bricks. It seems like every time I get up from something, I get knocked down with something else."

"It's called life. The phrase 'only the strong survive' wasn't created for nothing. These situations have been harder on you than me because you've never had to fight for your survival. It was always handed to you. If a problem did arise, you could generally handle it with a check or a trip to Bora Bora. Baby, I love you, but I don't think you could have survived in this world as a black man."

"I take offense to that."

"Why? It's true. I'm not trying to diminish your worth. I am speaking truth to power. You have no idea the struggle our men have had to endure just to put a pot of beans and Johnny cakes on the table. Having to watch their wife and children live in crime-infested neighborhoods and projects with dope dealers, rapists, and murderers because it was all they could afford. You don't know anything about that kind of life, Robert, and you should thank God it wasn't your experience. You're a good man with a decent heart, and a good man should find honor in admitting that all men are not created equal in the eyes of the law."

Pausing, Robert looked long and hard at Danielle. His eyes glowed. He raised his arms to caress her "You have opened by eyes to so many things and you've done it without prejudice or condemnation. I admire the heart that beats within you and the compassion you share with me and the rest of the world. You, my love, give meaning to life in a way I've never experienced before."

Danielle sprang to her feet and extended her hands to Robert. "Come on, baby, let's go. We have things to do. There's no time to debate who had a better life, and what role you played in the death of Camille. You must honor her life by not allowing her to remain in a morgue full of strangers. She not only has a name, she has a family who loved her dearly. You will honor her by taking her spirit home where she can rest in peace."

Robert found himself walking into the shower, giving thanks to Danielle for reminding him he was alive and financially able to honor Camille's life by allowing her to rest in peace and dignity.

By the time Robert joined Danielle in the kitchen, arrangements had been made for Camille's cremation and his airline ticket to New York. After his morning talk with Danielle, he was operating on full speed. Before Danielle could comment on his take charge attitude, he closed his eyes and planted a loving kiss on her forehead.

"Well, what got into you this morning?"

"Nothing got into me this morning, something got a hold of me last night, and oooh, it must be love."

Danielle found it hard not to be smitten with Robert. She flashed him a smile and said, "Remember, you need to make arrangements for Camille."

Robert was hilarious. He waved his hand like a magician. "Done!"

"Good," she said. "Well, you still need to make your airline reservations."

Waving his hands for the second time. "Done that too, little lady! I'm taking the last flight to New York on Sunday, and returning home Thursday morning."

Danielle couldn't stop laughing. "Well it looks like Mr. Kelsey has done it all."

"Looks that way," he replied. "Now what is Mrs. Kelsey going to give Mr. Kelsey for being such a take charge man?"

"Hmm! Mrs. Kelsey doesn't know, but she's going to think of something special for Mr. Kelsey."

"Mr. Kelsey knows what Mrs. Kelsey can give him."

Laughing hysterically. "I bet he does with his sexy self."

Just as Robert thought he was going to get a morning treat, Captain Bill walked into the kitchen. "Good morning, people."

"What's good about it?" Robert replied.

"Don't pay him any attention, Captain Bill. You came right in the nick of time."

Bill nodded his head up and down. "Ooh, I get it."

Flashing his pearly whites Robert replied, "Well, I didn't."

When Bill left Robert yesterday he was lost in sorrow, but this morning he was looking and acting as if he was given a new lease on life. One thing Captain Bill knew, the affect Danielle had on his friend, most men would never experience, not even for a day. This was real love, up front and personal.

Captain Bill grabbed a cup of tea as Robert stole a kiss from the love of his life. Both ran down the stairs with a bagel and cream cheese sandwich. Danielle waved goodbye and walked slowly to the terrace. Being pleased with Robert's ability to move forward while in pain and despair, she sat quietly in her chair meditating until the center of her being was calm and at peace.

When Robert retuned home, he was hot and sweaty. The sun was spreading its sizzling rays all over the grounds on the island. The trees were dry and hundreds of iguanas appeared on the open street looking tired and thirsty. The intense heat wave was taking its toll on the once vibrant vegetation of the tropics. Danielle had traded her long flowing sun dress for a pair of white shorts and a red Xtremely Hot tee shirt. The island wasn't the only thing on fire in Robert's view. "Isn't it hot enough? Seeing you in that outfit makes my temperature rise."

"You know I wore them just for you. I've been watching the waves in the Atlantic all day, trying to extract some much-needed relief from the blistering heat. Maybe I should leave. I wouldn't want you to get tired of seeing me."

Looking at her. "I will never get tired of seeing you, my love. You are a vision of beauty. Do you have a minute? I'd like to share something with you."

"Sure."

"I was thinking about our conversation about the governor possibly using my businesses for money laundering. How do you feel about me closing all three of the businesses?"

"That's an idea, but wouldn't you lose money?"

"Yes, but that's not an issue. We don't need the money, we have more than enough to live on."

"But what about the employees? What would they do?"

"Well, I thought I would give them a severance package, (to include a year's salary for each year they were employed with us), their health benefits, and two weeks paid vacation. That would give them adequate time to find a new job without disrupting their lives."

"It sounds good, but there are other things you need to consider."

"Other things, like what?"

"For starters, the push back you're going to get from the governor, and God knows who else. You will also have to pay the monthly rent on the spaces you were leasing."

Clearing his throat, "I look at it like this. I'm at risk whether I remain open or close. By closing the business, I will bring immediate disruption to the governor's operations. As for the monthly rent, I can either sublease the space or just negotiate a buyout of the lease. That's the least of my worries. My primary concern is our safety."

"I think that's a great idea."

"Great, because I'm going to need you to make it all happen while I'm away."

"As of tonight, we focus on what the total annual salaries and vacations will be for the employees, then you will need to contact George and have him work up the cost to maintain their insurance coverage for a year. You will need to accompany me to the bank, so we can get you on all the accounts. You can disburse checks the morning after the door locks are changed. You will not be able to do this alone. It will take at least three people to get it done. Hopefully, Robyn and Bill will help. Everyone will be assigned a location so when the employees arrive, you can tell them of our closing, thank them for their services, and give them their severance pay. By the time I return, all hell will start to break loose, but it's our first step in dissolving our association with Governor Gunn."

"I think it is a brilliant move, baby. I promise I won't let you down."

"I'm not the least bit worried about that. I know what an awesome partner I have." When he leaned forward to kiss her, she responded by returning his kiss.

Danielle removed her tee shirt leaving only her white lace bra exposed. "I hope my manner doesn't mislead, you Mr. Kelsey."

He gave an appealing glance and replied, "It's not your manner that concerns me, young lady, it's my emotions. As I recall, before I left home this morning you were thinking of ways to reward me. Now I've come up with an exceptional plan, which you, I might add, approved. I think I'm entitled to something very special." He stood directly in front of her, awakening her sensuality. He saw enough in her eyes to compel him to take her hand and lead her into a night that turned from passion to erotica.

Saturday morning, Captain Bill was in the city picking up Camille's cremains from Hawes Mortuary, when he heard the voice of Bonehead. "Hey man, I notice you've been sucking up to the rich white boy these days. You need to make sure you're being loyal to the right people. I wouldn't want to see you get hurt or nothing."

Being a man of few words, Captain Bill replied, "And you need to watch who and how you approach me. Don't let my lack of words confuse you, brother."

Captain Bill was nothing to play with. His cool demeanor was in direct contrast to the hell raising Rasta man he once was. He was known by his reputation as a man to be feared. It was only due to the loss of his twin brother, in a drive by shooting, that convinced the handsome Rasta man to change the direction of his life. For some reason, Bonehead didn't remember a pit bull never forgets how to fight. As one of the governor's bodyguards, he always displayed a tough presence when he was in character, but Captain Bill knew he was just a snotty nose punk. Nodding his head to Captain Bill, he took a few steps back and walked away with his mouth shut and his attitude in check.

A feeling of concern fell over Captain Bill. It was obvious that the governor was applying pressure on Robert, and he figured it would only be a period of time before he would be drawn into the confusion. With all that being said, Captain Bill made a mental note to stay strapped from this day forward. He understood it would be difficult to remain a man of peace when war was breaking out all around.

When he arrived on James Island, he carried the silver urn and placed it respectfully in Robert's hands. I thought it would be a good idea to let Camille enjoy the trade winds in her favorite chair on the terrace before she journeys back to the concrete jungle.

Robert smiled. "I think that is a great idea Bill."

Danielle listened attentively to the men exchanging stories about Camille and her bizarre and crazy behavior. As for Danielle she had only one encounter with her, and it wasn't very memorable, so she had nothing to add. Because of Robert's genuine love for Camille, she also had nothing to subtract. She gave them both the space they needed to remember the lady who threw more than her fair share of shade.

Sunday morning arrived early, and so did Captain Bill. Robert placed the cellophane wrapped silver urn snuggly in his suitcase. Watching Danielle's eyes beaming bright and intense, he whispered, "I love you in her ear." He kissed her goodbye and joined Captain Bill on the yacht. Danielle took her usual position on the front lawn waving goodbye to a man she watched leave so many times before. She was beginning to feel anxious and nervous, all at the same time. She had been given a new life, one which was filled with security and love, but she had also inherited a life of crime filled with murder, corruption, and uncertainty. Her faith was challenged daily, her body ravaged by a man whose appetite for love drove her to the point of insanity. His world and his island had drawn her into a life she once hated, into the life she now loved.

On the yacht ride over, Captain Bill shared his encounter with Bonehead. Robert was regretful that Captain Bill was now being drawn into his mess. "Look, Bill, the last thing I want to do is cause you and your family problems. As much as I value our friendship, I'll understand if you wish to sever ties."

Captain Bill chuckled. "Is that why you think I told you about my little run in?" No man, I wanted to let you know that things were heating up and it was going to be necessary to make some definitive plans on eradicating these clowns. I'm with you partner. You're a straight up guy, and believe me, they don't come around every day black or white. I am with you all the way. The love you have shown to Robyn and me is golden, not to mention the way you love and respect your wife. We are going to get through this mess one way or the other."

"I'm so happy to hear you say that. I left Danielle instructions to shut down all my operations on the island, and she's going to need your help to make it happen."

"You can count us in, man."

"Thanks, Bill. Another thing. Is it possible for you and Robyn to stay with Danielle until Maria returns on Tuesday? I should be back no later than Thursday."

"No problem."

When the two arrived at Red Hook, Robert took the safari to the airport to catch his flight to New York. He waved to Captain Bill. "Take good care of my baby for me."

"You got it, partner."

When Robert arrived at the airport, he recognized two of the governor's men standing by the ATM machine. He tilted his cap and walked straight to the doors to customs. After clearing all the hurdles in security, he took a seat by Gate 2, and waited for his flight to be called. Being concerned about Danielle, he placed a call to her.

"Hello."

"Hello, sweetheart, how's my girl?"

"Your girl is fine, baby. Is everything ok?"

"Yes, baby. I wanted to hear your voice and remind you to be very careful. I've asked Bill and Robyn to stay with you until Maria returns so you won't be alone."

"Thank you, baby. That makes me feel a lot better."

"Yea, me too."

"Look, sweetheart, I know everything has been a big mess since our first meeting, but I want you to know that if I had it to do all over again I would do it differently. I seemed to have brought so much confusion to your life, and that wasn't what I intended. Because of you, I am a better man and I promise you that if any one touches a hair on your beautiful head, I will hunt them down and kill them with my bare hands."

"It's okay, baby. We'll be just fine. I can feel it. I think the first phase of your plan will definitely make the governor understand that you are not going to be intimidated by him or his barbarians. I don't know witchcraft, but I know God, and I trust him to provide and protect us from the evil activities of Governor Gunn. We may encounter some more challenges, but I know we will overcome them together. Now, you stop worrying about me and go put your friend to rest, then hurry home to me."

"I will. That you can count on. Look, baby, it's time to board. I will call you when I arrive."

"I'll be waiting."

When Robert arrived in New York, he got off the plane and took a taxi directly to Camille's condominium. Robert always stayed there when he was in New York. He had his own set of keys and the personnel knew him well from his generous tips. There was only one time he didn't stay at the apartment. It was on his last trip to New York, when he asked Camille to leave his home. As he entered the lobby, he was greeted by Edward the night doorman. "Good evening, Mr. Kelsey, may I be of assistance to you?"

"You certainly may, Edward. It grieves me to tell you Ms. Kelsey is deceased. I'm here to bring her cremains home and pay my last respects."

Edward was stunned. "It saddens me to hear, sir. Joshua will help you with your bags. Please extend my condolences to your family."

Edward signaled for Joshua. "Help Mr. Kelsey with his bags, please."

"Thank you. I will be here for a couple of days tying up a few loose ends, so I would appreciate you notifying me if any packages or visitors arrive for me."

"I certainly will, sir. Again, I'm terribly sorry for your loss."

Robert placed his hand on Edward's shoulder, then turned and followed Joshua to unit twenty-three hundred.

When Robert entered the room, the huge painting of Magen's Bay Beach, hanging over the white oversized leather sectional, caught his attention. The spacious and luxurious apartment was immaculate. Robert thought it strange that Camille would never see her million-dollar view of the New York skyline again, she loved it so dearly. It seemed crazy that there was so much life in the city, but no life in the beautiful silver urn that housed her cremains.

Robert tipped Joshua and walked him to the door. "Well, goodnight, sir. Will there be anything else?"

"No. Thank you, Joshua. Goodnight."

Placing the security lock on the door, Robert poured himself a drink and immediately felt his body relax. He walked into the bedroom, where Joshua had taken his bags, and took the silver urn out and placed it carefully on the fireplace mantel.

He sat quietly on the edge of the bed, pulled his phone from his pocket and called Randall. The phone rang and rang until it eventually went to voicemail. "Hey, I'm here at Camille's place. Give me a call when you get this message."

Two hours later, Randall returned Robert's call. Robert was half asleep, but managed to grab the call on the last ring. "Hey, man, how was your flight."

Sounding harsh and annoyed, "As well as can be expected."

"Look, I spoke with Attorney Driskell. He wants to see you in his office in the morning at 10:00 a.m."

"Alright, will you meet me there?"

"No need. My name is nowhere in her will."

"Who is in her will?"

"I have no idea, all I know is you are the executor of her will, and you, my friend, have been requested to meet with Attorney Driskell in the morning. Give me a call after your meeting. We can grab a bite to eat, and you can bring me up to speed."

"Sounds good, brother. I'll check with you tomorrow."

Robert placed his phone on the charger, rolled over, and went right back to sleep.

The next morning, Robert was awakened by the sounds of the city. He stood up gazing out the window, watching the movement of the people on the sidewalk. Moments later the phone rang, it was Danielle.

"Good morning, baby. How are you? I fell asleep last night, waiting to hear from you."

"I'm sorry, sweetheart. It was a tiring trip, and when I arrived at the apartment I went straight to sleep."

"I understand. I just wanted to make sure you arrived safe and sound. What do you have planned for today?"

"First, I'm going to meet with Camille's attorney, join Randall for lunch, and then do the unthinkable; go see Mother."

"Oh, Robert, she can't be that bad."

"She's just like your Aunt Lucy, always wreaking havoc in everyone's life. The only difference between the two, other than skin color, of course, is Mother does it with her nose, and your Aunt Lucy does it with witchcraft."

Laughing. "I see you're full of jokes this morning. I'm happy to hear you lighten up a bit. Well, keep me abreast of things and try to relax."

"I will, sweetheart, and you do the same."

Robert took a long relaxing shower, got dressed, and took a taxi to Attorney Driskell's office. He arrived an hour early, so he sat quietly thumbing through African American magazines that laid on the wood and glass coffee table. The front desk was vacant, so he waited for the receptionist. A few minutes later a beautiful young lady appeared from Attorney Driskell's office introducing herself as Vermell. She looked a little flushed and half put together. Robert glanced up quickly, thinking to himself that his early arrival seemed to have disrupted a little office romance. In a sweet and sultry voice, she said, "Attorney Driskell will be with you shortly, sir. Would you like some coffee while you wait?"

"No, thank you."

Robert was sitting patiently when Vermell returned and escorted him into Attorney Driskell's office. As he entered, he couldn't keep his eyes off of the beautiful African art and statues which covered the rich mahogany walls. The side chairs were covered in black and white Mudd cloth. A large tiger skin rug covered the polished hard wood floors. It was obvious the man took great pride in his heritage. Attorney Driskell raised up from the large black leather chair and shook Robert's hand.

"I'm terribly sorry we must meet under these circumstances, Mr. Kelsey. However, we all know we have an expiration date stamped on our heads the day we come into the world. We don't know the day or the hour, which is the reason I feel it's imperative we each make good use of each day we are graciously granted."

Robert shook his head in agreement. "Eloquently said, sir."

"Well, Mr. Kelsey, let's get down to business, this will not take very long. Camille was a free spirit. I've been her attorney now for over six years and I'm sorry I will no longer be privileged to share her company."

"Thanks, nice of you to say."

"Oh, I mean every word. She was an exceptional and surprising woman. As for her estate, she named you the executor, and the beneficiary of her real estate holdings, which includes her condominium in New York, a $500,000 life insurance policy, which has an accidental death rider attached, and a 2014 black SXK 32 Mercedes Benz."

"By the way, she also had credit life on her assets and real estate properties, so everything is yours free and clear. I would suggest that you notify her credit card companies and her banks. I have a list of them right here."

"What? She left everything to me? I will contact the credit card companies and the banks immediately."

"Yes, that's a good idea. As free of a life as Camille lived, she was a very caring person. There is one other thing, she requested that you donate $100,000 every year to a charity of your choice, which fights against the exploitation of women and children in the Caribbean. That's right, Mr. Kelsey. You must have been an amazing brother-in-law and a great friend."

Robert placed his head in his hands and wept with dignity. "She left me everything she owned?"

"That's correct. She also left you a note she wanted me to read to you, if this day ever presented itself. I will read it for you now."

I've heard that in life, everyone has as a guardian angel. Someone who peeks inside the window of their lonely heart and give love when no one else will. Robert Kelsey, no matter how many times I flew into your nest with broken wings, you took me in and stood beside me until I could fly again. When I lost Randall, I thought I had lost you, my best friend and brother, but I didn't. You never took your love from me and you never lost hope that I would one day find myself in a place of love, peace, and solace. Well, my friend, today is the day. You can rest now, for I am not only at peace, I am flying high above the clouds. So, when you sit on your beautiful veranda on James Island, just look up to the sky and know you too have a guardian angel who will be flying over you night and day. Thank you for my wings, my friend.

I Love You, Camille

The sunlight ceased as rain fell from Robert Kelsey's and Attorney Driskell's eyes. The message was emotional and thought provoking, and gave each of the men a closure they both needed and deserved.

Robert left Attorney Driskell's office with a different perspective on how Camille lived her life. It was sad drug addiction entered her world, along with crossing paths with the man who brought about her untimely death. Robert had made a promise to meet Randall after his meeting, but he didn't feel it was a good idea. Randall didn't miss an opportunity to dog Camille, and he knew if he attempted to do so during lunch, he wouldn't be responsible for his actions. He decided to visit his mother instead. He hailed a taxi, gave the driver the address, and sat quietly in the back as the meter ran like a running faucet.

The radio was playing, "Ain't No Mountain High Enough," when the driver announced their arrival. "Nine twenty-two Park, sir."

"Thanks, buddy." Robert reached into his pocket, paid the driver, and entered the elaborate building of the rich and famous. As ridiculous as his mother and the other residents of the building were, he always felt comfortable when visiting. His mother wasn't aware he was coming, so he asked the doorman to announce his arrival in the event his company wasn't preferred. However, he could hear the excitement in his mother's voice, which gave him the validation he needed.

She opened the door and saw her handsome son. He was dressed in white linen slacks and a light blue shirt. "Good heavens, don't you look spectacular. What a surprise. It's so nice to see you, sweetheart. Before you say a word, allow me to apologize to you for misspeaking about your personal life. You are a grown man. I want you to know that I might not agree with your selection, but I do truly love you and will learn to adapt and behave accordingly."

"I appreciate what you're saying, Mother, and I know you would like to mean everything you're saying, but we both know you don't. I truly feel you would love Danielle if you met her with an open mind. She's beautiful, delightful, and entertaining."

"Oh, my dear Robert, so are cartoons, but I don't watch them. They're not acceptable for stimulating the mind. Enough small talk, darling. How are you? Randall told me about Camille. I tried to warn her that living in the jungle wasn't a civilized thing to do, but she never listened to me. Such a pretty girl, and all she wanted to do was run around in the jungle looking for Tarzan. I told her it wasn't safe to live there. I saw a movie where all of the servants got mad because their employer wouldn't give them more money, so they killed them and ate them for dinner."

"Mother, that's the most ridiculous story I have ever heard. Please don't ever repeat that. Someone would surely put you in a mental institution and throw away the key." Robert stood in the middle of the floor and gave his mother a big hug. "I think I'm going to head back home."

"Ok, son, but what time is the service?"

"It will be held tomorrow morning at 11:00 a.m. in St Anthony's Cemetery. Bishop Paul with be in charge of the brief liturgy."

"That's fine. I will see you in the morning." She leaned over and whispered in Robert's ear, "Another thing, I'm not worried about you. I know you're experimenting with the ladies, and it will only be a matter of time before you find a good girl, of your own kind, to settle down with. You know, my father always said—Dogs should marry dogs, and cats should marry cats. It's all about the pedigree."

Shaking his head. "Well, Mother, I'm not marrying a dog or a cat, but since we're on the subject, Danielle and I did get married."

"Oh, Robert why do you play these silly games with me?"

"I'm not playing, Mother. You're now the proud mother-in-law of a beautiful West Indian woman."

"Good Lord, Robert."

This time Robert left his mother standing in the middle of the floor with her tiny mouth wide open. He knew before he left the building, she would have taken two Xanax to calm her nerves. He laughed, but wasn't worried. He knew that if, and when, she met Danielle, she would fall completely in love with her, and if she didn't, it didn't matter. His love for her, and her love for him would be enough.

Robert hailed another taxi. As the vehicle moved at a snail's pace, Robert gave thanks he didn't have to deal with the traffic of New York City on a daily basis. When he arrived at the condo he retreated to the bedroom, and prepared himself mentally for the next day.

Morning came too soon. Robert rushed to dress for Camille's' service. He wanted to pay a special tribute to Camille, so he wore the Givenchy black linen two-piece suit she had given him for his 34th birthday. She always said he looked like a million dollars in it, and today was no different. The two-button designer suit gave him an edgy slim fitting appearance. When he looked in the mirror he smiled, knowing that she would have been pleased to see him out of shorts and tee shirts for a change. Out of respect for their friendship, he didn't even take the time to call Danielle. Today was Camille's day.

He grabbed his keys, placed his black Armani shades over his captivating, but swollen blue eyes. He collected the silver urn from the fireplace, and held it closely to his chest. He paused momentarily, then walked out the door and into a taxi.

When he arrived at St. Anthony's Cemetery, Bishop Paul met him at the door, and relieved him of the urn. He placed it gently on the table near the burning incense and the Easter candle. As the door opened, Randall and their mother entered. Edward, the doorman, was also in attendance, along with five of Camille's girlfriends. The sound of "Amazing Grace" flowed sweetly from the boys' choir. Bishop Paul stood directly in front of her family and friends memorializing her with God's tender mercy and compassion. He reminded the family they were celebrating her life and not the expression of grief. He closed the service with the following passage:

I have been deprived of peace; I have forgotten what prosperity is. So I say, my splendor is gone and all that I had hoped from the Lord. (Lamentations 3:17-18)

The choir sang, "Come to Her Aid" as the services ended with the Rite of Committal, where her remains were inurned in a crypt in the mausoleum.

Robert embraced his brother Randall after removing his shades to wipe the tears from his eyes. Randall whispered in his ear, "I loved her until death."

"I know," Robert said, "and she loved you."

Robert kissed his mother goodbye and returned to the condominium. Camille's life had ended and his had just begun. He had traveled home with her to pay his final respects; now it was time for him to return to James Island, and the life he now loved.

Chapter 20

The morning was full of sunlight and hope. Only the promise of positive expectations resided in Robert's mind. Danielle had completed his requested task of closing the businesses, and the thought of resting in her loving arms was becoming a reality as he got closer to LaGuardia Airport. New York was a city on fire, and the amount of people buzzing around the curbside check-in was mind blowing.

"Good grief, where are all these people going this time of morning?" he asked the driver.

"Where are you headed to, sir?"

"I'm headed home."

Laughing, the driver replied, "Some of them are probably headed home like you, sir."

Robert sunk into the driver's thoughts, realizing how very lucky he was to be returning home. Less than a year ago, he would return to a beautiful, but empty home. But all of that had changed, he was blessed with a beautiful wife, who was kind, loving, and supportive. He had loving friends and everyone was in good health. Were things perfect, absolutely not. In fact, they were a mess, but things could have been worse, so it was his decision to savor the moments of his good fortune, with the anticipation that eventually things would be better than they already were. Robert sprung from the taxi, tipped the driver generously, thanked him for the ride, and got lost in the sea of travelers.

When he arrived at the gate, he placed two calls. One to Danielle and the other to Captain Bill to tell them of his departure from New York. The trip to New York hadn't been as bad as he expected. It had been an enlightening experience. Even his mother wasn't as annoying as usual. He had taken his friend home to rest, and bonded with his brother. He discovered that as unconventional as Camille's way of living was, she was actually living a good conventional life; minus the drugs and the governor. He only wished she had given as much love to herself as she had given to others. Maybe then she would have found peace in her life.

As the plane descended into St. Thomas, Robert was looking out the window with the same thoughts he harbored each time he returned back to the island. What if the plane hit the big mountainous boulder which sat at the end of the runway. And each time, the plane would land safely, and he would rejoice in being home again.

He grabbed a safari taxi, and embraced the tropics as he traveled to Red Hook Marina. As they approached the area near Bovoni, Robert noticed the area was plagued with police cars. Turning to the driver, he asked, "What's going on?"

The driver replied. "The signs of the times, sir". The driver pulled over to check things out. "I'll only be a minute, sir."

The taxi driver overheard the officers' talking. "We first need to determine her identity, which isn't going to be easy without a head. So where do we go with this?"

Minutes later the governor arrived on the scene, cautiously making his way to the investigating officers. "What do you think, Chief?"

"Well, I'm not sure what to think, but I do know she wasn't murdered here. She was dumped here. I've already assigned the case to Detective Hart. He'll get the body identified, then back track her steps. We'll need to know with whom she spent her last hours. It's not going to be easy."

The governor replied, "Oh, it may be easier than you think."

Chief Patrick nodded in agreement. "Maybe." Then walked towards his patrol car. A group of curious spectators were pushing and shoving behind the crime scene, trying to get a glimpse of the body as the paramedics rolled the gurney to the ambulance.

Baller shouted, "Stand back, people, haven't you seen a dead body before?"

A young man yelled back, "No, not without a head."

Chief Patrick looked around and shook his head, signaling Baller to step forward. "We don't need your help in controlling the crowd. What we need to know is if you have any information regarding this murder."

Baller didn't answer at first, then he said, "I'm just looking around, Chief. I don't know nothing about no murder." Baller didn't say another word. He walked away and slipped quietly into the governor's limousine. The chief decided he would keep an eye on Baller. He was positive he knew more than he was saying.

The taxi driver returned to the safari, looked at Robert with bulging eyes. "Someone placed the body of a dead woman in the dumpster last night."

"That's horrible."

"No. What's horrible is her head was cut off."

"Oh, dear God. Do they know who she is?"

"'Not yet, I guess that's the reason they cut off her head. It's hard to identify a faceless person."

"I guess you have a point. Not that it matters, but was she black or white?"

"Neither one, sir. She was Hispanic."

Robert exhaled deeply, his voice in a low whisper, "That's a shame."

"Yes, it is. Like I said, it's the sign of the times. My beautiful island is going to hell in a hand basket. I've lived here for over thirty years, and I've never seen so many murders in my life. Between this young generation and the corrupt officials, we're fighting a losing battle. Neither of them has any respect for life. They only worship money and power. I call it Caribbean greed. It's sad because they are willing to kill and die for it."

"I totally agree, but it's just not in the Caribbean, my friend, it's all over the world."

"Well, sir, we're here. Have a good evening."

"Thank you. Robert tipped the driver and stepped off the safari, making his way to the dock.

"Welcome back. Boy, it seems like all I've done for the past few months is welcome you back. You've done plenty of traveling, my friend."

"Yes, I have. It's good to be back and it is great to see you. Now get me home to my beautiful wife, please."

"Laughing, Captain Bill replied, "None stop, sir, none stop.""

When they arrived on James Island, Robert ran up the steps and into Danielle's arms. Maria stood there smiling from ear to ear. "Welcome home, Mr. Kelsey. I'm so happy to see you again."

Robert smiled. "I'm happy to see you too, Maria. Danielle tried to starve me while you were away."

"I don't believe that, Mr. Kelsey."

The family was reunited once again. Their separation only heightened their commitment to each other. None of them had any regrets. Robert took Danielle's hand into his and took a stroll through the beautiful lush garden, where they sat lovingly in each other's arms and watched day turn into night. Maria brought Danielle a bright yellow shawl to ward off the evening chill, and carried Robert his favorite glass of brandy to warm his spirit. Life on James Island was back to normal.

That evening Robert and Danielle were engaged in conversation, when Robert asked, "Did you hear about the dead body they found in the dumpster near Bovoni?"

"No, I didn't. I bet all of your money Governor Gunn was involved."

"I know he's a slimy kind of guy, but I don't believe even he would decapitate a woman."

"You stay there!"

"What does that mean?"

"It means believe what you want. I know better."

Danielle wanted to bring Robert up to speed on the closing of the stores, but he only wanted to savor the presence of her company. She was enjoying his company as well, but knew it was imperative for him to know, especially about the comments made by Lidia. If he could talk about dead bodies with heads missing, she could surely discuss the closing of the stores. Going against his wishes, in her sweet seductive voice. "Baby, you should have been there to witness Lidia's behavior and her remarks. I really think it's important that you know, then we can escape back into life as we want it to be."

"Okay, sweetheart, let me have it."

"Well everything went as planned. Captain Bill, Robyn and I were all present at each store as you wanted. Of course, they were all disappointed to lose their jobs, but when they opened their checks, they were happy as a child at play. Everyone but Lidia. She looked me in my eyes, and said, "Bitch, you have no idea what you have done.""

"What? And what did you say?"

"I said, bitch, yes I do. I got rid of your crooked ass for one, and whatever else comes—bring it on."

Laughing, Robert remarked, "Good for you, Ms. never say a bad word." He pulled her into his arms closer and planted a kiss on her forehead. "I knew you could handle it, baby. Now I think you deserve something special."

"Your something special always have us ending up on the beach or the bedroom."

Closing his eyes, placing his head on her shoulder. "Which do you prefer?"

Squinting girlishly at him. "I don't want sand in my panties tonight."

Robert couldn't refrain from smiling. "Then the bed it is, my love."

"Come with me," she said. "Would you like to die a happy man?" Without even waiting for his response she led him into the house, and to the chamber of love.

"Is there anything else you can do to make me love you more?"

"Do you really want an answer to that? Or would you prefer to find out for yourself?"

Looking into the beautiful eyes that captured his attention and his heart, he fell into her arms where they nestled together without saying a word. Suddenly the phone rang. Robert answered it quickly. It was Captain Bill.

"Hey, man, sorry to call so late, but there's something you need to know. The dead woman they found in the dumpster was Suzi Rose."

Shocked beyond belief, Robert sat straight up. "What? Good God."

"Yes, I can't believe this shit. Didn't you put her on the plane?"

"Yes, I did, and I saw it take off into the sky."

Danielle, lying patiently still, was waiting for Robert to end his conversation. Her imagination was getting the best of her. Robert placed his hands over hers rubbing it back and forth, trying to calm her, as well as himself. It was always nonstop drama in their lives and, he was getting to a breaking point.

Still searching for answers. "How do they know it was her?"

"The rose tattoo on her breast. Molinda, from Club Lacey, identified the body."

"What about her head, where is her head? This is some crazy shit. Man, it looks like everyone on the island needs to get a tattoo; driver's licenses are becoming obsolete for identifying a person."

"You think I don't know it. I just wanted to let you know, because I feel this was a warning. I would say get some rest, but I'm sure that's not going to happen."

Robert gave a deep sigh. "Ok, man. Thanks for letting me know."

Robert placed the receiver on the phone.

"What's wrong, baby?

"The body they found in the dumpster was that of Suzi Rose."

Losing herself in sorrow, she cried, "Oh my God, Robert."

It was impossible for either one of them to get any rest. They both grabbed a robe and retreated to the kitchen to make a cup of hot tea. Moments later, Maria emerged. It was apparent she too was unable to sleep. Robert looked at Danielle. "We need to tell her."

"Tell her what?" Maria asked.

Robert took a deep breath, and murmured, "Suzi Rose," under his breath.

"What about Suzi Rose?"

"They found her body in a dumpster today."

Maria fell to her knees, as Danielle rushed to her side to steady her. "Who did that to her?"

"We don't know," Danielle replied. "I'm sure they will catch the maggot who killed her. There's something else, Maria. They removed her head."

The last bit of information was too much for Maria, she instantly fainted in Danielle's arms. Robert rushed over and helped Danielle lay her on the sofa. They gave her smelling salt and placed an ice pack on her forehead to revive her. Maria was disheartened by the news, and had nothing to say. They both remained by her side. Replacing the ice packs until she quietly fell asleep.

After a while, they both felt the presence of Governor Gunn hovering over them. Was this a warning or did he have something more sinister in the works? It would only be a matter of time before their question would be answered.

Danielle's face had the appearance of discomfort. It was she who had told Lidia to bring it on, and within hours of her remarks the Kelsey family was once again in defense mode. Danielle now understood why her father told her never to dance with the devil. His analogy was correct: he would never stop dancing until all the music had been played. Governor Gunn was the devil and he had no intentions of stopping the dance.

When the sun opened its eyes, everyone was sleeping in an unconventional way. Maria was stretched out on the sofa, and Danielle and Robert were curled up together on the large blue chaise. Danielle prepared a pot of lemongrass tea, and fried a pound of bacon. The aroma of bacon always brought the family together, and she felt they needed each other more than ever. When Maria joined her in the kitchen, Danielle embraced her lovingly, assuring her the three of them would weather the storm together.

Robert sat by the window, which overlooked the Atlantic Ocean. The window was framed with stately palm trees and bougainvillea flowers of bright red. The day was warm. However, the trade winds were blowing doubts and uncertainties. He truly was at the crossroads regarding his relationship with the governor, when the phone rang. To his surprise, it was Governor Gunn himself.

Reluctantly and in a disapproving way he answered the phone, "Good morning."

"Good morning, Robert. You sound like a man that found a headless friend in a dumpster."

"You son-of-a bitch," Robert replied.

"Careful son, you're already grieving the loss of two. And if the stores are not reopened, I will make it three. You're causing me a great deal of stress."

"It's you causing the stress; making it necessary to close the business. I have no desire to operate business in the territory any longer, and that's not a crime. But killing people is."

Clearing his throat, in an authoritative voice, "You have until Monday morning to reopen the stores or else."

"Or else what?"

"Or else, all the money in the world will not keep your ass out of prison for the murder of Suzi Rose."

"You've lost your freaking mind. I didn't kill Suzi Rose and you know it."

"I know it and you know it, but the law doesn't know it. And if my memory serves me correctly, you, my friend, was the last person that saw her alive."

"The ball is in your court, white boy!"

Robert slammed the receiver down. "That son-of-a-bitch is trying to frame me for Suzi Rose's murder."

With a panicked look on her face, Danielle screamed, "What? What did he say, Robert?"

"He said I had to reopen the stores or else the authorities would arrest me for the murder of Suzi Rose."

"This is too much. That's ridiculous. You didn't kill Suzi Rose. You weren't even on island. He's just trying to frighten you."

"Well, he's doing a damn good job of it. I have no idea what he's capable of after this. He's the governor, and my simple white ass is on an all-black island. The odds are definitely against me."

"I'm not trying to pick a fight with you, baby, but this is a good teachable moment."

"What's the lesson in this shit?"

"Sadly, discrimination."

"Where are you going with this, Danielle?"

"I'm not going anywhere with it. It's right here in front of your face, blatant discrimination. You said it yourself. You're in a predominately black environment, and you fear the odds are against you being treated fairly. Not because you're guilty, but because you're white. The sad thing is you're right. It is how blacks live their lives every day, but luckily you have a black wife who knows her husband is innocent, and understands the laws of this land. We will fight fire with fire. I'm not saying we won't feel the heat, but I promise, sweetheart, we'll not get burned. You see how the chain of events are presenting themselves merely because you closed the stores. I can only imagine how much more we would be subjected to if we complied with his request. He would have your balls in a vice grip for the rest of your life. Now, there is no doubt in my mind that he killed your father."

"You're right. I believe he did too. And to think a few minutes ago I was giving that bastard the benefit of the doubt, saying he wouldn't cut off a woman's head. Man, he's a real sleaze ball, isn't he?"

"Yes, he is, but I have access to his kryptonite."

"What is his kryptonite?"

She turned toward him, took his hands, and replied, "Aunt Lucy."

"Oh, shit, the witch?"

"Yes, the witch," she replied. "You can't fight evil with good; you must fight evil with evil."

"But aren't you afraid of your Aunt Lucy?"

"Yes, I am, but my mother isn't."

"But you're not speaking to your mother."

"I will be, when the time presents itself. It's going to take a village for what we're going to up against, baby. I just need you to remain strong, and know you made the right decision. Sometimes you just have to cut your losses, put on your boxing gloves, and fight like you're Muhammad Ali."

The weekend was quiet on James Island. Everyone nestled in a corner by themselves mourning the death of Suzi Rose. It was apparent the news had placed a damper on the happy mood they were previously enjoying when Robert returned.

Robert had no idea what would transpire on Monday, when he didn't reopen the store. But not wanting Danielle to be faced with additional pressure, he thought it was time to tell his brother just what he might be facing. He picked up the phone and dialed his brother's number, to his surprise Randall answered.

"Hello."

"Hello, brother, you got a minute?"

"Yes, what is it? Don't tell me you won the lottery and we're going to be rich?"

"No, I didn't win the lottery, and we're already rich."

"Oh yes, I forgot. Seriously, putting all bullshit aside, what's up?"

Robert took a deep breath and gave Randall a quick overview of the chain of events that was currently plaguing his life. He listened to his brother in total silence. It was hard to believe the things he was saying. It was like he was listening to a bad movie script. He knew his brother always held his own and never sought his assistance on any matter, which was confirmation to him that his baby brother was in a world of trouble.

After Robert finished sharing his dilemma. Randall asked, "So how can I help?"

"I might need you to come and help Danielle navigate through any legal problems. I don't want her to deal with this alone."

Even though Randall was the older of the two brothers, he was also the comedic one. Taking Robert's entire conversation into consideration he replied, "Look, man, I love you and I feel the pressure you're under, but realistically it doesn't make sense for me to come there. Then they would have two white boys they could kill. Mother would have a heart attack, especially when you tell her the governor's cutting off people's heads and Danielle's aunt is a witch who puts spells on people.

Sounds like the perfect family. Man, our whole family could be wiped out in a flash. Your father's already dead, I feel the best thing I can do is send money."

"Randall, I already have money."

"Okay, then I've run out of options." Both men laughed. "Seriously, I repeat. I'm not bringing my white ass down there. Besides, I don't speak Swahili."

"Randall, they don't speak Swahili. They speak English."

"Then, I don't see the problem, talk to them. Let them know you have lots of money."

"Now I see you have real serious issues."

"I tend to differ with you, little brother. You, on the other hand, seem like the one with the issues. My wife and I are doing very well in America. You might want to consider living here, and pretty damn fast."

"That's the most sensible thing you've said all day. I think relocating might be a good idea, and we do have Camille's condo. But I'm not sure Danielle would want to leave the islands; her family is here."

"Oh, you mean, her pimp mama, governor machete, and her fire breathing aunt. Didn't you say her life was in danger?"

"Yes, unfortunately, it is."

"Do I need to remind you it is your responsibility to protect her?"

"Man, you sure know how to shift the narrative. As insane as this conversation has been, you've unbelievably given me some good advice. I never thought about relocating. I guess I was focused on staying on my beautiful island. This is my home."

"The hell with James Island. Do you have any idea how many islands are for sale in the world? You've been hanging with the wrong people. You keep forgetting you have money and money will buy you another island, if you can manage to stay alive. Which is not going to be a problem for me. Trust me, I'm not coming down there, not even for your funeral. I have one last thing to say before I go. RUN!"

"Goodbye, man."

How strange it felt to be laughing at himself and the situation he found himself in. However, Randall was not only a comedian, he was very serious. He knew his brother wasn't stepping one foot on the island of St. Thomas or James Island. Robert stepped out on the terrace and found a pair of faded swimming trunks. He stood naked facing the sun while pulling up his trunks. Danielle watched him from the window, and as he jumped into the pool she immersed her naked body beside his. Robert was glad he had made the call to Randall, it took the edge off of a very stressful day.

The water was too warm for Danielle. "Why don't we go down to the beach and take a bath and a nice swim before dinner?"

"It's the same sun that warms the ocean, my love. The temperature will probably be the same."

"That's impossible. Do you see the amount of water out there? There is no way the sun has the power to set the whole ocean on fire, like it did this pool."

"You have a point, I'll try it. You get the towels, and a bathing suit. I wouldn't want the paparazzi to catch you in your birthday suit; it's for my eyes only."

Danielle ran to the room, slipped on a suit, and returned with some towels, which she gave Robert to carry.

The couple took their normal stroll along their private beach. This time they extended their route, due to observing a large black bag under a bush along the shoreline. Robert reached down to pick up the bag to examine its contents, when they heard a boat coming their way. They immediately hid in the bushes adjacent to the bag. When the boat passed the large rock in the ocean, it became visible. Robert recognized it as a fiberglass Picuda. One of the fastest drug smuggling boats in operation. As the boat moved closer to the shoreline, two men jumped off the boat and picked up two large black bags while two other armed men stood guard. The men tossed themselves and the bags aboard the boat, leaving at a rapid speed toward the British Virgin Islands.

Just as he thought things couldn't get any worst, they did. Not only was the governor using his business to launder money, he was using his private beach to store and smuggle drugs. Robert and Danielle's interest in taking a swim and making passionate love on the beach was gone. They gathered their towels from the other side of the beach and returned home.

"Dinner's ready," called out Maria.

"We're not hungry."

"What do you mean, you're not hungry? Every time you two go swimming on the beach you come back with your belly's hungry and full of passion."

Robert gazed over at Danielle. "You're right, Maria, that's exactly what it is. We're going to retire early tonight. We'll see you in the morning."

"Okay, I'll slice some roast beef to make sandwiches, in case you get your appetites back."

In Danielle's most native tongue she replied, "Bread butter on both side yo no."

Scratching his head. "Why did you tell her to butter the bread on both sides? You know I don't like butter on my bread."

"That was a West Indian proverb. I told her we had it good."

"Okay, I get it." Robert said nothing more. He chuckled and following his proverbial speaking wife to the bedroom, where they found themselves again conversing about the criminal life they had both been drawn into.

Without hesitation, Danielle looked sternly at Robert. "Do you know how serious what we observed tonight was?"

"Yes, sweetheart, I'm aware. Now I'm beginning to understand why my father lost his life, and why our lives are now in danger. If the money laundering wasn't bad enough, we've now added murder and drug smuggling."

"Robert, the boat we saw tonight is the same one that's been cruising around the island. It seems like I bought the camera and binoculars for nothing, because I sure as hell don't want to know who the owner is."

"I understand. Believe me when I say that model boat costs a shit load of money. It's a fiberglass Picuda. The body stretches 38 feet long and is equipped with not one, but three two-hundred horsepower engines. It's a drug smugglers dream."

"I'm happy you're fascinated with its features, but I'm more concerned with how we are going to escape these covert actions."

"Listen, sweetheart, I was speaking with Randall this afternoon and he made a great suggestion."

Danielle gave her pretty girl face look. "And what was that?"

"He suggested we sell the island and relocate back to the states."

"Okay, there's not enough time to sell the island. Who do you think is walking around with thirty-five million dollars to buy on such short notice? Secondly, why would I want to move to New York? Did you ask Randall that?"

"A matter of fact, I did."

"And?"

"He said if you didn't want to leave the island, then you must have a death wish."

"Is that supposed to be a joke?"

"Maybe, but I don't think he was joking. Baby, both of our lives are at risk. We could leave temporarily until things cooled down. We could use the time and space to determine what's in the best interest of our family. We already have a home there."

"Who has a home there?"

"We do. Things were moving so fast, I failed to tell you Camille left her estate to me, which includes a condo, a car and a life insurance policy. We don't have to remain here and drown in this cesspool of a life."

"I guess it's true that money attracts money. You're right, we don't have to remain here. I just don't know if we have enough time to get off island before the governor drops his next bomb."

"We can at least try."

"Okay, on two conditions. If Maria comes with us, and if Captain Bill and Robyn can join us, if they choose, or at least have them visit us twice a year."

"That's not a problem, baby. I thought you had a really difficult request. Your conditions are as pleasing to me as they are to you. Thank God we have the resources to make it happen."

Danielle immediately called Robyn to tell her of their plans. Afterwards, she added, "Look, my friend, I'm going to need you to think about you guys joining us in New York if we decide to stay."

"Girl, I'm not leaving the Caribbean to spend winters in the snow. Have you ever seen the amount of snow New York City gets in the winter? I'm not freezing my happy butt off for no one, not even you. I'll come visit you in the spring. Anyway, I'm glad you're getting off the rock for a minute. You two are like magnets, drawing all types of deadly shit to you and me. I've been stressing out like a crackhead without a pipe."

"Robyn, stop it. You know you're going to miss me."

"Yes, I am, but I'd rather miss you knowing you're safe in New York, than to visit you in the cemetery. You know how spooky that place is. I'm sure your Aunt Lucy has an apartment in there somewhere."

Laughing hysterically. "I love you, and I'll be counting the days until we see one another again."

"Likewise, my sister, likewise. Hey! Don't forget to call me at least once a week."

"I'll call you every day."

"There you go, sucking up all my time again."

"Girl, goodbye."

Danielle sat quietly thinking about how much she was going to miss her friend when Robert entered the room. "Hey, baby, due to our time constraints, I was thinking we should just lock down the house and leave. Eddie can oversea the property. I can have Bill store the yacht and keep it maintained. That way both of them will remain employed and draw a salary. We've already closed the businesses, so that's not a concern. We could spend tomorrow packing, and take the 1:00 p.m. flight to New York. Better yet, why don't I just charter a private flight with Bushwhackers Charter. That would give us the opportunity to carry more luggage."

Unfortunately, Robert didn't know that Jeff Pride, the owner of Bushwhackers Charter, was in partnership with the governor?

"That sounds great. I'm so excited. I've never been on a private plane, and I've never been to New York."

"Well, sweetheart, there's a first time for everything, and it looks like you're getting two for one. I can't wait to take you shopping, you're going to lose your mind."

"You know, Robert, I almost feel like we're on the run; like fugitives."

"We are," laughed Robert. "The difference is, we haven't committed a crime. When we get to the mainland, we can speak with the authorities there and see if they can offer some suggestions on resolving our problems. All I know is I'm sick and tire of the governor's lawless ways, and always being on his emotional roller coaster ride."

Playfully, Danielle, flipped her hair up and stuffed it under Robert's baseball cap. "Do you think we can get in the witness protection program once we turn state's evidence against the governor?"

"I don't think that will be necessary. Something tells me that the governor is going to mess with the wrong people one day, and all of Aunt Lucy's magic potions won't be able to help him out."

"I don't know, Aunt Lucy has some pretty powerful stuff. Remember she's a Luciferin."

Robert just shook his head and laughed. "I don't care what her religion is, I'm not stepping one foot in her church."

Slapping her hands together, Danielle laughed and gave him a reminder. "Don't forget we might need to call upon Aunt Lucy one day."

Robert said, "Let me make myself perfectly clear. I'm not stepping in her church, and I'm not calling her on the phone. I'm emphatically not interested in coming face-to-face with the witch from 666 Eastside bay."

The family spent the next two days packing and cherishing their last days together. At 10:00 a.m. Monday morning, the beautiful island of James Island was about to be void of the Kelsey family. Captain Bill was there to help Robert load the luggage on the yacht, while Maria stood in the distance, tears streaming down her beautiful face.

Danielle walked over and placed her arms around Maria. "Don't worry, you'll be joining us in two short weeks. We just need you to make sure everything is closed up properly."

"I know," replied Maria. "I will take care of everything for you. Please be safe and call me when you two get there." The two ladies embraced once again. "I love you, Danielle."

"I know, and we love you, Maria."

Robert ran up the stairs, took Maria in his arms and whispered softly in her ear, "See you in New York."

Maria smiled and waved goodbye as The Wanderer made it last trip to St. Thomas with the Kelsey's.

Chapter 21

Time was passing swiftly. Everyone was excited, hoping to find some semblance of peace along the way. Robert wondered why it took Danielle so long deciding what to wear. But he understood when she stepped out looking like a million dollars in a beautiful yellow chiffon dress which captured the essence of her beautiful brown skin. Her matching chiffon scarf was wrapped elegantly around her head to protect her long silky hair, adding to her undeniable femininity. Robert looked back gazing at her with total admiration. He was elated Danielle had given in to his request to journey to the mainland. He knew the distance from the island would give them a much-needed break, and give Danielle an opportunity to see New York from her eyes, and not through his. She was excited and he was happy, a combination of emotions both deserved to experience. Their love had been tested over and over again, and each time they were stronger in love. Danielle inhaled the fresh ocean breeze as they sailed fearlessly on the open sea. In just a few short hours they would be away from the narcissistic and evil ways of Governor Gunn.

When they arrived at Red Hook Marina, Robyn was waiting at the dock. "Did you think I was going to let you leave without saying goodbye?"

Danielle wrapped her arms around her dear friend and whispered in her ear, "Without true friends, life is not worth living. Thank you for loving me in spite of myself."

Robyn did everything to hold back the tears, but to no avail. She surrendered and allowed them to run gently down her face.

Robert stepped in between the two. "Come on you old crybabies, you'll see each other sooner than you think."

The men grabbed the luggage and placed them in a safari taxi Robyn had reserved. She turned and jumped in the back and rode with them to Bushwhackers Charter. Upon their arrival, the driver parked near Lindbergh Bay and carried the luggage to the main office. Danielle and Robyn were having their last little chat, when Robert observed three police cars, lights flashing like a slot machine, heading in their direction. He told the driver, "Looks like they are headed to Fortuna Mills. He wondered what was going on as the police cars got closer. They stopped and pulled into Bushwhackers. Four officers jumped out of the car demanding Robert to place his hands above his head.

Danielle ran towards him screaming, "What are you doing?" Her body began to tremble causing her to fall to her knees. "Leave him alone."

One of the officers body blocked Danielle. "Miss, I'm going to ask you to step back or I will arrest you for interference."

Shocked and out of control, she cried, "Why are you doing this? He hasn't done anything. If ah lie ah die."

Robyn rushed over to Danielle's side. "Come on, Danielle, we must haul een de door."

The second officer slammed Robert against the car, placed his hands in cuffs, and patted him down. "Robert Kelsey, you are under arrest for the murder of Suzi Rose."

Robert was scared and confused. "What? I didn't murder Suzi Rose, I'm being setup."

As the officers placed Robert in the patrol car, silence hung between him and Danielle. They stared hopelessly in each other's eyes. Not sure how things would turn out and not wanting Robert to lose hope, she cried out, "Don't worry, baby. I will fight for you. I know you wouldn't hurt a fly, and I will never let the governor get away with this."

At that very moment the governor's shiny black limousine drove by. The left rear passenger window slid down slowly. The governor stuck his head out of the opened window, howling with laughter. "Going somewhere, Mr. Kelsey?" It didn't matter how wealthy or how impeccable Robert Kelsey's credential were. He was being handcuffed and taken to jail for the murder of Suzi Rose, like a common criminal, just as the governor had planned.

Danielle and Robyn were furious and disgusted. Danielle rolled her eyes at the governor and said, "You bastard. If I saw you burning in hell, I would throw gasoline on the fire. I hate you."

The governor blew out a puff of smoke, and spoke in an irritating manner. "Careful pickney, if you're smart you'll stay in your place."

As the police car drove passed Danielle, she shouted out to Robert, "Don't worry baby, I will take care of this."

Danielle was a nervous wreck, but Robyn was busy plotting their next move. After putting Danielle in the safari taxi, she collected their luggage, and returned back to Red Hook. After picking up the car, she and Danielle headed into town, while Captain Bill transported the luggage back to James Island.

As Danielle and Robyn drove to police headquarters, they couldn't believe how the chain of events had unfolded. When they arrived at the station, they weren't allowed to see Robert. However, they did run into Helen Hughes, an old high school classmate. She explained to the ladies Robert had been arrested because of circumstantial evidence that linked him to the murder of Suzi Rose. She told them Robert had already been read his Miranda rights, and was in the process of being booked, and had refused to answer any questions until his lawyer was present.

She looked directly at Danielle and stated, "You need to contact your attorney, and fast. Things don't always go as they should with some officers. Sometimes the telephone isn't available, if you know what I mean."

Helen's words didn't make Danielle feel any better. She knew the governor had some crooked cops on the inside. It was hard to determine who was actually working for the good of the people. Two thing she knew for sure, the flat-footed pot-belly governor wasn't one of them, and Robert needed a good and honest attorney. Having no idea who to trust, she remembered making a mental note of attorney George Hall, Robert's business attorney.

Danielle placed a call to his office. "Good afternoon. You've reached the law office of George Hall."

"Hello, this is Danielle Kelsey. Could I speak to Attorney Hall, please?"

"I'm sorry, Attorney Hall is on another call."

"I'll hold, this is an emergency. Please tell him I'm calling for my husband, Robert Kelsey."

The receptionist placed the call on hold, and a few minutes later, a man answered. "Attorney Hall, how may I help you Mrs. Kelsey?"

Nervous and in a frantic state of mind she murmured. "My husband has been arrested for murder, and he needs you."

There was a moment of silence. "I'm sorry to hear that, but I can't help him. What he needs is a criminal attorney. I practice corporate law. I can refer you to my brother Shelton Hall. He's an excellent defense attorney, but he's off island until tomorrow morning."

"Tomorrow?"

"Yes, unfortunately. Mrs. Kelsey, this is a serious matter and you don't want just anyone representing your husband. Look, your husband is a good man. I've done business with the family for over ten years. Let me handle this. I will contact my brother as soon as he returns in the morning, and we'll see what can be done to get your husband released from jail. I'm sure you've had a stressful day. Why don't you go home and try to relax? Remember, Mrs. Kelsey, night always brings day."

Wiping the tears from her eyes. "Thank you, I appreciate your words and your help."

While Danielle was trying to find a lawyer, Robert was in the process of being booked for the murder of Suzi Rose. As he stood in the dimly lit room being photographed from left to right to center. He realized life as he knew it was fleeting right before his very eyes. His manicured hands were now being rolled from side to side on a large messy ink pad, where his prints would be recorded with numerous criminals from all walks of life. It was humiliating to utter his name and date of birth for this inhumane process, but it wasn't until he was searched and his personal property catalogued, that he sunk into depression. For the first time, he wanted his meddling Mother, but he couldn't bring himself to humiliate her as he had been.

That day, Robert exchanged his navy-blue slacks and pinstriped cotton shirt for a bright orange jump suit. He was escorted down the hall to a dingy jail cell, without being allowed to make a call. He had laid down with dogs, and now he was covered with fleas. The only thing that kept him sane was knowing that he had Danielle on the outside, fighting for his release. He couldn't bring himself to lay on the stained dirty mattress. After a while his tired body surrendered, and he found himself looking at the ceiling wondering what he had done to deserve such treatment.

Danielle returned home to James Island. Maria met her at the door and walked with her to the villa. When she stepped into the room she saw their luggage sitting in the floor. All of a sudden, the flood gates opened and she balled up in a fetal position and cried herself to sleep. Morning came fast.

She was awakened by a knock on the door. As she struggled to open her eyes, which were swollen shut from crying, she saw Robyn walking towards her with a cup of bush tea. "Come on girl, we have things to do, and people to see. Get moving, your husband needs us, so chop! chop! No time for shedding tears. You can do that later. Right now, we have an innocent man in prison and we all know how things go in the world of Governor Alex Gunn."

Danielle, sipped the bush tea, then headed to the shower. She stood there allowing the cold water to run over her swollen face. Robyn was the strength and motivation she needed. Like Robert, she had always been a fighter, but the governor had begun to wear them both down. Still she had to muster the will power to fight. She knew her husband was depending on her, and she promised him as he was taken away, that the governor would not get away with framing him for Suzi Rose's murder. The more she thought about what he had done to destroy their lives, the angrier she became. Danielle stepped out of the shower, slid on a pair of denim jeans, a crisp white shirt, slid her white sneakers on, pulled her long beautiful hair into a ponytail, and placed a white rhinestone cap on her head. She was ready for action.

When she arrived on the terrace, Maria, Captain Bill and Robyn rallied around her, feeding her bagels and crispy fried bacon, and a huge dose of moral support. Danielle looked around her table of friends. "Cum wha cum; cum big oh cum small." Everyone smiled and raised their glass to signal a victory. The three stood up from the table and headed to the yacht departing for Havensight Marina, which was closer to town and to the judicial complex.

When the three arrived at the courthouse, Helen revealed that Robert's attorney had arrived and he was currently speaking with his client. Danielle, was relieved. She was hopeful that once Robert explained everything to the attorney, he would be released, and they could go home.

Attorney Shelton Hall entered the interrogation room. "Good morning, Mr. Kelsey. Your wife has asked me to represent you. Do you understand why you were arrested sir?"

Holding his face in his hands, he replied, "They're trying to pin a murder on me," raking his fingers through his blond wavy hair, "I'm being setup."

"Alright, Mr. Kelsey. I need you to tell me everything you know."

Robert cleared his throat. "I'm a prisoner of circumstance."

"Everyone is a prisoner of circumstance when they're arrested, sir. I'm interested in learning the circumstances, so I know how to structure my defense. I need you tell me exactly why the authorities feel they have probable cause to arrest you for the murder of Suzi Rose?" Looking over a document in his hand, he continued, "Let me help you out. It states here that you abducted Suzi Rose from Club Lacey and held her hostage. Then traveled with her to the Dominican Republic, where you subsequently returned with her two weeks later on a private plane you chartered. She refused to remain with you, so out of jealously you killed her. Is any of that true, sir?"

Robert took a deep breath. "Some of it is."

"Alright, Mr. Kelsey, tell me your version of what's true."

Robert was sweating profusely. "I met Suzi Rose at Club Lacey. I was told she had information regarding the death of my father, so I wanted to speak with her. When I found her, she was intoxicated. I carried her home with me, hoping to speak with her after she sobered up. The next morning, she answered most of my questions. She was frightened and told me that because I had taken her from the club, she was now a dead woman. I felt bad, so I kept her on the island until I felt it was safe to send her back home. She was happy the entire time she remained with us on the island. I gave her money so she could get settled once she got home and my fiancée provided her with clothing. I purchased an airline ticket for her and me, so I could accompany her to the gate to make sure she boarded safely. I watched her board the flight and take off. After watching her wave goodbye, I returned home. There are people who can verify this. That was the last time I saw her, I swear."

"Mr. Kelsey, you said someone is trying to set you up, do you know who and why someone would want to do that?"

"Yes, it is Governor Gunn. He's the one who is setting me up, and I am pretty sure one of his boys killed Suzi Rose and Camille."

"Whoa hold your horses! We were talking about one murder, now you're talking about two. That is a pretty tall leap. And who is Camille?"

"Camille was my sister-in-law. They found her body floating in the ocean a couple of months ago. After I was contacted by a private investigator I hired to locate her. He called to tell me there was no movement on her since her arrival to St. Thomas. He suggested that I contact the authorities. Which I did, only to have to identify her body. I had her cremated and carried her cremains home last week. I wasn't on island when Suzi Rose was murdered. I was in New York, and I can prove it."

Robert talked nonstop for two hours. His nervous behavior and fear of prison was compelling. He knew he had nothing to lose. He was fighting for his life. He shared everything with Attorney Hall he thought could possibly clear him of any wrong doing. When he finished talking, Attorney Hall leaned back in the chair. That's quite a story, Mr. Kelsey."

"It is not a story, it's the truth. You have no idea how many layers of criminal activities that are going on in connection with Governor Gunn. When I discovered I was indirectly involved, I pulled back my association with him. I tried everything to distance myself, and that is when pandemonium erupted. Just last week my wife and I were on our private beach taking an evening stroll before dinner when we spotted a fiberglass Picuda, one of the fastest drug smuggling boats in operation, pulls up and throw two large plastic bags onto the boat. Two men with assault weapons were guarding the men picking up the bags. We were scared to death they would kill us if they knew we were there. We kept our hands over our mouths afraid to breath or move, then we saw them steering the boat towards the British Virgin Islands. Look, man. I am in real trouble here, and I need your help. I don't know who to trust or where to turn. There are a lot of people involved in this criminal enterprise. And, speaking frankly, I'm scared to death that you might be too."

Attorney Hall gave a questionable look. "Believe me, Mr. Kelsey, I'm not involved in any type of criminal activity. Listen, I believe your story. There has been some talk over the years about the possibility of the governor's involvement in a few unsavory things, but as far as I know there was never any concrete evidence the investigative agencies found. It was impossible to get anyone to roll over on him. The first thing we need to do is to try and get you out of here, but based on what you know, it might be safer for you to remain in jail. But, that's entirely up to you. You are going to be arraigned. This is where you will be advised of your rights. We will enter your plea of not guilty and request that bail be set for your release. I have no idea who is in the governor's pockets, so it's hard to determine what amount the bail will be."

Robert exhaled. "It doesn't matter how much, I have the money."

"Ok. The first thing we need to do is get you in court."

Robert exhaled a sigh of relief. He shook Attorney Hall's hand. "Thank you for believing me." He sat quietly with a sad demeanor, hanging his head like Tom Dooley, until the officer prepared to escort him back to his cell.

Nodding his head, Attorney Hall replied, "You are welcome, Mr. Kelsey. Now all we need to do is get the court to believe you, which we will do. I need to speak with the District Attorney about the alleged drug smuggling on your property. If what you say is correct, it will help support your theory about being framed, which will add a little more fuel to the fire."

He picked up his files, placed them in his briefcase. "Goodbye, Robert. I will see you in the morning."

While Robert was speaking with his attorney the three friends decided to part ways temporarily, all needing to attend to business. Danielle was optimistic about Robert's release. She gave Bill instructions to meet her by the yacht at 5:00 p.m. She hugged her friend's goodbye, then walked down Main Street to the library to continue her research on the governor.

Robyn and Bill returned home.

Once her research was completed, she realized the three of them would need protection, and only one person could provide it. She immediately called Robyn.

"Hello my friend, I have something I need you to do?"

"No problem, I got you girlfriend. What do you need?"

Holding her breath. "I need you to go to Aunt Lucy's and pick up three bottles of dead snake eye potion." A long pause ensued. "Robyn, did you hear me?"

"Yes, I heard you. Danielle, you know how I feel about you, and you know how I feel about your Aunt Lucy. I'm not taking my scary behind to Aunt Lucy's and pick up nothing."

"I understand, honey, but this is a matter of life and death. I need you to do this."

"A matter of life and death for who?"

"For you, for us?"

"What the hell you talking about, Willis?"

Danielle breaks out in laughter. "Girl, pull it together. We have some serious and incriminating evidence, and the governor has already set Robert up for murder. Logically, we're next in line. We need protection. I'm not chancing anything happening to you and Bill. We all need to be covered in snake oil for our protection."

Robyn inhaled and released. "Okay, you want me to have your old crusty evil aunt cover me in snake oil for protection. Who's going to protect me from her? Oh, hell to the no! Come on, Danielle, I'm not going over there by myself. I'm scared of that woman, and she knows it."

Laughing uncontrollably, Danielle replied, "Ok, scary cat, I'll go with you, but we don't have much time. I'll grab a taxi and meet you at your house."

Robyn was shaking in her shoes. "Listen to me, Danielle Kelsey. When this is over. I'm getting some new squeaky-clean friends. No more of this mumbo jumbo voodoo crap.

I'm only riding with you on this because I have no intention of dying at the hands of Governor Gunn."

Danielle grabbed a taxi in front of the library entrance and rode straight to Robyn's. Once she arrived, Robyn, who was struggling with her fears, reluctantly got into the taxi. Looking nervous and sideways at Danielle, she immediately started to laugh. "Girl, I guess now you're a member of the demonic elite club?"

"No," Danielle replied, "I'm a member of the save yourself and everyone you love club."

When the two arrived at 666 Eastside Bay, Robin stared squeamishly at Aunt Lucy's house. It had the appearances of an abandoned home. White paint was peeling off the exterior walls, a yard full of old doll parts, broken dishes and glass jars lined the make shift walkway. Two old mangy dogs, serving as protection, laid viciously on the dirt covered yard. The entire house was surrounded by a weather-beaten fence covered in bright red bougainvillea. It was the only true sign of life that resided there. Danielle asked the driver to wait. However, shaking his head in total fear, declined. "This is far as I'm going lady, and this is too damn far."

Robyn looked around at the house. "I'm with the man, this is as far as I'm going too. That house doesn't even look like someone should be going into it. Danielle, you can't think of another solution? What about prayer, can't we just pray for protection?"

"I do pray, but you must remember. Sin run afta sin."

The driver turned to the ladies. "Look, you're going to get out or stay in?"

"We're getting out." Danielle exited the cab and pulled Robyn out with her.

Robyn saw Dasheen peeping out the window across the street. "I got it! Ask your mother to get the snake oil eye potion for us. It's her sister. She would do it for her, and your mother would do it for you."

"But I'm not speaking to my mother."

"Well I think it's time you talk, because I'm really not comfortable going in there or spreading snake eye oil over my body. What the heck is that supposed to do anyway?"

"The eyes of the snake watches over you. The venom, mixed with sacred oils, represent the bite of the snake, which attacks those seeking to harm you."

Robyn eyes rolled to the back of her head. "Girl this is 2017, they have guns for protection now. They have a red light that marks the target, and a bullet that kills the person trying to bring harm. But if you feel comfortable with some greasy ass oil and a pair of snake eyes, then please go speak to your mother."

As the ladies continued their debate. Danielle couldn't help but observe the contrast of where she came from and where she now lived. As she gazed at the front door of her childhood home, Dasheen stepped out of the shadows and into the streets where they were standing. She walked straight to Danielle with caring eyes. "Hello, Danielle. I know you hate me, and I probably deserve it, but everything I did, I did for you baby. I never meant to bring you harm."

Danielle stood still, trying not to cry. "Mother, all my life I trusted and believed in you, even when I didn't agree, I honored you. What you never understood was it never mattered to

284

me what we didn't have. What was important to me was what we did have, which was each other. I know life has been hard on you, but you lost your way. You believed that the material things in life would bring joy and happiness, but it doesn't. Mother, I married Robert Kelsey, and thank God he's a good man, because if he wasn't my life could have been a total disaster. Even though we have money, we don't have peace and happiness. The same man who helped sell me into a life of slavery, has now framed my husband for murder. All because of his insatiable greed. When will it stop? So, Mother, the happy life you said you wanted me to have has been filled with lies, drugs, death, and destruction. Where is the joy in that, Mother?"

Dasheen looked like a beaten woman. She had no idea that the governor was wreaking such havoc in their lives. Staring in to her daughter's sad and desperate eyes she asked, "What can I do to help?"

Robyn was elated. Without hesitation, she blurted "For starters you can get the snake eye oil from Aunt Lucy, so I don't have to look in her face again." Robyn was so busy talking she did not notice Aunt Lucy standing behind her. Danielle was shaking her hands trying to stop Robyn from talking, but she just kept on rambling. "I simply don't understand why my best friend, in all the world, wants me to be in the company of a woman who spits fire, buries people alive, and plant worms and insects in the bodies of others. I mean who would want to be around someone like that?"

Danielle dropped her head as Aunt Lucy spoke to Robyn in a demonic and penetrating voice. "Who? You say who?" Stepping directly in front of Robyn, fingers raised and pointed at her. "I should curse you and your tongue for it is eviler than the eye and the cross. I will spare you only once. For you have shown love and friendship to my blood of blood."

Robyn stood there shaking in her shoes. Moving her tongue from side to side, making sure the evil witch hadn't ripped it from her mouth. All she could think about was how she found herself; face-to-face with the spirit of evil again. And all for the sake of friendship. When Robyn regained her footing, she stepped backwards, slowly distancing herself from the mouth of fire. Danielle stood next to Robyn, taking her hand into hers squeezing it tightly. "I love you, my friend. No harm will ever come to you, for Aunt Lucy sees the fear you have for her, and the love we have for each other. You are protected from the dark side of life."

Robyn rolled her eyes at Danielle. "I will save my comments until we get back to the light side of life."

Dasheen and Lucy walked through the weathered gate, passing the mangy dogs and onto the spider infested porch of the torture chamber. After a brief conversation, Dasheen returned with four bottles of snake eye oil. Her hands were shaking as she handed the bottles to Danielle. "I brought an extra bottle for Robert. Fear not, my daughter. All is well. The scorpions shall rejoice at the feast of the enemy. The light of darkness shall protect you, my child. Dance unto the kiss of death, as it shall fall upon the hearts of the wicked."

Leaning her frail body into Danielle's she whispered softly in her ear, "My love for you lives beyond boundaries."

Wiping an escaped tear from her eye. "As mine for you, Mother."

Out of nowhere appeared the taxi driver. His car came to a screeching halt. "Ladies, going my way?"

The pair jumped in the taxi." Why did you come back?"

"I didn't wat your blood on my hands, so I came back to make sure you ladies were alive and well."

"Thank God for that," replied Robyn. "Now, please, get me the heck out of here."

The radio was playing "Stepping Out," by Steel Pulse, one of Robyn's favorite reggae bands. Suddenly the song was interrupted by a breaking news report. The driver said, "Did you hear that? A missing head was discovered on the estate of Robert Kelsey, the New York resident, who was arrested for the murder of Suzi Rose. The man said the woman's decapitated body was discovered in a dumpster located on the east side of the island. White people do some weird things, mon. Why the mon cut off her head? Well, they'll be arraigning his ass tomorrow before Judge James."

The taxi driver looked in the rearview mirror and said, "Now that some sick shit. Some psycho cut off a woman's head and threw her body in a dumpster and then buried her head on his estate. I tell you, the local government always inviting a bunch of criminals on our beautiful island, and look what they do."

Shocked to the core, but maintaining her composure Danielle replied, "A person is innocent until proven guilty."

Robyn placed her right hand over Danielle's. "It'll be okay, you have your snake eye oil, and I have my faith in God. Take us to Havensight Marina, please."

When the pair arrived at the dock, Captain Bill was waiting. "Did you hear the news? This is getting out of hand pretty damn fast. It doesn't matter what they found on James Island, we all know Robert didn't kill Suzi Rose."

Crying hopelessly. "I know, but we can't prove it. Governor Gunn is trying to destroy Robert, and so far, it's working."

"Come on, Danielle," replied Robyn. "We don't have time to surrender. We have to take this bastard down. Someone has to know who planted Suzi's head on James Island."

Both Danielle and Robyn had an ah ha moment. "The eyes, oh my God! Robyn, we can prove who planted the head." They all jumped simultaneously on the yacht and headed to James Island.

"I bet that fat-bellied creep didn't see this coming. We'll get the evidence and take it to the authorities. Wait, we need to put the evidence in the right hands. This is some serious CSI stuff, girl."

"Danielle, calm down. You're right. We must plan our moves all the way around. Who can we trust? Other than ourselves?"

Danielle meditated for a minute. "We have an attorney. If we can't trust him, we can't trust anyone. We need to contact him so he can tell us what to do."

Danielle regained her composure and placed the call to Attorney Hall. After jumping through hoops with the receptionist, she finally put her call through. "I know my husband didn't commit this murder, and I can prove it."

"Alright, Mrs. Kelsey. If what you say is true, you need to proceed with caution and bring the evidence to me. I will present it to the Attorney General." Clearing his throat, "Mrs. Kelsey, if the evidence you have can prove your husband is being setup, then I'm positive he will be going home with you tomorrow."

Feeling a sense of relief. "I sure hope so, sir. I will see you tomorrow morning at 7 a.m. And please call me Danielle."

"I'll be waiting for you, Danielle."

When the yacht docked on James Island, yellow tap covered the entire garden area. A large police dog proceeded two police officers carrying two black bags in their hands. Confused and hysterical Danielle cried, "Officers, what are you doing here?"

Detective Hart spoke firm, but politely, "Mrs. Kelsey, you will need to find somewhere to stay for a while. Your housekeeper has already been escorted to St. Thomas. Unfortunately, James Island is now a crime scene."

Danielle regained her composure and spoke to the officer in a raspy sultry voice, "Officer, all of this has taken me by complete surprise. Will you please allow me to get some personal items from the house?"

Looking at the Caribbean beauty with lust in his eyes. "Sure, Mrs. Kelsey. Take your time, but your friends must remain outside."

"Thank you, sir."

"Sir, isn't necessary. Just call me Kevin."

Danielle gave a pleasant smile. "Then, Kevin it is."

Another officer walked over to Detective Hart. "You want me to go in with her?"

"No," he replied. "The poor woman has been through enough. She's one of us."

Danielle went immediately to the bedroom and grabbed her tote bag, which was already packed. She saw the yellow chiffon dress and matching shoes she was wearing the day

Robert was apprehended. She removed a few items to allow room for the dress and shoes. She rushed to the kitchen to remove the tapes from the pantry. She placed all three tapes in a Ziploc bag and laid it between her articles of clothing. She saw the officer watching her in the kitchen, so she took a six pack of Ting from the refrigerator and handed it to Captain Hart. "Kevin, you and your men look a little warm, so I brought you a cool drink."

He smiled, and handed her his card. "Thank you, that was very thoughtful. If you need me for anything, and I do mean anything, please give me a call."

"Thank you, Kevin, I will."

Captain Bill took the bag from Danielle's hand. Watching her every step, Captain Hart turned and said, "Mrs. Kelsey, I'll have you back in your home real soon."

Smiling sheepishly. "Thank you, Kevin. I appreciate your thoughtfulness."

Captain Bill helped the ladies aboard, as Detective Hart waved goodbye to Danielle in admiration. Robyn was busting at the seams. "You hussy—Thank you, Kevin, I appreciate your thoughtfulness. That old sleaze ball is trying to put Robert in prison so he can bang his wife on her private island. I don't trust that man at all. He broke all kinds of protocol."

Danielle laughed. "I could care less about him or his protocol. I did what I had to do to get the tapes, so my husband can get out of jail."

All three, feeling a sense of relief, headed to Robyn and Captain Bill's home where they could rest for the evening. For the moment they all felt safe, and Robyn was relieved that Danielle was not alone.

The next morning, Robyn made Danielle a cup of tea and carried it to her. "Good morning, my friend. Listen to me. That old nasty potbellied Governor Gunn is not going to get away with this. We are going to fight him tooth and nail."

Danielle jumped out of bed, slipped on a pair of jeans and a top and started for the door. Robyn stepped in front of her. "Hold your horses missy. First of all, you're not running out of here looking like a prisoner of war. You look a hot mess. Remember, never let them see you sweat. You're going to get your husband from jail. He's looked at enough nastiness to last him a lifetime. When he sees you, he needs to see a vision of beauty."

"You're right. I've got plenty of time and I have the perfect outfit to rewind time." Danielle walked back to the bedroom and returned a vision of beauty, wearing the beautiful chiffon dress she was wearing the day their trip to New York was interrupted.

Robyn smiled. "Now, that's what I'm talking about."

At 6:30 a.m., Captain Bill accompanied Robyn and Danielle to Attorney Hall's office to deliver the tapes. Attorney Hall had already placed a call to the attorney general advising him he would be presenting him with some very compelling evidence. When Danielle arrived, she was escorted to the conference room where she was joined by District Attorney Roy Edwards and Attorney Shelton Hall. She pulled the three tapes out of the Ziploc bag and placed them on the table. All three set there, with their eyes focused on each frame that appeared on the screen. Danielle was getting nervous as the first tape revealed nothing but the gardener grooming the lawn. She held her breath, praying quietly to herself, when suddenly two unmasked men were caught on camera. Digging a hole in the same discovery place of the disposed head of Suzi Rose. Everyone set there in total awe as they saw the men place a duct taped black bag in the garden and bury it. Tears streamed down Danielle's face. "I told you my husband was being setup. He's a good man and wouldn't hurt a fly. Now, can he go home?"

"It's not quite that simple," replied the district attorney. "Your husband's arraignment is set for this morning at 11:00 a.m. I will ask the court for a motion to dismiss, and if all goes well, as I expect it will, he will be processed out and you can take him home."

Filled with excitement Danielle picked up the tapes. "One minute, gentlemen, I need a copy of the tape before I leave this office. I simply can't take any more chances with my husband's life. We are dealing with some deep-seated corruption, and I have no idea who are all the players."

"That's not a problem, Mrs. Kelsey. I can duplicate the tape right in front of your beautiful eyes." District Attorney Edwards pulled a blank tape from the drawer and duplicated the tape that would gain Robert Kelsey his freedom. She placed the tapes in her bag and joined her friends in the reception area. Her face was void of emotion as Robyn and Captain Bill waited for acknowledgement of victory. She lowered her head and smiled. "We got it guys, the eyes have saved us all."

Robyn punched Danielle lightly in the side. "I can't believe you kept us in suspense like that. I should give you one big cuff."

Danielle updated everyone on the scheduled arraignment, and what the procedure would consist of. As they headed towards the court, they spotted Maria standing at the bus stop in Sub Base. Bill pulled over and Maria looked in the car with tears streaming. "Take me to Mr. Kelsey, please." The family was almost back together. The four laughed and cried all the way to Territorial Court.

As they were going through security, Danielle spotted Governor Gunn walking into the court room accompanied by Detective Hart. She knew the victory they thought they would claim today would soon be replaced with the realization that bad guys don't always win. Her only desire, other than Robert's freedom, was to observe the cunning and evil grin wiped completely off of the governor's face. She made it a point to sit in bird's eye view of the despicable Alex Gunn and the disgusting Detective Hart.

The bailiff was bringing Robert into the courtroom the same time as Danielle entered. All eyes were on her, including Robert's, as she radiated like the morning sun in the same elegant yellow chiffon dress and matching pumps she was wearing the day Robert was arrested. Her long silky hair framed her beautiful face perfectly. She was truly a vision of beauty.

Everyone was directed to rise as Judge Kenneth James entered. "You may all be seated," he echoed. "Case number 4567, the territory of the Virgin Islands Government versus Robert Kelsey."

Before the judge could ask the defendant if he was aware of the charges being brought against him, the district attorney asked permission to address the court. "Your Honor, new information has come to our attention that clearly shows two unidentified men planting the evidence on the property of the defendant. I find that an in-depth investigation was not done, which has proven to be a deliberate cover up to frame Mr. Robert Kelsey for the murder of Suzi Rose. Based on my findings, I'm entering a motion to dismiss, requesting all charges be dropped against the defendant."

Judge James announced, "Motion granted, as it relates to Mr. Robert Kelsey. The charges are dismissed and the court declares Mr. Robert Kelsey factually innocent of the murder of Suzi Rose."

Governor Gunn, shocked beyond belief, dropped his head and snuck quietly out of the courtroom. Danielle, Robyn, Maria and Captain Bill all jumped for joy as they rushed to Roberts's side. Tears running down his face, he whispered lovingly in his wife's ear, "This is the best day of my life, other than the day I married you."

Attorney Hall shook Robert's hand and told Danielle, "Once we get him processed, he's all yours. Thanks to you, Danielle, your husband is a free man. You have rectified a grave injustice today, and trust me, things are just getting started. There are some very frightened people on the island that's about to have their hands in cuffs and their day in court."

Danielle grabbed Robyn's and Bill's hands and said," The family has rectified a grave injustice."

It took all of three hours to get Robert processed and released, but this was the first day since Monday, that time didn't matter. When Robert walked out the door and inhaled the sweet smell of freedom he looked up to the sky and said. "Thank you, God, thank you."

The entire Kelsey family boarded the yacht, while Captain Bill stood proudly at the helm navigating The Wanderer with Robert, Danielle, Robyn, and Maria back to the beautiful James Island. A place they always celebrated with great food, laughter, and love.

Robert stood on James Island once again, lost in thought as he held Danielle passionately in his arms. He looked out at the beautiful Atlantic Ocean realizing that without Danielle, his freedom could have been lost forever. This shy, soft spoken young lady, whose mother had plotted to sale into slavery against her will, had blossomed into a beautiful and radiant woman. A woman who put her life at risk in order to fight for his freedom. For the first time in his life, he had everything money couldn't buy. Happiness with a woman he loved and cherished.

Chapter 22

When Governor Alex Gunn walked out of the courtroom he was in complete and total shock. Like so many of his victims, he found himself exposed and vulnerable. His entire political career had been comprised of sex, drugs, murder, and witchcraft. Even though he had been elected to lead the people of the Virgin Islands to prosperity, he had done just the opposite. He had taken his people and the beautiful Caribbean Island down the corrupt road of death and destruction. Now his plan to destroy Robert Kelsey had backfired. His greed and egomania persona had extended far pass his ability to reign it in. There were no limits to the extent that the governor had gone to acquire wealth and power.

The rich American he had thought of as young and foolish, had found his legs with the young girl he had sold to him. How could he know the two would fall in love and forge a union that would one day wreak havoc in his life? The other thing he didn't count on was the unbridled fear of Danielle being left alone on the James Island. A fear so real that a surveillance system was installed for her protection. A system that not only foiled his plan to frame Robert for the death of Suzi Rose, but recorded the faces of the men he contracted to do the job. He knew he couldn't afford to risk his freedom by allowing them to run free where they would eventually provide information to the authorities.

Both men were babbling idiots, and he knew he had to make sure they didn't have a chance to implicate him in anyway. There was only one thing and one person he could depend on, his wife, Lucy Gunn. She always knew exactly what potion was needed to make his troubles go away. It was obvious he had underestimated the rich American. Whatever the case, Governor Gunn understood that the target was now on his back. He knew it would be only a matter of time before the authorities would be knocking on his door. He needed time and a new plan to escape from the islands before the feds converged.

Even though he hadn't actually murdered anyone. He had contracted the services of others to carry out numerous crimes. His body became enraged with anxiety, the more he thought about his current situation. He needed a place to hide and be inconspicuous so he could maneuver on the thirteen-mile island without notice. He instructed his driver to carry him to Club Lacey, where he could think things over without interruption. He then directed him to drive the limousine to his office and park it behind Government House.

When he walked into Club Lacey, Molinda was sitting at the bar dressed in a long slinky black dress. Her hair was uncombed and mascara was running down her tear-stained face. The sound of Santana was piping from the speakers that lined the graffiti painted walls. The smell of last night's cigarette smoke lingered in the air as she lifted her head looking the governor directly in his face. She turned her back to him in disgust. "You are a terrible man. You care about nothing but money and power. Do you have any idea how it felt for me to identify the headless body of Suzi Rose?"

Puffing on his cigar he looked Molinda squarely in the eye. "You of all people talk to me about money and power. Did you forget that it's you who transports young girls from their native countries, in poorly vented containers, selling their bodies to drunken strangers and perverts? You have no room to discuss anyone's moral character. As for Suzi Rose, I saved her life once for you, but it wasn't enough. She just had to come back to this shit hole of a place. Did you ever ask yourself why? Well, I did, and the answer I came up with was to squeeze me for the murder of Robert Kelsey's father."

Crying uncontrollably. "You think you know everything. You're not so damn smart. Suzi Rose didn't come back to put the finger on you. Suzi Rose came back to be close to me. She was my baby sister. I was all she had in the world. You didn't just kill my sister, you cut her head off, and made me identify her body. I don't care what happens to me, but I do care what happens to you. I hope you rot in hell. Another thing, if you don't want me to testify against you, you might as well kill me now. I swear to you on Suzi Rose's grave, I will do whatever I can to bring you down. I don't know how you sleep at night."

"The same way you do, bitch. With my eyes closed, and if you keeping talking shit, I'll have you taking a nap in a second."

"You don't have the heart. You get others to do your dirty work. Remember, Governor, you're not the only one with a gun, and if you want to live a little longer, I suggest you get your fat ass out of here."

The governor walked through the door of Club Lacey and took a safari to 666 Eastside Bay.

Lucy Gunn was sweeping the dirt in the yard when the taxi pulled up to the house. When she realized she was getting a visit from the governor, she immediately tried to knock the dust off of her tattered clothes. Regardless of what others thought about the governor, she loved him, and had remained a loyal wife for ten years, with the promise of him returning home once he had obtained the wealth required to live a good life. She couldn't believe her eyes. She rushed to the gate to greet him. "Alex, you've come home, just like you said.'"

Having no place to go, he couldn't jeopardize being rejected by the ugliest woman in the world. He glanced at her reptilian leathery like skin and her chameleon changing eyes and wondered how he would survive being with Lucy long enough to arrange for his and Audrey's (his lover) departure from St. Thomas.

"Yes, baby. Daddy has come home. Let's go into the house. I don't want anyone to see me. We have a lot of things to talk about."

As the governor entered the living room, he couldn't help but notice the room was decorated with fruit jars filled with eye balls, black spiders, fingers, and snakes. Not an ideal place for a man who suffers from acrophobia. He took a seat by the window, where spiders had spun their webs in the corners of the glass window panes. Lucy was filled with excitement. Wanting desperately to make the governor comfortable, she attempted to straighten the house as best she could. She grabbed a container from the refrigerator. "Would you like a cool drink?" she asked. "It's passion fruit. I know how much you love passion fruit."

Thirsty, but skeptical of accepting the offer. "No. Lucy, I really need your help. There are some people who know information that can hurt me. We need to make sure they are unable to utter one word about me to the authorities. I need to waive their right of speech. Do you understand what I need to have done?"

"Yes," she replied. "What are their names?" She handed him a piece of paper and instructed him to right the names on the paper and place it in his shoes. She then instructed him to walk around the table three times as she chanted the rites of the silent storm. He scribbled their names down, and placed the paper in his shoes as Lucy chanted. "Ishano Ishadam from tongue to cheek, I shall not speak. Ishano Ishadam, house the words within. Words unspoken brings no sin. Ishano Ishadam, bring forth the blood of the lamb."

Without warning, Lucy loss consciousness, falling to the floor next to the governor's shoes. Lucy had succeeded at tying the tongues of the enemy. The governor picked her up from the floor and laid her on the small cot and covered her with a blue checkered blanket.

His mission was accomplished. Now all he needed to do was contact Audrey so she could make the necessary arrangements for their flight from St. Thomas. He placed a call to the woman he loved, and with whom he planned to spend the remainder of his life. When she answered the phone, he hesitated momentarily. "Hello Audrey, it's your man."

"Hello, baby, I've been worried about you. Where are you?" The police arrested Bonehead and Baller. Tiny said they are looking for you."

The governor whispered hoarsely, "I'm at Lucy's. I'm putting things together so we can get off this damn island. Thanks to Robert Kelsey, shit is falling apart. Look, baby, I need you to take all the money from the safe, buy about 20 trac phones, then make arrangement with Bushwhackers to fly us to Brazil. You need to pack us both a bag to hold us over for a minute. I'm going to hide out in this godforsaken shack of a house until Lucy completes silencing all of our loose lips. We should be ready to leave the island 8:00 p.m. tomorrow night. One more thing, I love you, and be careful not to let anyone see you."

"Ok, baby. I will pick you up tomorrow at 8:00 p.m."

"Audrey, I won't be calling you again in case the feds are tracking my phone."

The governor looked at Lucy's limp body, not knowing she was fully conscious and had overheard every word he had spoken. A few moments later he saw her move. "Oh good, you're awake. Come on, baby, we have more work to do."

Feeling betrayed, she sulked, telling the governor she didn't want to do any more unless he allowed her to prepare him a welcome home dinner. He agreed, reluctantly, and Lucy began preparing her husband a dinner he would never forget. The governor kept his suspicious eyes on her the entire time she was cooking. He had to make sure she didn't drop any crispy critters into the pot. As she cut provisions and seasoned the chicken, she thought about all the times she closed her eyes to the governor's women and business dealings, but not today. She knew that in order to keep her husband by her side, she would have to reduce his metabolic rate and his ostentatious character.

He sat quietly as she placed a spotted phosphate rock in each hand calling forth the metamorphic serpentine. His body began to relax and soon he was in a calm state of mind. Suddenly and without explanation she began rubbing her hands over his bald head. "I am your wife, there will be no one before me, and no one after. In your heart, I may be void, but in your head I will forever live."

She led him slowly to the cot. The removal of the multicolored rug, that laid under the small wooden table, exposed a secret door. She carefully lifted the door, took the governor by his hands and led him down the squeaky steps to a private hell beneath the kitchen floor. It was in the confines of his new space that she fed him a cup of broth made from the man pot stew she conjured up, containing a dash of Datura and puffer fish venom.

No longer did Lucy worry about losing the man she loved. And no longer would the governor worry about being arrested for his hideous and violent crimes. The life he deserved to live had come to pass. In a conscious state of mind, the underbelly of the world he served stretched over his paralyzed body. In his zombified condition he was surrounded by spiders and snakes, and held captive in the arms of the woman he feared.

LINGUISTICS PROVERBS

"The Interpretation of West Indian Proverbs."

When I began writing the **DAUGHTERS OF DASHEEN** series, I knew I wanted to weave the Islands linguistic proverbs and thought-provoking phrases throughout the pages of my novel. My intention was to preserve the richness of the West Indian culture and the genius behind their philosophical way of thinking. I sincerely hope the knowledge shared in **THE CHOSEN ONE** is readily understood, and found to be entertaining, as well as enlightening.

The colloquial language of the Caribbean Islands is as beautiful as its people and as breathtaking as its majestic ocean views. Their colorful proverbial language is intricately woven together with elements of sarcasm and sweet memories of yesterday. Even though life in the Caribbean is constantly changing, the linguistic proverbs spoken by its ancestors continue to provide warnings to those who seek wise counsel.

My ability to share important aspects of the past would be impossible if not for the great people of the Virgin Islands and beyond. Today, I pay love and respect to Ms. Sandarilla Farrington, Mr. John Sewer, Mr. Larry Hodge, Mr. Roy Stout, Rev.Cornelius Turner, Mr. Tito Morales, Ms. Chola Kean, Mr. Eddie LaBorde, Ms. Helen Sookwah, Mr. Monroe Farrington, Mr. Victor Sydney, Ms. Eunice Duggins, Mr. George Goodwin and all who shared knowledge through conversation or stories. Special recognition to Mr. George Seaman, author of *Not So Cat Walk*, and Mr. Lito Valls, author of *Jumbie Jamboree*, both who masterfully preserved important aspects of the West Indian culture through their publications.

GLOSSARY OF INTERPRETATIONS

- ***A kick from the mare does the stallion no harm***: Maybe a little uncomfortable, but man will endure.
- ***Ah know wha' yoh comin from***: To understand what someone is saying.
- ***Ai put mi name in de mout' of de public***: Gossip about someone.
- ***Babylon***: America.
- ***Bread butter on both sides***: To have it made.
- ***Cane no grow like grass***: Things are not as easy as they appear, it may be more difficult than one expects.
- ***Cum wha cum; cum big oh cum small***: Facing life's problems regardless of the size.
- ***Dog run fo' he character, hog run fo' he life***: Poor pig is running for his life, while the dog is running for prestige.
- ***E buy it:*** He had it coming.
- ***Ebr ' body think ah dollar is ah dollar, but ah dollar ain ah dollar***: Money's not everything.
- ***E head to close to e' tail***: He too short.
- ***Eye 'fraid eye***: Being wary of someone.

- *Ebery shut-eye no sleep*: Don't be taken in by a person who appears to be sleeping, they may deceive you.
- *Haul een de door*: Put an end to things.
- *Fo' night bring day*: Bad times don't last forever.
- *Hot lub soon cool*: Too much passion dies soon.
- *If ah lie ah die*: So help me.
- *Jumbi*: A ghost or spirit.
- *Pickney*: A child.
- *Sew up you mout*: Shut your mouth.
- *Sin run afta sin*: Evil begets evil.
- *Tis wha' yoh hole deh in yoh eye*: Ugliness is in the eye of the beholder.
- *Wha' yo' do me nobody see, wha' i do yo'eberybody see*: Passing judgment on a person's character.
- *Wha' eye don' see heart don' grieve fo'*: You can't miss what you didn't have or see.
- *When yoh hear de shout*: Getting to the center or heart of a matter.
- *When rat see cat he nebber laugh*: Never ignore those who can cause you harm.
- *Yoh* : Your day will come.
- *Yo' no hear yo' feel*: If you refuse to listen, you feel the pain.
- *Yoh kin expect trouble when marine butt up wid sailor*: No use in avoiding the inevitable. You have to fight until you get tired of fighting, then get up and fight some more.
- *Yoh know how ah stay:* Knowing a person's position on a matter.
- *Yo' thro water it run, thro blood it settles*: Blood is thicker than water.

ABOUT THE AUTHOR

DAUGHTERS of DASHEEN
The Chosen One

Sandra Davis is a former communication executive, and mother of one based in Georgia. Since early childhood she has recorded hundreds of poems, proverbs, and short stories. Her ultimate dream was writing fiction with a hint of realism, which would one day evolve into blockbuster movies. Her enthusiasm of such was fueled  by the desire to create movie roles for her beloved African American actors. After countless years of placing her dreams on hold, she finally allowed the characters who resided in her head to appear and speak life into her first series; DAUGHTERS of DASHEEN—The Chosen One.

Made in the USA
Lexington, KY
25 September 2018